PRAISE FOR
RALPH PETERS'

"An excellent . . . novel of political intrigue."
—*Cleveland Plain Dealer*

"An uncommonly intelligent and exciting caper, with a likable hero. . . ."
—*Publishers Weekly*

"Told with pinpoint clarity. Peters writes with a style that is lucid and so direct that it seems to be almost effortless."
—*San Diego Union*

"Peters has an acute ear. . . . So many of the passages come off so well that one knows this is a serious writer. . . ."
—*The New Republic*

Books by Ralph Peters

Bravo Romeo
Red Army

Published by POCKET BOOKS

BRAVO ROMEO

RALPH PETERS

8 3.95
1 4.00 *matrix*
1 0.95 1 N S W
2.95 1 N S W
1.00 1 N S W
14.39 GAS
13.?
127.24

POCKET BOOKS

New York   London   Toronto   Sydney   Tokyo   Singapore

This book is a work of fiction. Names, characters, places and incidents are either the product of the author's imagination or are used fictitiously. Any resemblance to actual events or locales or persons, living or dead, is entirely coincidental. The views expressed in this book are those of the author and do not reflect the official policy or position of the Department of the Army, Department of Defense, or the U.S. government.

Excerpt from Homer, *The Iliad,* translated by Robert Fitzgerald, copyright © 1974 by Robert Fitzgerald. Reprinted by permission of Doubleday & Company, Inc.

POCKET BOOKS, a division of Simon & Schuster Inc.
1230 Avenue of the Americas, New York, NY 10020

ISBN: 0-671-68166-4

First Pocket Books printing August 1990

10 9 8 7 6 5 4 3 2 1

POCKET and colophon are registered trademarks of
Simon & Schuster Inc.

Printed in the U.S.A.

For the ASIC boys

Ah, cousin, could we but survive this war
to live forever deathless, without age,
I would not ever go again to battle,
nor would I send you there for honor's sake!
But now a thousand shapes of death surround us,
and no man can escape them, or be safe.

—THE *ILIAD*,
translated by Robert Fitzgerald

PART
ONE

1

Thorne leaned back against the building, bare arms folded across the chest of his tennis shirt, waiting. The fresh darkness made the drink-craving more manageable, the cooler, better air was half satisfying. Down through the black treetops, he could see shining puzzle pieces of Glifada and the bright spread of greater Athens beyond. Slivers of the bay caught neon pastels from the beachfront clubs and restaurants, a lean French cruiser was strung with a carnival of lights. The sailors had been all over the city that afternoon, in dress whites, well-behavedly snapping photos. They were very different from the military types Thorne was used to.

Every few minutes, a commercial jet roared in low overhead on the approach to the international airport. Thorne was familiar with the approach pattern. When you lay on the beach at Vouliagmeni, the big shadows swept over you and the incredible noise broke off your conversation. Still, Vouliagmeni was all right. The best of the women jiggled along the water's edge and

3

there was an outstanding tavern close to the sea. When you were locked tight into Athens, Vouliagmeni was the best you could do. It was a shame there was never any work out on the islands. The islands were always on his own time. Where the eager northern women came to roast their merry asses and the water was clean.

Another jet **thund**ered overhead and Thorne watched the landing lights float down. The American airbase was down there, every so often the angry young locals blew up some dirt-poor enlisted man's car. Thorne fought down a surge of anger and impatience. He'd worked out of Athens for the past two years, rotating in and out of the Mideast, and he liked the Greeks whenever they weren't making him furious. They were warm and fundamentally decent people. But they were not very good at accepting responsibility for their own mistakes, and Thorne was tired of hearing the CIA accused every time the plumbing broke down. He knew very well how tame that particular beast had become.

A match flared a few meters down the hillside. One of the sentries. They'd looked like prison guards to Thorne, not military types. Dressed in blue dungaree uniforms, sawed-off shotguns and pumps interspersed with the automatic weapons, they'd been sitting almost casually on the sandbagged rims of their positions when the captain drove Thorne into the compound. It was too dark to see them now, but Thorne imagined them in the same relaxed postures, weapons held easily across the lap. He wondered what they thought of all this, how much they told their wives and friends. They had to know. It didn't take a genius to figure it out. Screams, even those shut in a basement, carried at night.

Maybe they were all fascists. Perhaps there was a secret conspiracy of fascists none of the spooks had picked up on yet. Maybe the next generation of colonels was only awaiting the high sign from Mount Olympus. Thorne frowned at his fantasy. More likely, these men were simply well paid and wanted to keep their jobs.

That was part of the trouble. You could spin the threads forever, what you were told, what you saw, what you felt, and never once lay your hand on the steady rail of reality. Thorne often considered the possibility that there was no reality in the intelligence world, only the convergence or collision of separate visions.

But no. The screams, whenever they came back, were real. Human suffering was real, it was the base you started from.

Yes, Thorne thought sourly, I am here because I am resolutely opposed to all the unnecessary suffering of this world, loafing quietly in expectation, while this torture is being inflicted for my benefit.

He desperately needed one he could believe in, an assignment where he could saddle up his white horse again. It had been too long between good ones now, too long between justifications, and he was not the man to deal diplomatically with the enthusiastic torturers and hired guns.

If it didn't get better soon, he'd have to walk away from it. Go home. And he was still afraid of that. He hadn't solved half the problems yet. He didn't want to go back until he could touch down with the hopeful wonder of the stranger. And that was still a long way away. It was the sort of thing you could never talk about, it was too embarrassing to love and hate a mere country so fiercely and naïvely in the nineteen-seventies. It was like being the last child after all the rest of the world had matured.

Definitely, Thorne thought, I'm due for a clean one.

The screams came back again, suddenly, pleadingly, only to hide in the rush of another big jet. Standing firmly behind Thorne's shoulders was the building with the mandatory basement room, and past the building waited still more guards. Beyond those guards and the wire, another slope ran down to a small bay. Across that bay, only a few hundred meters distant, was the Astir Palace Hotel, opulent, over-priced and ever crowded. They would be serving grand platters of seafood just now, with the appropriate wines, to the rich and their apprentices. The Cream of the West. Still, you could almost live with it here. Even the ditchdigger with his squawking family crammed into a tiny flat in Kessariani was on the way up. But Thorne had served in too many countries where the discrepancies were not so easy to live with. The countries with the incredible mortality rates and the higher birth rates and humanity rotting. He often considered how easily he could've ended up on the other side. He loved so much of what they said. The problems arose over the things they actually did.

But it was often a very near thing, this balancing act of ultimate justice in conflict with interim human decency. The plane was gone now, taking the latest ache of screams with it. But Thorne could picture the close, bright room, he could feel its pulse and smell it. He'd been there. He knew the shot-up apartments of Beirut and the loathsome cells in Persia. Iran. The thought of the place stopped him for a moment. The country was a plague pit of writhing, vengeful corpses, and any day now they were going to rise up. And nobody wanted to hear.

But that wasn't his problem anymore. They'd pulled him off that one. He hadn't been able to provide the comfortable answers. The memories sickened him. He'd thought—hoped—that they'd learned. But they'd learned nothing.

Now his problems centered around this unseen basement room and its miserable sweat of pain that ghosted in his nostrils. He could see clearly the alternate looks of hopelessness and determination and blunt suffering. He knew the various faces of agony the way a conscientious tourist knew cathedrals. Sometimes there were clever tools. Other times just the trusty old fist. You came almost to expect it in the Middle East. But, until this evening, he'd believed that the business had been shut down in Greece along with the dictatorship. Then this captain—this man who identified himself as a captain—had been waiting in his air-conditioned Mercedes outside the gymnasium.

It had been stupid to answer the man's call, more foolish still to get into the car. That was the sort of thing that had so nearly shut the big door on him in Cairo. Besides, his cover was going all to shit and so many of his fellow experts had been turning up in car trunks. He had instantly disliked the captain as well, distrusting the classic sunglasses and the tailored safari jacket. The understated manners and elegant facial features had been too perfect. But Thorne had dropped into the passenger's side without a single test question, just as he had followed the man with the promise and the knife into the City of the Dead. Our strengths were also our weaknesses.

And now he stood outside, not permitted inside where he could witness and maybe even control the situation himself, excluded from all but the screams, unable to trust anything but the reality of those screams, shut in this compound by wire and the guards in their dungarees. He wasn't afraid. Someone was going to far too much trouble to impress him to just blow him away and drop him on the beach. But he was getting tremendously pissed off at the archness of the whole situation.

A door opened back around the front of the building, and brisk footsteps hunted across gravel.

"Here you are, sir. Good." The captain. He'd taken off his safari jacket, and his pale shirt moved luminously through the clear night. When he stopped, within breath range of Thorne, the glowing shirt revealed a dark sprinkle across its disarranged belly.

"Terribly sorry to keep you waiting," the captain went on. "You understand how these things are, sir."

Thorne waited, making no commitment. Neither to the insistent sirring nor to any shared understanding of anything. He'd already waited a long time.

The captain turned half away, toward the distant

thrill of lights, making a show of breathing in a full chest of the cooling air. He had a tastefully athletic build, the look of a horseman.

"A lovely evening. There is nothing finer than a summer night in Greece. The tourists come for the sun, of course, but we Greeks treasure the summer nights. So many of the most important things happen after the sun dies." He turned fully back to Thorne. "As a poet, you must certainly appreciate that, sir?"

"Captain," Thorne said, "could you please tell me what this is all about?"

The captain met Thorne with an assured smile that remained more felt than actually seen.

"Naturally, sir. Sorry to have kept you in such suspense, but you know how these things are. As a fellow soldier, you understand the need for absolute certainty in these matters."

Another jet roared over them, dumping noise. Thorne felt his patience beginning to crack wide now, the dirty little show had been effective after all. Maybe he wasn't the grand and patient master he thought he was. I am no longer the right man for this, he told himself. Never was, really.

"I believe," the captain picked up. in his bothersomely fine English, "we may, inadvertently, have stumbled upon a matter of concern to your people. The . . . subject we've been questioning . . . has been involved in arms trafficking. Nothing on the grand scale, but he made the mistake of stealing from the Greek Army. That he is a fellow Greek makes it all the more inexcusable." The captain smiled. "I'm afraid my countrymen sometimes become too industrious for their own good. Still, all this seemed to be strictly an internal matter—until we learned that this . . . criminal . . . had recently made a business trip to the Federal Republic of Germany. To the town of Bad Sickingen."

The captain paused, milking the tension. Thorne knew the name, of course. He'd even been there years before. And the captain had correctly assumed that he'd know it. Thorne granted him, or the people behind him, another point.

The captain inched closer. "I asked myself, why should this particular town ring a bell? I consulted maps, and was reminded that Bad Sickingen is the headquarters of a U.S. Army division. The Sixty-fourth Infantry Division, Mechanized, I believe. Now, perhaps this is purely coincidental, but our subject has been trafficking in a variety of demolitions equipment, and, as we all know, the U.S. Army in Europe has been something of a preferred target for leftist terror groups."

"Can I see him?" Thorne asked.

The captain backed off into the darkness, eye-gleam and pale shirt. "I'm afraid that would be impossible, sir. He was taken ill during the examination. But he did offer us a bit more. His place of contact was a tavern, the Soonwalder Hof. He claimed he didn't know the name of his actual contact, it was a passive meet, nor did he give us more than a weak description of the man. German, dark hair and a beard. Not very much, I'm afraid. We did try all the photos of known and suspected terrorists circulated by the German government, but without success. Cigarette, sir?"

"No. Thanks."

"Yes, of course. An athlete as well as a poet. And the damaged lung from the war. All in all, an interesting man."

"Captain, do you believe everything your subject told you?"

"Oh, yes. In this instance I can virtually guarantee the validity. A certain amount of pressure was applied during the interview."

"Then why are we playing games?"

"Games?" The captain seemed distressed now, but only at Thorne's lack of finesse.

"Why the theater? Why leave me standing out here while you bust some poor joker's nuts to provide me with a sound track? You must've had all this information before you tracked me down this afternoon."

The captain eased a long taste off his cigarette, untroubled. He was good at this. Thorne almost had to smile in admiration. Dude, Thorne thought, if I had *you* in that little room . . .

"Sir," the captain began, "I mentioned earlier the need for absolute certainty. We would not want to pass along any information that was not one hundred percent dependable. We wanted you to be very clear on that point. In reference to any exceptional means applied during the interview, we understand that your people are presently somewhat squeamish on the subject. So your exclusion from the examination room was strictly in your own interest. It wouldn't really have done for you personally to have violated your country's human-rights policy, would it have?" The captain gave a moment's attention to his waning

11

cigarette, then added, "As for tracking you down, sir, it didn't involve much. We are thoroughly in control of our own country."

Thorne thought of the unintelligent-looking gunmen in their workshirts and jeans, the sandbags and barbed wire.

"All right," Thorne said. But it wasn't all right. He was reeling in professional doubt. First of all, intel people didn't give anything away free. "But why take the trouble to pass this information in the first place? The love affair's been on the rocks lately. Especially with your military."

The captain lowered the smoldering tip of his cigarette, laughing a cocktail-party laugh. They waited for another jet to pass.

"Oh, yes," the captain said in an indulgent tone, "arms, the Turks, Cyprus, oil in the Aegean. Personally, I think you're foolish to give anything to the Turks. They are an ungrateful people. On another level, I understand. *We* understand. The Turks have more to offer you on a strategic level. The common border with the Soviets, as well as a side door into the world of Islam. But whatever indignities you may subject us to, there are nonetheless those who realize our unavoidable dependence on you, those who have little sympathy with the dangerous games of the left. Let's say that certain parties wanted you to know that there remains a strong conservative tradition here in Greece."

"Captain? May I please see the man? For a few minutes?"

The captain savored a last stingy taste of his cigarette, then flipped the butt onto the gravel.

"I'm afraid that's impossible, sir. As I mentioned, the last interview was unexpectedly disturbing to him. I don't think you'd find him very responsive." The captain grasped Thorne suddenly, startlingly, by the arm.

Thorne flashed back to the stumbling dark violence of Cairo, the recent near-death, and came within an instant of hurting the captain badly. Full seconds after the shock of the touch had passed, Thorne's fury was still on a thin leash.

"Shall we be getting back into town?" the captain asked pleasantly.

Thorne had the captain drop him off by the university and from there he strolled back to Syntagma Square. The street was dependably lunatic with taxis and private cars with smacked fenders, and the bright sidewalk cafés boiled over with tourists. Thorne browsed down a clothespinned line of international newspapers at one of the kiosks until a seat opened up along the rear rank of tables, then he moved determinedly for the brown, cushiony lounge chair, *Le Monde* tucked under one arm. Rival Palestinian factions gunning each other down in Paris, maybe someone he knew.

A plump harried waiter took Thorne's order without actually stopping on his dash between the tables, and Thorne tried to concentrate on the names of French streets and Arab assassins. But he had too much on his mind, he was still holding in his anger at the Joe-Slick captain, at his own failure to grasp control, and it was like trying to hold in fiery piss. Then, in the chair flush with the left side of his, a hard-jawed northern woman of maybe forty began lecturing her younger Greek companion in kindergarten German. How fortunate he was, she said, to live in such a gorgeous and good-natured land. Instead of the cold, strict north.

Where the jobs were, Thorne thought, where bored wives casually hopped a jet.

The woman drew herself a long cigarette from a shimmering case, and her companion bent immediately to light it. He was a graceful and agreeable young man.

But it all went back to Nam again. The lessons learned the hard way. You never really knew who was doing the exploiting. The pudgy waiter dropped off Thorne's beer. Amstel. Thorne drank half of the bottle quickly, answering his long thirst, drinking through foam. To mutual exploitation, and mutual gratification. He stood up, laying his newspaper on his chair, and went inside to an open public phone.

When he got through, the familiar female voice said, "Apollo Impex."

"East here. I'd like to speak to Fritz."

There was a pause, a black silence on the other end that meant the phone had been keyed off. Thorne watched an old man slice fruit pies. Then the line hummed back to life.

"Fritz isn't here right now, but we're expecting him. In about an hour. Oh, and Hafez was looking for you."

"Any bargains?"

"Nothing that won't keep. He wanted your advice on a deal through the Paris office."

"I think I know which deal he's talking about. I'll get with him in the morning."

"And Fritz'll be expecting you."

"In an hour."

Thorne rang off and went back outside, crossing trails of energy left by the waiters. These were not typical easygoing Greek waiters, and Thorne half expected to find that his half-finished beer had been swept away.

But the bottle and the glass were waiting, and he poured the rest. He'd been told it was all the same batch with different labels, but the Amstel never tasted as good to him as the Fix. Thorne respected a good beer, he had once lain three days in the jungle, caught in the wrong place at an utterly wrong time, pissing down his leg because any movement would've cost it all, then thirsting unbearably and remembering in turn each of the great beers of his life, the sweet Mex beer at the sex shows in Juárez when he was young enough to turn his heart completely off or the fresh morning bottle of *Pils* while hiking in the Alps with a clear-eyed, clearheaded companion. The beer was finished now, a few webs of foam clung to the sides of the glass. He flagged the waiter. Another bottle. There was time.

The German woman and her Greek had been replaced now. By an English woman and her Greek. The national industry. It was both easier and harder to take with the English woman sitting perfume-close to him, because she was not so obviously in control and her clothing was not so bluntly expensive. In fact, when she spoke she sounded very unsure about the situation. Then her Greek friend leaned closer and stroked her hand and spoke confidently to her. Thorne couldn't quite hear what the man whispered, but she replied that she didn't know, that she really didn't know. She sounded positively afraid. Thorne opened his paper wide in front of him, displaying a sudden Frenchness, not wanting to give her the least cause for embarrassment. When the waiter delivered his beer, Thorne paid him off with an exaggerated tirade in his best Saigon Parisian, thoroughly confusing the old man.

After the second beer and a brief trip downstairs to the delightful plumbing facilities that were his favorite in Athens, Thorne set himself in motion. He turned down past the American Express office, then right, away from the Plaka. He followed back streets, much better for the beers, slowly curling his direction back on itself. The black alleys between the major arteries held a special hush, the night wore an Oriental thickness, and sound choked. But this was not the Orient, nor the Mideast, and, as he listened for company behind him, Thorne thought how good it always was to be back in Europe, even this halfway Europe. Most of the places he worked did not have dark side streets where northern men could walk without fear. He imagined he could feel ice along the slithery trace of his knife scar, his peacetime wound. It had been bloody, but not bad. A short, curved blade, a slashing blade, skittering along the hard, wonderful bone of a rib. Then the fireworks, and the Egyptians, not very wisely, yanking him out. Now everyone knew what he'd suspected for a while, that he was pretty well blown in the Mideast, that he wouldn't do much more than sift stale news or die chasing after some third-rate scrap. He'd done a lot of hustles in a couple of quick years, been lucky and on the move. But it was over now. The Mideast was no place to hang on, not even manning a desk. It was too full of grudge fighters with long memories. The knife business had been a grudge hit. Just thank God for the Egyptians with their new fondness for Americans.

Thorne eased up into the Plaka from the northwest, passing the first cluster of noisy restaurants, their small tables spread right out in the middle of the sloping street, the waiters pitching the virtues of their establishments in a contest of languages. Thorne smiled them off, waved them off, finally marched through their persistence. Winding into the crowded alleys that terraced the hillside, he lingered to admire an occasional windowful of handicrafts or junk, watching back after the pretty North American college girls in their jeans and sandals or swaying Indian print skirts, using the splendid trail of their rumps as an excuse to make sure nobody had picked him up. Overamplified bouzouki music clanged and the restaurants spilled thick fragrances, oregano and thyme and frying olive oil, the cheaper or tired oil reeking. The whitewashed steps of the steep alley that served as the Plaka's spinal column were almost invisible under the August swarm. Tourists of a hundred varieties tried to make a wise choice from the profusion of incomprehensible menus, between the contests of screeching, happy music and identical female singers. The throaty girls not only sounded but even looked the same, dark-eyebrowed blonds Thorne called the thousand and one daughters of Melina Mercouri. It

17

was a reassuring treat just to walk through all this, enjoying the life of it all and the solvency. It was so easy on the soul to be where everyone had enough to eat, even the bluejeaned, bearded beggars wolfing down their *gyros*. And the Greek hustlers were vivid and exasperating and undeniably entertaining. Not like the gaunt Egyptians, their bellies taut with river worms.

A pair of life-shakingly lovely young women toured by, all northern height and health, in cotton dresses that teased between their thighs as they walked. They brought to mind all the other, pleasanter lives there were to lead; Thorne longed suddenly to sit them down and talk peaceably with them until a favorite emerged. To turn his back on all the rest of it and be untroubled by everything except the small dilemmas of men and women growing intimate. But he soldiered on.

He turned back into the less traveled side streets, aiming back toward Syntagma again, wondering it all out again, how much of the captain's story to believe, who might be grinning behind it, and what exactly to report.

Briefly back on a tourist street, he passed the city's piss-poor, overpriced Japanese restaurant and a succession of antique shops. Then he turned once more into the gloom, and on a half-lit corner he paused to look into a display window full of rusting crap of the sort that fired a well-to-do grandmother's soul. He glanced behind himself one last time. And he slipped in by the side door.

Inside was jungle dark, the little paleness from the front window didn't reach. But Thorne was a night-walker from way back and he went playfully between the fragile displays.

You were supposed to wait, to stand in one place until you were challenged. But Thorne never did. He always moved quietly out of the lines of light, the lines of fire. They'd taught him that early on and he refused to forget his training now at the bidding of clerks.

In a few seconds an anxious female voice whispered:

"Nikos?"

"East," Thorne replied. He had come closer than she knew and he could feel how he'd startled her. You learned to read the vibrancy of another human being close by in the dark. Just as the flowery, unsexy perfume conjured the rest of her from memory.

A red-hooded flashlight flicked on, lighting the prescribed trail along the floor. Thorne played the game now, following the slant of light through a doorway into deeper darkness.

The woman shut the door behind them and turned on the overhead light.

"How's the war, Julie?" Thorne asked. He expected her to complain, as she usually did, about his sneaking around the shop.

But she only smiled welcome tonight. Clean, plain and thirtyish, the classic librarian, liberated now into the overrated world of intelligence, become a librarian of classified documents. "Oh, we're winning, Jack. How're you?" Then her senses homed in, cataloguing his mood. "Christ, don't you look pissed off."

"Don't ask."

The woman shrugged, a friendly okay, whatever, and led him down to the basement. The first room was littered with more of the cluttering junk that was actually sold during business hours. Ship's ornaments, corroded weapons from the Turkish occupation, old dolls, dented copper, musty piles of bridal gowns from the mountains. Thorne followed the woman back to a low doorway, stooping through into a small lamplit chamber where a young man in a rugby shirt stood cradling an M-16, protecting a gray vault door. He was blond and blue-eyed, all university sports, and seemed uncomfortable with the sexy black weapon. Better a football.

"Good evening, sir," the kid said.

"Howdy," Thorne told him. He'd never seen this one before. "Put that fucking thing on safe. Please."

"Sorry, sir."

"God, you *are* in a mood," the woman said, amused.

The kid turned his broad back to them and rang the buzzer on the wall beside the vault door. A Mary Renault paperback was stuffed into one of his back pockets.

Definitely new in town, Thorne thought.

After a peephole check, the vault door opened. An older man in his shirtsleeves, open collar and dangling tie, stood in the wedge of flat light. He had a permanently weary, malarial look. The Congo, Laos and Nam, Biafra, back to Nam, then Angola and Savimbi. The long slide down. Leedom of the civilian sister: CIA. They'd met a long time before, in Nam, when Thorne was still an infantry line officer and Leedom was involved in a filthy rural-pacification program. Years later, when Thorne first went on special assignment, they met again, which wasn't remarkable considering how few operatives the various intelligence agencies actually fielded in these days of concentration on electronics. For the last handful of men out on this quietest of battlefields, there was a great deal of ground to defend against an enemy who was numerically far superior. The Military Intelligence boys and the CIA types had to work together, though both organizations often had mixed feelings about it. And Thorne and Leedom had become cautious intel-world friends, trading tales, generally with significant omissions, and sharing the usual if-you're-ever-stuck-there tips.

"Jack," Leedom said, welcoming.

"Lee." Thorne nodded and shook the man's loose-skinned hand. Inside the drab vault there was only a tinny desk, two gray GSA safes with thermite grenades rigged on top, and the soundproofed secure-line booth. "Fritz up?"

"On the line." Then Leedom smiled with the small malice of the overworked. "I'll bet he's thrilled. They don't keep Med hours up there."

"The nighttime is the righttime," Thorne said.

"Hey, I read your piece on Alexandria. Good stuff. You really ought to quit this business and write for a living."

Thorne grinned. "I *do* write for a living, remember?" This was a routine they went through periodically.

"I mean really. Not just as a cover. Get clean. Live a life of leisure."

"I'd be bored. Besides, you can't live on what they pay for that travel garbage."

"So do news."

"Too responsible."

Leedom shook his head like a wiser older brother, almost like a father. "That was almost an honest answer. If you meant that you're too responsible. You know what the truth is? You're the last man on earth who gives a shit." Then he turned to the woman, including her for a charitable moment. "Don't you think he should get out and just write, Julie?"

"I think he should just write his poetry," Julie said, trying her way into the friendship. "Jack, you write like an angel."

"I couldn't keep myself in coffee. *Po*etry don't pay zip." He was flattered, but getting tired of the conversation. It was hard enough to reason with yourself. He turned back to Leedom. "Ever run across a Captain Katsovakis?"

Leedom immediately put on a business look, reviewing his mental files.

"Says Army," Thorne tried. "Horsey, rich-boy type. Drives a silver Mercedes sedan." Thorne looked over to Julie, who didn't have a Greek boyfriend and who stood quietly, with professional good posture now. "Speaks number-one Brit, with the occasional dash of American adviser. Sly little prick, good, extremely right-wing, if he's playing up front."

"Sounds like I should know him." Old Leedom, with his yellow cheeks that had been pestered by a billion flies.

"That means you don't?"

"I'm not sure, Jack. Let me run a check."

"Please. It could be important." Thorne looked Leedom in the eyes and curled a smile at himself. "That, or somebody's making a big-time fool of me."

"Want to read me in?"

Thorne made room for two in his smirk now, all comradely cynicism. "I can't wait. You're going to love this one. Just let me talk to Fritz and get that over with."

Leedom nodded toward the booth.

Thorne shut the padded door tightly behind himself, force of habit, and keyed the receiver. He waited until the scrambler finished whirring up, then said:

"Wie geht's, sir?"

He waited as the other scrambler cued in response. Then came the tiny voice, still recognizable as Ferry. An honest, passed-over lieutenant colonel with whom he'd served on a wild-goose chase in Berlin.

"How are you, friend?"

"Good as new," Thorne said. "I get you out of bed?"

"No, I was out on one. Nasty business, too."

"My apologies, anyway. I got ants in my pants."

"Something hot for us?"

Thorne took the mental deep breath. Probably . . . he shouldn't have called. Much ado about chickenshit. "Maybe. Probably not, though. To be perfectly honest, it's a foxtrot-six. I mean, something's going on, but I'm not sure just what. I'm hoping you'll be able to tell *me* something, give me a thumbs up or down."

"All right. Shoot." But the distant voice sounded slightly annoyed now. Tired, after all.

"I've got a reported case of arms trafficking, to include demolitions equipment passed to possible tangos in the U.S. Victor Corps area."

The other scrambler whistled anxiously in Thorne's ear.

"Where in V Corps?"

"Bad Sickingen," Thorne said.

The other end rushed him again. "When did you get this?"

"Two and a half, three hours ago. You sound interested."

"Positive? About the time frame?"

"Two and a half is closer than three."

"I'm glad," the tiny voice said, not sounding glad at all. "For the sake of your peace of mind. I'm glad you weren't off lying on a beach, mulling this one over. A bomb went off in the Bad Sickingen commissary this afternoon. A big one. It caught the after-work crowd. Christ. We were just now down there. Worst thing I've seen since Nam." There was a pause, a hard thinking. Then Ferry said, "Hold one, I'm going to see if I can catch the Chief. He's taken a personal interest in this one."

Maybe it was just coincidence, Thorne thought, maybe this perfect, terrible timing and all the rest of it was nothing but a great big playful coincidence. He clutched the sleeping receiver. And, even if that little rich-boy cocksucker captain had not dicked around playing his goddamned theatrical games for several hours, it wouldn't have prevented anything. We wouldn't have moved on it, there would've been no real reason, no clear direction to move. We would've begun another piss-ant eternal investigation in cooperation with everybody but the Texas Rangers, and this thing would've happened just the same.

But it burned in him.

The fragile voice came back from the northern end: "Still with me?"

"Roger."

"It sounds as though you have some interesting friends down there. Got anything else on it?"

"A little."

"Good man. Listen, the Chief wants to talk to you."

"It's your dime," Thorne said.

"No. I mean here. In Germany. Tomorrow."

=== 2 ===

The white Mercedes taxi fought its way through the downtown. On the sidewalks, well-dressed men and women went swiftly about their business under a gray standard-issue sky. Office buildings in the international corporate style soared above their street-level luxury shops. Frankfurt had the most efficient ongoing propaganda campaign of any city in the world, calling both tourists and businessmen to a colorful and congenial rendezvous. In reality, it was a mean muscular bastard of a place, with bad food, the coldest whores in Europe and the same anything-but-cheap thrills as Fifth Avenue. Its shameless display of riches always embarrassed him, these were his cities, the cities that owned half the world and bled the other half to death. He watched the taxi meter tick off the Deutschmarks, already past the price of a cab all day in Athens. Then he caught the driver disgustedly inspecting him in the mirror.

Thorne smiled, picturing himself through the German's eyes. The loose curls, the beach bum's tan, the

26

faded and fraying *chemise* Lacoste. Not an especially promising fare.

He told the driver, in the dependable German he kept up by reading and practicing on vacationing secretaries, to let him off at the next corner. He still had several blocks to travel, but a short stolen walk and a quick beer could only build the better man. He was uncharacteristically nervous about the coming interview. Normally he was unimpressed by rank and position. He'd seen the bowels of the mighty. But he wanted this assignment, he craved to stand once more indisputably on the side of justice, to fight the good fight against bad men.

And he took a mischievous pleasure in completing the taxi driver's picture of him. He even took his time counting out the astounding fare, paying exactly the amount on the meter, though it wasn't coming out of his pocket anyway. Then he watched in good humor as the fine machine launched itself back into the shining glut of traffic.

He hoisted the strap of his travel bag onto his shoulder and strolled down the sidewalk in an easier mood. Thrilled by the pale, grand women. Social guilt and outrageous prices notwithstanding, there were advantages to being here. He always had mixed feelings and good times in Germany. He was, in the end, a northern man. Greece, the islands, were first a dream, then a pleasure, next a habit, and, at last, just a bit of a bore. He was not, and didn't really want to be, one of the northerners who could give it all up and snooze on a beach forever. The Aegean made for a terrific vacation, even a very extended one, and a gorgeous hideout. But the soul finally craved the nourishment of worry and hard deadlines, the fierce achievement of the cities and the stirring bitter winters on the land.

He'd never written well on the islands. Their lulling qualities made for poems that were pretty, thoughtful bores. He needed conflict, trouble of a certain kind. The periodic horrors of the Mideast didn't meet the requirements either, filling him only with the spectator's sorrow, the observer's outrage. To his irritation and shame, he moved through this terror that belonged to others in a protective shell. It wasn't his fight. This unwilling detachment made for superb operational effectiveness, but not peace of mind. Or poetry.

But his earlier poems, the Nam poems, those first jagged lines written when it all started going uncontrollably to bits, and then the strict verses from the discipline of pain and hospitals—those lean lines— and later the full blooms gathered from his sorrowful, divided, brilliant homeland in the closing days of the war, were worthwhile. He had accomplished that one firm thing in his life. Then the "activist" reviewers, who had never been to Saigon or the Highlands or the Delta, who'd never smelled it, who'd never been pierced, who didn't realize how complicated the horror was, how innocent so many killers were, how susceptible to evil every last swinging dick became, had taken him up, thrilled at the political statement that wasn't really there. Even when he'd tried to explain, they hadn't believed him. They'd had their own answers prepared for their own questions, they led legions of college girls who wanted to kiss his scars. They described him as haunted. But he never had nightmares. Only clear memories. He slept well, greedily, at night. It was the days that were a problem. When he wrote:

We killed them all to keep ourselves alive

it hadn't been a confession, only a still-astonished statement of fact. Not even of regret, since he would've done the same thing again under the same circumstances, but of *fact*. And perhaps of wonder, bitter as rust soup. But they'd read it from their creaking tradition of perceptions. When a man wrote such a thing, it meant he felt a certain way. And it was the young professors who were the worst, men themselves of soldiering age, who hadn't gone to the war. They managed to write of his ordeals in a way that made them seem very brave for not sharing them. They co-opted tasty amounts of his pain. Where were you, he'd wanted to scream, when *we* were lost and dying? These bright young men should've been the platoon leaders. But they'd left the job for the Calleys. Then they complained when the job was done badly. The liberals had abdicated their responsibility early on. They left the Army to the conservatives and the uneducated, then complained because they had an uneducated, conservative Army. They had abandoned the war to those incapable of expressing the experience to the folks back home, and the war had gone on, while the bright young men piled up degrees. And Thorne, who had so nearly been one of them, had written his poems to keep his sanity and to remember and honor the decent dead boys he'd left behind, poems that were his anchors and their gravestones, and the stay-behinds had shit intellect all over them and ended by making Thorne feel like a scummy fucking profiteer. With all their pitying bravos.

He'd been ready when the Army he'd so hated called him back to active duty. After the misery of Southeast Asia, the splendid comfort of his homeland was impossible for him. And the Army had come back to him as anxious to exploit him as everyone else, but with a seemingly better offer.

Help us, they'd said. You can help us. It's very special work. No more Vietnams, ever. It's all going to be different now. We need a different breed of man.

And he'd believed them.

Thorne turned off the sidewalk into a businessman's bar. The empty gloom inside gave the impression that the place was closed for the break between lunch and dinner. A hefty, miserable-looking blonde stood behind the bar washing up glasses. Thorne asked. Open, grudgingly admitted. He parked his bag beside a booth and slid in. When the woman started out around the bar with a menu, he saved her the trouble. Just a large beer. She didn't answer, only moved back to her position and took a clean glass down from the shelf. She wore a cheap-looking dirndl that had no more to do with this part of Germany than sombreros had to do with the Pennsylvania coal towns where Thorne had grown up. Schizzy Frankfurt. But the advertised beer was Paulaner, genuine Bavarian goods. That, at least, would be a treat.

Thorne calmed back against the wooden booth,

soothing out the haste and grubby feel of a day in motion. Then he remembered that he was in Germany, that there would be, by law, clean facilities, and he got up to wash his face and give his bowels the option.

The way led back through a dining room decorated, in plastics and laminated woods, as a medieval wine cellar. But the sinks and shitters were a scrupulous heaven of white porcelain. Scrubbed. Thorne considered, happily seated, all the grim places he'd parked his ass or just hunkered down over the years. Now, that was how you could tell when you really knew a third-world or especially a fourth-world city. When you knew all the bearable places to drop your load. What a guidebook that would be, and a worthy one too. They always told you where to eat, then left you bursting with the aftereffects. Thorne's Bwana-Sahib Toilet Directory. A friend to the civilized bottom. After shitting vigorously in jungle, desert, swamp, forest and field, in gutter and drain, hillside slum and grand hotel, at sea and in the air, the wanderer found that the true comforts of civilization still touched a soft spot. He considered for a moment whether that might finally be the determining factor in the paying of his allegiance. Maybe he was just on the side of the good, clean johns.

He shuddered at the thought.

"No, sir," Thorne said, "that's about it. But, if it's all on the money, it gives us plenty to move on."

He sat in the paneled twilight of an office that was serviced by a private elevator, surrounded by sales charts handsome as good modern paintings and by watercolors of late-model cars, facing two men in business suits. Ferry, alias Fritz, was the younger of the two, a fortyish lieutenant colonel, yet he seemed older, decidedly less potent, than the Chief. Thorne had never met the Chief before, he knew him only from increasingly frequent news pieces: NATO's current god, a man who'd slipped deftly out of the ruins of the White House. A briar-smoking iron-ass with the snow-capped aristocratic features democracies preferred in their general officers. Lately, he'd taken on the crisp look of a candidate as well.

The Chief was unhappy today. The final body count at the commissary had been twenty-two dead. The bombing, as he put it, looked very bad for the Army.

For the candidate too, Thorne thought. But he drove on earnestly with his pitch: "As you can see, sir, the bombing validates at least a portion of the information. Seems to, anyway. The only thing that still bothers me is the why. I don't trust freebees. And it was all so *arranged.*"

"I'm not worried about that end of it," the Chief interrupted. "The Mediterranean male always confronts life in a theatrical manner, Major." He had sober violet eyes that locked on their target. But the mighty stare had an acquired rather than a God-given feel to Thorne. "Information—*intelligence*—must, of course, bear the closest scrutiny. But we must also exercise great care not to allow our own ingrained cultural traits to bias our evaluation of foreign peoples."

You incredible bastard, Thorne thought. If you'd only believed the last part fifteen years ago. If you only really believed it now.

"Yes, sir," Thorne said calmly. "That's why I think we should move out on the info we have."

"Major Thorne has worked up an operational format," Ferry explained. "I feel it's worth your attention, sir."

"Fire," the Chief ordered, swiveling back to Thorne. Blood and thunder, hit the leather, on to Moscow. He grounded his pipe and leaned back, and a wing of light from the smoked window dutifully strafed his hair. He touched the points of his fingers together, thoughtfully, before the lower half of his face. Two points of light tracked Thorne under thickety eyebrows.

"Sir," Thorne said, "I'd like to go in on this one myself. My German's adequate, and I even have some prior knowledge of the AO." His thoughts glanced back to a younger man, a boy-man, an unscarred Airborne pirate let loose on Mainz while awaiting orders to Vietnam. "Of course, I'm not known there —certainly not in my present capacity. And my cover's made to order for this one. The Exile slash Expatriate retracing his bitter younger years, simultaneously getting a perspective on the land of the capitalist warmongers through the catalyst of a society just as evil and repressed, et cetera. I can go right into the den of thieves on that one, sir."

The Chief went into a thoughtful pause. Just long enough to exhibit evaluation without hesitation. Then he dropped his pressed fingertips to chest level and leaned slightly forward in his chair.

"All well and good, Major, all well and good. However, this isn't your area of operations. I took a look at your file—I hope you don't mind? You're one of our big guns down in oil country. I'm not convinced that we wouldn't be misusing our assets."

Thorne wanted this one. It was the closest he'd come to black and white in a long time. Tracking the sick fuckers who blew up small-timers and innocents. He wanted this assignment, and now he felt he needed it.

He met the experienced gaze of the stern, carefully constructed man on the other side of the desk. God save the American electorate. Had the mad bombers' league taken out a roomful of men such as this one, Thorne wouldn't have been nearly so interested.

But they hadn't. They'd arbitrarily blasted the buck sergeant's high-school-dropout wife into the hamburger counter. Some revolutionary act.

"Sir," Thorne said, packing his voice with all the persuasive energy he had, "I'm all but finished down there. Even the Egyptians knew who I was last time out. *They* were using *me*. Next it'll be waiters and cabdrivers." Thorne held up for a moment, swimming against a flood of images, Cairo, Beirut like a pretty woman raped and cut up, the Kurdistan they swore didn't exist, Athens and the islands. Goodbye to all that. "I'm blown down there," he concluded. "Besides, sir, I've been called up here on less."

Maybe too much, Thorne thought, they don't like displays of emotion. He waited in the pricey quiet of the fine, high room.

"He's slated out of there, sir," Ferry put in. "It'd be a few months' difference at most."

I owe you one, pal, Thorne thought.

"Be that as it may," the Chief said, and now he had

put on a tone that had decided to be difficult, "be that as it may, it seems to me Major Thorne has some unfinished business down there. This Captain Kazantzakis or Katzenjammer or whatever his name is. That has to be followed up. Immediately."

"There's a good man on it right now, sir," Thorne said. He turned to Ferry. "You know Leedom, sir? Charlie India Alpha–type?"

Ferry had no chance to reply. The Chief jumped. *"Ma*jor, are you telling me the CIA's been read in on this already? This is an *Army* project. *Damn."* He grasped the edge of the desk, scanned its top as though looking for a weapon. "Damn." He stopped his search and looked hard at Thorne, at Ferry, back to Thorne. "We don't need any help from those clowns in the damned CIA."

Thorne kept it very cool now, steering through the storm. "Sir, down there we all have to cooperate. Things have been scaled down considerably, as you know. And, to be perfectly honest, they've got a better line into the Greek military than we'll ever have. They've still got a lot more money than we do."

Then Ferry came more strongly to his aid; Berlin had been worth something tangible after all. "Sir, I believe Major Thorne's our best bet for this one. His background would appear to be tailor-made for this kind of infiltration, and, unless this group's plugged directly into the PLO, his cover should hold."

Thorne picked it up. "A series of my poems have just been anthologized in German, sir. Well-circulated left-wing pub, at that. It couldn't be better timing."

35

"Oh . . . yes. Yes, Major." The Chief sat back, the executive decision-maker relishing his role once more. Thorne had no doubt that this man and every interchangeable one like him had their exact doubles in like positions on the other side. "Your poetry. That was in your file, too."

"Sir," Ferry interrupted, returning bravely to Thorne's aid, "it's my considered opinion that Major Thorne's our best shot on this."

That, Thorne considered, gratefully and sadly, is why the poor sucker never made full bird.

There was a long, worrisome silence. The Chief was not accustomed to being interrupted. Thorne felt himself reduced to childishness with wanting. Beyond the tall tinted window a 747 climbed the sky.

"Oh, hell," the Chief said abruptly, "go ahead. Run your show, Ferry. I'm just an old infantryman. I don't understand the sort of bugger who blows up a commissary full of women and children and simple honest soldiers. I'm just an old line doggie, not a damned psychologist." He eased considerably now, smiling heroically, savoring this image of himself. "You go ahead, run your show." Then the wary political beast sneaked in. "Are you planning to read the Germans in?"

"I hadn't planned to, sir," Ferry said. "Not until we surface something. They're like a sieve."

"All right, all right. It's your show. And it'll be your ass." He turned his final attentions to Thorne. "But, Major?"

"Yes, sir."

The Chief stared into him. The mighty, weathered, Yankee-patriot stare that made such dramatic magazine covers, that wilted underlings. But Thorne didn't back off, he met the violet eyes head on. And, as a reward, he glimpsed the genuine anger of the man.

"You get those bastards."

3

Thorne took his time. He spent his first few nights in
Bad Sickingen in a bed-and-breakfast in the oldest
part of the town, where the Turkish *Gastarbeiter* lived
many to a room and the Germans hid their few fellow
citizens who'd been passed over by the economic
miracle. He made himself visible, hunting a room to
rent, walking the streets, sitting in the park with his
notebook, wearing a washed-out denim shirt and
forgetting to shave. He drank beer and inexpensive
white wine in the workers' bars and took an attic room
with the toilet closeted in the hallway. He picked up a
used typewriter and splashed the room with the few
possessions he'd brought and an accurate selection of
books. He let a glass of flowers wither and pinned up a
few photographs. And he waited.

Every night, he went to a different taproom, hunting
down the cobbled alleys for the haphazardly furnished
front rooms where a glass of beer was a few pfennigs
cheaper and the regulars marked a stranger's visit and
hushed for long minutes. Where the barmaids

scratched the number of his drinks on cardboard coasters and never really smiled. Where the police came in suddenly, stared menacingly, and left quietly. And when he had, by virtue of his own quiet, blurred a bit into the thick light, the men would laugh their loud, exclusive laughter again and drink relentlessly. Finally he would be asked, abruptly and demandingly, from where he'd come. When he told them he was an American, they were puzzled. He clearly wasn't a soldier from the U.S. Army *Kaserne*. Neither was he one of the dollar-sloppy tourists who came to visit the wine country for a day. Then it would be his turn to brood, instead of leaping into the opening, because friendship with these men—these men who reminded him of the huge, decent miners of his childhood—was not part of the role. And the men hitched up their baggy workers' corduroys in disgust and turned their curiosity back to the bar. Thorne behaved ignorantly, and it was not his usual way, and it saddened him. But he was outside now.

By day, he hunted through the stores in the crowded, traffic-free shopping street, playing at bargain-hunting in this wealthy, bargainless country, drifting among the unsmiling housewives with their dreadful legs. They amazed him, these German women. They were so strictly divided between the slender shopgirls and secretaries, hair short and hennaed this year, who floated on their platform sandals and wore their jeans so tight it must've slaughtered their crotches—between these calculating blossoms and the gross wives with their suspicious piggy eyes and ape's calves. It seemed that the only thing they all had in common was their determination to ignore the increasingly shabby, unshaven man in their midst. Once in a while, Thorne caught one of them offguard, found the eyes appraising his tough, half-bared chest or his face that was still brown. But they quickly retreated into their ambition. He knew them, remembered them. He'd had them, when he was clean-shaven, athletically naked and interestingly scarred, on narrow strips of beach, when they were fiercely anxious to have their money's worth of their vacations, when they were thrilled at the thought of their own bared bodies, all greedy self-provoked lust. But here, at their duties, clothed to a colder climate, confronted by a ragged gypsy a few years too old to be stylish in this context, a man who clearly had nothing material to offer them, they were maddeningly, amusingly, pathetically other beings.

The indifferent end of August passed to a clear, golden September. In the mornings, Thorne went to the town library, looking for meaningful dates in old newspapers and town histories, anniversaries that might be used for symbolic strikes at the local military installations. His search didn't turn up much of pertinence, no obvious symbolism connected to the commissary bombing. But, in passing, he learned the life of the old town. The pomp when the Prussians came with their glittering, clattering cavalry, and the bent wives in the vineyards. The hungry years after the first war, then the now carefully edited puffing up of the national chest. Town bullies in Sam Browne belts. Then the photos from war's end, women scuffling through the ruins with loads of bricks. A French garrison, replaced by the Americans. And the incredible, determined, almost frightening leap from recovery to abundance. It was not a comfortable history to consider. He took it with him into the long afternoons, walking up out of town into the hills.

Bad Sickingen was a spa town, an affluent community even for Germany. Only the unrenewed old quarter, where Thorne now belonged, and the *Kaserne* area cordoned off by a fringe of industry had missed out on the good life. By the grand *Kurhaus*, promenades led through fanatically neat rose gardens, along a swan-patrolled river. The municipal park was bordered by nineteenth-century mansions, their driveways proud with Mercedes sedans and low Porsches, and, beyond the fountains and lawns, a web of gravel paths let the clinic patients and hotel guests stroll exactly as much of the countryside as they chose.

And the countryside was a sea of wine. The surrounding hilltops were crewcut with vineyards, long rows of vines ripening late after a moody summer, their pale-green grapes hanging in tight clusters. Above the orange and gray roofs of the town, immediately beyond a ruined castle haunted by a tacky modern restaurant, the vine dominated, clutching the sunny southern exposures and the leveled crests to where the northern slopes fell away in buff patches of grain and cut cornfields. Chains of villages disappeared into curling, hazy valleys; along dark woodlines Thorne monitored the irregular pulse of secondary roads. Until his time sense was restored by a booming training flight of NATO Starfighters. The camouflage-painted darts played supersonic tag up and down the river valleys, each afternoon was punctuated by their explosion of invisible barriers. Thorne always imagined the pilots chuckling. Pilots were great big kids, they had to be. Then he went peaceably on his way over the ridges, granting himself the slight sanity of fresh air and time out, a full ration of the stingy German sun and this inadequate bit of exercise his role permitted him. A few hours on the hoof, quiet push-ups and sit-ups morning and evening. His body already craved the tough workouts and long runs it was accustomed to. He trained hard between missions, at every opportunity, in no rush to age physically and still fighting wounds. But it didn't fit the role now, and this one was too important to him.

He'd also gone, carefully, by the *Kaserne*. The streets nearing the barracks complex went slutty with GI bars and used-car lots. Shop windows offered pimpish outfits on credit plans and plenty of loan and insurance offices promised low rates, their signs misspelled in English and Spanish. The sluggish reek of frying sausages hung in pockets between *Schnell-Imbiss* stands. Peepholed discos, dead by day, had their windows barred with iron and patched with cardboard. Even in the middle of the duty day, soldiers in sloppy green fatigues prowled the gloomy entrances and alleyways, looking to score or just hanging loose. It was all instantly familiar to him.

Across the street from the rip-off joints, behind a stone wall with a barbed-wire collar, rows of decaying barracks stood formation. Like virtually all of the U.S. Army facilities in West Germany, these billets were pre–World War II vintage, on their gables they still bore tile Maltese crosses, victory wreaths and swords. Only the swastikas had been removed or painted over. When Thorne had served his first tour up in Mainz, his platoon's billets had been so grim they wouldn't have passed as a stateside prison. Other barracks he'd seen, in Gelnhausen, Fürth, Mannheim, Fulda, Graf and Wildflecken, had been worse. A few had been halfheartedly modernized by the German government. But the best were still abysmal. The U.S. Army had never been able to justify spending any serious amount of money upgrading the living conditions of its soldiers in Germany, because they were there only on a temporary basis. For more than thirty years, the U.S. Army had been in Europe on a temporary basis, and the sons of today's privates would undoubtedly live in the same dungeons, and, when the President or his proxy came to inspect combat readiness and enlisted life styles, they would steer him to one of the two or three showcase installations, where the plumbing worked.

Thorne watched the young soldiers come and go through the main gate. Somewhere between stoics and zombies, abandoned in a snooty foreign land they could no longer afford, living in trashbins the Germans wouldn't have, feeding their families Kool-Aid and starches, bitter at the outrageous emptiness of all the promised benefits, they counted the days to home. Thorne knew them, felt himself an indebted brother, cared hopelessly about these boys and men. Now, in the peacetime, undrafted Army, the great nation he grudgingly loved had gathered together, through coercion and deceit, the poor of the nth generation, the worst of the minorities and the socially defenseless. Hadn't Marx scribbled something pertinent? That, in the final mad fit of free enterprise, the capitalists could buy a willing ally in the *Lumpenproletariat*?

Yes, the *Lumpenproletariat.* The Untouchables of the Marxist caste system, one of the unacceptable flaws. Thorne watched the parade of unexpressive faces, the tired walks. These boy-men who had been designated to stand outnumbered and ignorant on the border, the delay-and-die crowd, while back home the educated and affluent entertained themselves with the cheerful neuroses of the moment. Yes, Thorne thought, remembering how, even with the draft, the front-line grunts who'd got themselves shot up beside him had rarely been the middle-class college kids. There had been a few odd pilgrims, but society's expendables had done the big-time dying.

Above the busy main gate, an arched sign, flanked with absurd wooden cowboys, proclaimed the *Kaserne* to be the headquarters of the 64th Infantry "Trailblazer" Division. Yes, Thorne thought, I have run the long miles, combat boots in the Georgia sun, and I went through the Nam craziness and the drab garrison life and the desperate paydays that can't have changed much since the first cave got itself designated a barracks. I've been ripped off with them and I will never forget the sputtering rides in prayer-powered choppers or the dumbfounded look of the semi-retarded, McNamara's Hundred Thousand, with their bellies splashed all over a jungle trail, too dumb to know they're already dead. Yes, he thought, there are some things I'm bitter about. And that was how it was with the commissary. The charred façade of the building was guarded by an MP. But it was wasted duty. There was nothing left to guard, and the MP knew it. He looked bored. The blast had been a big one—much more powerful than the most lurid newspaper accounts or even his briefing from Ferry had led Thorne to expect. The entranceway gaped; the glassless window frames showed splintered beams and daylight where the roof had collapsed. A few plastic tarps billowed and gasped, useless as Band-Aids pasted on a man who'd been blown apart. Thorne strolled around the side of the ruin, keeping his distance, only to be met by the shrieking laughter of a half-dozen kids who came running out of a gutted side door, grabbing at each other, faces camouflaged with soot.

The damage was even worse in the rear. The back wall of the building had ceased to exist. Thorne was stunned by the extent of the wreckage. He'd seen the results of plenty of terrorist bombings: banks, buses, airline offices, gendarmerie posts. There was always a lot of glass, with infernal amounts of paper. And perhaps a bundled body or two. But the commissary looked as though it had been hit by an air strike. He'd never seen anything like it in a country at peace. Twenty-two dead. The figure was only beginning to come real to him. Those were battle casualties, and heavy ones. In Beirut he'd seen company-sized elements fire each other up all day long, with each side losing at most two or three killed and a handful of wounded. In Nam there'd been major firefights with far lower body counts. Twenty-two dead. He poked closer to the blackened brickwork, thinking how it must've been.

There'd been two separate bombs, he could see that from the way the roof had dropped. Christ, they'd known what they were doing, they'd known the construction of the building from the inside. The newspapers had been screaming Baader-Meinhof, *Roter Mor-*

gen, radical youth trained in Palestinian guerilla camps. If they were right, it meant the quality of instruction was improving. To say nothing of the quality of the demolitions gear. The bombing had unquestionably been the work of experts. Yet the newspapers had made it sound like a crude job, another in a long line of terrorist incidents. And they hadn't made any mention of two bombs.

Ordinarily, he could understand the newspapermen getting it wrong. But this time they'd been quoting police reports. And the *Polizei* weren't stupid. Besides, they would've been working with the U.S. Army on this one. And the U.S. Army had men who knew how things were blown up.

He wished he could talk to Ferry, to find out what the follow-up reports had said. The operation had gotten under way so fast that he hadn't had access to any technical data. Probably by now there were leads he knew nothing about, details they were keeping from the general public. It was the only reasonable explanation for the misinformation in the newspapers. Over and over again they'd quoted German police reports. Thorne ached for the chance to shuffle through Ferry's in-box. But he couldn't risk breaking his cover before the job had even begun. He wished he at least had access to a secure line. But there was nothing. He was on his own.

Twenty-two dead. Thorne stepped over a burn-cancered beam. He had to have a closer look. Anyway, the lone guard was at the other end of the building. And he could always fall back on the Germans' reputation for ghoulish curiosity. Roast brick and garbage crunched underfoot. After nearly a month, the fire smell and the tang of rotting food still rose sharply at the least breath of wind. If you looked closely, you could still make out the pattern of the aisles, like streets in an excavated city, rows of black ash speckled with bits of color. The beginning of one aisle was littered with shreds of cereal boxes that had been burned, then soaked with rain. Tony the Tiger's grin was still recognizable in the faded jigsaw pieces.

The gang of kids swarmed back in through a breeched wall. They were happy, the ruin was a fascinating place to play in. They kicked cans, poked piles of filth and yelped. Thorne waited for the MP to poke his head around a corner and tell them all to beat it. But the gleaming helmet never appeared.

The kids skirted Thorne, quieting a little when their chasing brought them within a certain perceived range. Now and then they glanced at him with curious eyes, until a stumble brought their attention back to the clutter underfoot.

Some of the victims would've died directly from the blasts, of course. Crushed, torn, hurled. Others would've burned. And when anyone was badly burned, you could only be grateful if they died on the spot. It hardly seemed worth the vast pain to hang on for a few weeks in a burn ward.

Why? Why had men done this? If the bombers had known the layout of the building so well, they must've known who used it. Mostly wives, pushing carts and tugging their rug-rats. Maybe a few loitering soldiers. But if you wanted to take on the Army, why not go after the brass? Hit a headquarters. Or go after a weapons storage area. Or even a barracks. Something *military*, for God's sake. But not this.

Of course not even all of the blasted or shredded would've died right away. They would've remained there, in their snapped-bone postures, gasping in the hot smoke and dust. Their eardrums would probably have been smashed, though they wouldn't have realized that right away. The conscious ones might've wondered whether help would reach them before the fire did. Of course none of them would've seen much with all the smoke, and most likely they'd wasted their last thoughts on the dullest things. Worrying about dinners that wouldn't be ready on time, or a bowling tournament that would have to be missed. Surely one or two of the more analytically minded would've tried to figure out exactly what had happened. And some would've felt pure joyful gratitude that they were still alive after the holocaust, rejoicing right up until the moment the fire touched them or their hearts suddenly stopped. No. No, that wasn't right. They would've all been worried about breathing. In the furious smoke. The inability to suck in enough oxygen focused your attention pretty hard. Had it been like drowning? In hot dust? Had the Jesus fans managed to wedge in an instant of prayer? Bleeding and gagging and burning alive on a bed of Oreos and Saltines.

Thorne had firm beliefs about terrorism. Those terrorists who struck at the heads of state, at the captains of industry and the hanging judges, whether you liked their politics or not, had some claim to be revolutionary soldiers. They chose targets who bore real responsibility for the state of affairs the terrorists stood against. And it wasn't enough to reply that Moro or Buback or Schleyer or Ponto or any one of them was a civilian. In these days of total war, of total systems, the leaders of every category had willingly accepted the rewards of their responsibilities, and they had to accept the random penalties as well. Tough shit. Thorne had no sympathy for them.

But the scum who machine-gunned crowded restaurants, who burned packed theaters, who blew up planeloads and busloads and commissaries full of dumb followers, of bit players, slaughtering the at-least-relatively innocent—these true terrorists deserved payment in kind.

The kids were playing hide-and-seek now. Three of them flushed squealing out of their cover, then disappeared again.

A stick tapped Thorne's shoulder.

Startled, he turned more quickly than he would've liked. He expected to meet the MP. But it was an old man in a gray Bavarian-style hat. A red-white-and-black *Bild* newspaper stuck out of his raincoat pocket. He was very short and his entire face was nicotine yellow. He'd touched Thorne with his cane.

He smiled conspiratorially and gestured for Thorne to follow him. He led the way back along the aisles, poking the rubbish with his stick.

"The children don't know how to do it," he said. His voice might've been continuing a conversation with an old friend. "They don't know where to look. During the war, we knew." He chuckled. "We had many opportunities to practice. We made wonderful games out of it. Horrible to think about it now, the things we used to find."

He stopped without warning, and Thorne nearly walked into him. The man poked deep into the ashes with his stick.

"They give up too easily," he said. "Just after it happened, the people were here in swarms. But even the older ones don't remember how to search properly. They've gotten fat. They've forgotten."

Down in the frothing ashes Thorne glimpsed hard white. At first he thought it was true bone, but an instant later the old man had uncovered a plate of false teeth.

"There's a great deal more," he said. "It's a treasure house, if you know where to look. I come here every day. For old times' sake. During the war you got so you could find food in the most extraordinary places. Like the miracle of the loaves and the fishes. Now they've bombed the Americans. The Amis didn't listen to us. In 1945 we said to them that it was time to settle our differences and fight the Russians together. But they wouldn't listen. Now look at this. The Communists want to kill every man, woman and child who has a decent life. Together we could've finished them off—driven them from the face of the earth. But it's too late now. We have no discipline anymore, no leaders. Everything would've been all right, if only the Americans had listened. We could've swept the Communists from the face of the earth. Now look at this."

The kids came screaming through again, howling in mock terror. They bunched and raced and collided.

The old man looked at Thorne, and Thorne saw that he wasn't even so old. It was only that all the vitality was diminished, as if by creeping disease. His eyes were as yellow as his skin.

"They don't know where to look," he muttered one last time. But he was obviously talking to himself now. Thorne had ceased to exist for him, and he turned his back, shaking his head in disgust. He went poking his way with his cane, stopping now and then to jab fanatically at a likely spot before moving on in disappointment. Thorne watched him for a while, trying hard to feel something decently human. Then he gave it up and turned away himself.

Heading back down the blighted street, he watched a team of resigned junior enlisted men policing up butts and candy wrappers from the sidewalk by the main gate. None of these young soldiers could know him, and, even if any of the older men he'd brushed up against in his uniformed days were to come out of the headquarters, he doubted they'd recognize him. But, despite the longer hair, the bristling beard and the denim, he remained one of them. He'd always hated the U.S. Army, he'd never wanted to be in it, he'd never planned to stay in it. But he felt helplessly responsible for it. It was like a bitch-wife crippled in a car wreck. You couldn't leave. Somebody had to empty the bedpan.

From a trash-peppered alley, a young black soldier called softly to Thorne in ungrammatical but effective German, asking if he wanted to score. Thorne almost answered in English. Then he thought better of answering at all and walked on.

He went back through the now improving neighborhoods, past the last small factory and the railyards, into the neat and lovely town, past the brilliant shops and busy restaurants, across the river, into the medieval alleyways that were scenic to wander down but pits to live in. Up in his room, he sat by the opened window, line of sight commanding sagging rooftops spiny with antennas, and wrote in longhand.

It came quickly, the way the best and worst of his poems did, and a few crumpled or corrected sheets later he'd finished, for better or worse:

In Garrison

Is any loneliness comparable
to that of the soldier?

In this foreign land,
worried by the hard, odd tongue,
where men are briefly decent
for a price,

and the women are schooled in ice,

a dream of other years
climbs inevitably
from bad wine.
They breed slow time here.

In the wind-chewed night,
on the eastern wall,
the bundled guard fights sleep.
There is a half-remembered
trust to keep.

If only the barren dawn
leaked threats of sudden smoke
a march away! What heart
would be afraid
of those sweet
barbarian hoofbeats?

He made himself a cup of instant on the hot plate and relaxed, reading the piece through to the renewal of the caffeine. He couldn't judge the quality yet, but he knew it was a finished piece. And he'd meant this one, more truly than he'd meant any of them in a long time. He would've liked to hang on to it, to read it again after the lapse of a few days, to test its worth. But these lines certainly were not part of the role, and he burned all the drafts in the ancient wall sink.

4

That night, he went to the Soonwalder Hof. He'd already scouted the location, it was tucked down a stale alley not far from his room. You turned in between a row of fermentation tanks and a decaying open-front stable that now sheltered a gutted Ford Taurus stranded on cinder blocks, stepping carefully in the poor light because of missing cobblestones and the abundant dogshit. The way led between cramped rows of glamourless old houses. Rugged shutters leaked blades of light, and swift voices complained in a stew of southern languages. The wandering dinner odors were different here, instantly familiar to him. He recognized the chime and slither of the music cranked to distortion on cheap portable tape players. Above one doorway, a crude sign the size of a license plate announced, with crescent and star, the Turkish Social Club. A tiny grocery shop offered a windowful of Middle Eastern canned goods and bottled fruit drinks, all the labels printed in harsh, inaccurate colors. The shop's door had been plastered over with pictures of Bulent Ecevit and Mustafa Kemal.

Suddenly German, a weathered inn-sign showed a mounted hunter in pursuit of a leaping stag. Shadows on curtains turned conversationally to one another, and a spray of deep laughter invited the passerby inside.

The Soonwalder Hof.

One evening during his get-acquainted period, before he was ready to move, he'd heard a strummed guitar and a strong voice from inside, an old folk song about a robber with two pistols. He'd almost gone in then, drawn from his solitary walk to the glad community of music. The time hadn't been right, but it had been difficult to pass by, he'd had to give himself marching orders. He'd always had trouble with music. As a brand-new butterbar at Ranger school, he'd rappelled unflinchingly down shit-liquefying cliffs, he'd leaped out the cold doors of C-130s by night and he'd spent a sleepless eternity in the swamps, moving through the crotch-high broth in thorough blackness while the slithering residents flirted by, now and then bumping into your thigh with heart-stopping suddenness. Each morning another poor bastard had been dropped from training with a leg swollen so severely they had to cut away his trousers. But he'd marched through all that with acid in his guts and his soul locked on target. Only to come triumphantly and exhaustedly into garrison, then break down crying outside a barracks window because they were playing a dull-witted song about going to San Francisco with flowers in your hair. San Francisco was one assignment he had definitely not been earmarked for, and the song possessed him as unutterably tragic and beautiful, under the circumstances. He'd leaned against the wall in the darkness and shrubs and shadows, listening and crying quietly, very much in doubt, certified that day as one of the best-trained killers in the world. Later, in Nam, he'd understood the crazies who risked their lives by going out on patrol with a transistor radio plugged into one ear. He'd never been one of them, and he'd smashed enough pocket transistors to open his own PX. But he'd understood.

The front door had an old lever-and-latch handle, then there was a hallway, with another door to the right marked *Gaststube*.

"Abend," Thorne said, entering the smoke, the murmur and body warmth. A few cursory replies acknowledged his greeting, a couple of stares tracked his progress. But, for the most part, the conversations and the hands of skat continued. He immediately sensed a different atmosphere here, an exceptional coldness. None of the tight camaraderie he'd imagined from outside while listening to the folk song. Neither was there a genuine communal reaction to his stranger's intrusion. It felt as though people remained strangers here, the tables seemed grimly separate. There were a few clusters of the standard-issue laborers winding down, and a regulars' table of ancient men in dark suits. But fully half the crowd wore long hair and beards, jeans and pullovers. A kid with purple welts on his face and a small gold earring sat on the edge of a conversation, rolling his own cigarette. A big, plain girl in a bulky gold turtleneck sat calmly at a

noisy table, reading what looked like a textbook. The coat racks were loaded with hooded NATO jackets and secondhand U.S. Army field jackets. No other Americans, though.

Thorne hung his leather jacket on one of the communal racks and sat down at the vacant end of a long table. A moment later he reached down along the burn-speckled tablecloth for a newspaper that lay abandoned.

Nothing radical, just the local edition. Another spy scandal in the Bundestag, an anxious rabies warning. Dead fox found on Mannheimer Strasse. There were no menus, he simply ordered a glass of dry white from the tubby proprietress. She promptly returned with a small water glass full of surprisingly good wine. Worn wooden floors, old chairs, an old coal stove in the middle of the room reminded Thorne of the bitter coaltown winters of his childhood. Classic leftist joint, if ever there was one.

Laughter crackled from one of the tables like hostile fire from a woodline. Thorne recognized it as the same laughter that had sounded so hearty and inviting from the alley. The surrounding tables ignored it.

Thorne examined the crowd in greater detail now, taking his time, dipping in and out of the paper. He ruled out the worker types, at least for the present, and a table of rotten-toothed young drunks. But he was left with plenty of possible suspects who fit the ridiculously vague description. Long hair and a beard. Christ, it was the national uniform. Thorne felt an anxious chill. There was no interest in him at all here, he wondered just how in the hell he was going to break into any of the small, private groups, let alone the right one.

The door opened.

It was the police. Two of them, one a huge orange-haired monster with a Vandyke beard. Thorne had seen the monster around, it was impossible to spend any great amount of time in Bad Sickingen and not notice him. The other cop was of medium height and build, but looked runty by comparison. They both wore peaked hats and green leather coats. And nine-millimeter automatics, Thorne knew.

The room had immediately gone quiet, dividing itself between those who watched every move the cops made and those who were determined to appear to ignore them.

It was truly a hard crowd. Thorne could read it now, he'd felt this kind of chill before. In those same coaltown bars, when the cosmic weather was wrong. And in Beirut, in a joint frequented by unholy Christian militiamen and gunrunners.

The smaller cop positioned himself just inside the door, monitoring the crowd, hand on his holster now. The monster plunged in between the tables, eyeing faces until they turned away. *He* was enjoying himself. Thorne had acquired a clear feel for bully boys. There were so many, on both sides.

Suddenly the monster stabbed a paw out to one side and grabbed a huddled kid by the hair. He yanked him backward over the chair, virtually lifting him, splashing the room with beer. He drew the kid to his tiptoes, then slammed the side of his face down on the tabletop.

"Not a move," the monster said.

The kid obeyed. The entire room obeyed. The kid's face was turned in Thorne's direction, white indoor skin and terrified eyes. He drooled and blew pink spittle, he gasped and the veins throbbed like fat worms in his temples. The monster cuffed him, making it hurt.

Motion erupted from the next table down. A girl— the textbook girl—was on her feet, sweeping a wave of beer up across the big cop's face.

"Ass-licker," she shouted, "fascist." She stood facing the startled cop, leaning sharply toward him in her too-big gold sweater, as though she were about to leap across the table at him. She drew in enormous breaths like a bull.

Thorne expected the monster to shoot a hand into her long loose hair, to yank her down, too. You didn't fuck with the *Polizei*.

But the big cop was surprised, the world held still between them. Thorne looked to the backup man, who stood tensed in the doorway, fingers nervous on leather, then looked back at the girl.

She was good. Gutsy, for sure. She was no beauty, but she looked awesome now, a big peasant girl standing alone against the oppressor, the stuff bad, stirring paintings were made of. A heroine for the barricades, and, maybe, his ticket inside.

Her tableload of long-haired companions had frozen. There was one genuinely rough-looking dude in the bunch, a muscle-boy with a Zapata mustache and a big steel cross on his chest, but even he was either unwilling or unable.

The girl's face was still set hard, but her breathing faltered now. She'd obviously surprised herself as well as the monster. She blinked a few quick times and Thorne thought it was over. The shock was draining fast, he expected the big cop's hand to strike out any moment now. Beer beaded and dripped down his face and into his whiskers.

On the tabletop, the cop's prisoner shut his eyes, tightly, as if expecting the storm to break over his head.

Thorne stood up. Slowly. He didn't want to panic the backup man. He stood up, stepped delicately away from his chair, and started walking. The big cop shifted sideways now, the step almost a boxer's dance, sure of his center of gravity.

He's not a bully, Thorne thought. He's a killer.

Thorne squeezed between the tables, keeping an obvious distance. He looked the big cop directly in the eyes.

And they were powerful, intelligent eyes, Nordic blue. The big cop wasn't a dumb beast. The eyes commanded Thorne to stop, to retreat, to give up whatever he was doing. But Thorne put one foot slowly in front of the other. The big cop's eyes were clear and furious, a bit crazy.

A killer, Thorne thought, with imagination.

He worked determinedly toward the girl, stepping through the minefield. He had the feeling of repeating an act for the thousandth time. He could've closed his eyes and felt the flickering of leaves on his cheeks, the tug of old roots gone mad. You held your rifle out vertically before you, testing the blackness, and you lifted your feet and placed them ever so carefully down. Here, amid men and light and smoke, a civilization away, it was the same.

They were out there, deadly, waiting for your mistake.

He arrived, finally, at the girl's side. The monster had followed Thorne's progress with his entire body, traversing as smoothly as the gun on a tank, keeping Thorne fixed in his field of fire.

Wait it out, man, Thorne thought, just wait it out a little longer.

Thorne laid his hand on the girl's shoulder, on hot wool.

"Sit down," he told her.

For a long second, he thought she was going to ignore him. He pressed slightly.

And she sat down. Without looking at him, without taking her eyes off the cop. Then, abruptly, she broke the stare, and the worst of the tension. She dropped her head confusedly and pushed back her hair with a shivering hand.

Thorne looked back to the cop, expecting to find the furious eyes waiting for him.

But the big cop had lost interest in him now. He was looking down at the girl from on high. Something that was almost a smile spread his set whiskers. He leaned down toward the girl, as if bowing, and said:

"Fräulein Burckhardt."

It was a greeting, as nonchalant as though he'd met her passing in the street. He watched her a moment longer, hunting a response. But the girl wouldn't look up at him now. Her fear was as definite in the air as the reek of the hurled beer.

The big cop returned suddenly, energetically, to his

job. He yanked his prisoner to his feet and rammed him toward the door. The kid skidded and rushed, struggling to keep his balance, with the monster shoving him open-handed, hard enough to knock the wind out of his lungs.

The backup cop had the door opened, waiting. The monster herded his prisoner out into the hallway, thumped him sickeningly off the wall and disappeared with him into the night.

The backup cop swept a last rearguard scan over the crowded room, then backed out into the hall. At the sound of the street door clacking shut, the girl smashed both her fists down on the tabletop. She was crying and shaking now. She beat the table again. Then she twisted her fists into the tablecloth, loony with nerves, making no effort to hide her tears.

Tables competed for the attention of the proprietress. The place drained. No one said a word to the girl, or even looked at her. Her own tableload of friends faded off in tattered field jackets. Except for Zapata the tin-crossed muscle-boy. He drew out a pouch of tobacco and began preparing himself a cigarette. Either he wasn't very experienced at rolling his own or he was near panic.

Thorne stood over the girl, wondering if she were a killer, waiting for her to finish crying. He had to wait several minutes before the vigor died into sobs and a wet nose, till the pressure of the fists eased slightly. It went on too long, and he began to feel clumsy standing over her. He put his hands into the pockets of his jeans, and just then she turned her face up to him. Asking what he wanted. She had brown eyes, washed almost green now, the whites all muddled and flushed.

"Are you all right?" Thorne asked, and added quickly, "May I sit down?"

Her male companion had remembered a little toughness now, and he cut the girl off before she could answer. He smirked up at Thorne.

"Fuck off, you old shit."

5

The girl stood up. She had a wide, graceless face that was all sorrow now. She retreated slightly, hardly an inch of physical movement, but it read as though her companion had insulted her and not Thorne, as though he'd slapped her.

"Uwe," she said. "Don't. It's bad enough."

Her friend turned on her, yelling, nervous, savage. *"You.* You're crazy. You crazy bitch. You're *crazy."* He lifted himself up off his chair as he spoke, snarling at her like a chained dog. The cigarette he'd been rolling so painstakingly was mashed in his hands now.

"Uwe. I'm sorry. I'm so sorry."

There were tears in her eyes again, just buds, not anger or frustration or fear for herself now. She laid her hand on Uwe's shoulder, gentle as a mother with a sick child.

He shook it away, slapped at it. He threw his mess of failed cigarette off the table and began again. But he couldn't hold the papers steady enough to lick them. He threw them away, flinging them toward the girl.

But the paper shreds had no weight, as soon as they left his hand they fluttered back toward him.

"Go," he shouted at her. He twisted to face her, couldn't quite meet her eyes. "Go. Get out. Get *away* from me."

"Uwe. Come home with me."

Uwe shut his eyes tightly, tremendous violence compressed into the miniature slamming of bits of skin. His face lost color, as though sudden sickness had gripped him, then he sighed. He fit his face in his hands, leaning wearily on the tabletop now.

"Just go," he said. "Please go, Maria." He lifted his head just enough to expose the eyes to the light, hands prayer-folded over his nose and mouth. "I'll come in a little while," he said peaceably. His eyes were faintly watery, spacey now. All the toughness was gone. When he spoke again, his voice was sad, defeated, sick with the failure to act when his lover had needed help most. "Your friend here," he inclined his head slightly toward Thorne, "can take you home." He snorted. "Shit. You'll be safer with him."

The girl looked her man—her boy—over. A big, wide girl. Not fat. But not one of the world's beauties, either. She looked lovingly, maternally, down at her man, eyeing him up and down as though making sure he was dressed warmly enough to go outdoors.

"I'm going now," she told him quietly. She picked up her textbook. And she went, simply, with no fuss, shutting the door behind her with just the slightest snap of anxiety.

Thorne was left standing over Uwe. The kid had given up on rolling a cigarette now, he sat thoughtfully, then looked up at Thorne. At first, anger tightened the skin around his eyes, but in a moment the expression loosened into calm contemplation. Then the eyes opened to a despair that looked right through Thorne.

"Shit," Uwe said softly.

Thorne turned away, the last soldier standing unscathed amid the casualties. The girl had maybe half a minute's lead.

He caught up with her at the Turkish Social Club, in the faint reach of a streetlamp. He'd come up behind her with an unintentionally quiet step, the habit of long years, and he spooked her. She turned sharply toward him, eyes huge, hands half lifted to fend off an attack.

Thorne stepped back. "Are you all right?" It was still the only approach he could think of. "I was worried about you." He tried a friendly smile on her.

The fear still owned her for a few seconds after she'd recognized him, but while he was speaking it clicked off. He could feel the intelligence spark back up in her.

She looked at him with curiosity. "You're not a German, are you?"

"No."

Another, slighter fear thrilled through her eyes, an odd response, then that became curiosity, too.

"Who are you?" she asked. A stranger on a train.

"Jack Thorne." He had her name from the cop and her lover, but he let her tell him.

"Burckhardt. Maria Burckhardt. You're English? American?"

"American."

She giggled. It was a strange, grown-up sort of giggle, a tiny laugh at herself. It trailed into sad eyes and a twisted mouth.

"So that's why you came to help me," she said. She was unmistakably disappointed. "I should've known, should've thought . . ."

"Thought what?"

She turned casually back into her stride, but the feel of the action hadn't excluded him. He fell in beside her.

"Oh, nothing," she said. "Obviously, you don't know the German police. It could've been very bad for you."

"And for you?"

She giggled her little self-kidding laugh again. "Oh, that's my problem. It wasn't your fight. You don't know me, you don't know the circumstances. But you were quite brave. I admit that, and I admire it. Whether you knew the German police or not. You were very good. Everyone's so afraid these days." She let a pause go by, a thought, a death. "Who are you really?" she asked.

"Why, Jack Thorne, madame. Poet, traveler . . . cosmic beast of burden . . ."

She passed over his humor. "A poet?" she said seriously, doubtfully.

"Well, I suppose that's not the humblest possible way to introduce myself, but it's what I do."

She remained completely earnest, his humor simply wasn't there for her. "But no one reads poetry anymore. How do you live?"

"Not terribly well, I'm afraid. But I get by. A few

people do read poetry, a loyal handful. And I do magazine pieces. Lot of travel stuff. If you're going to Izmir, and that kind of thing."

"You're a writer, then."

"I honestly prefer to think of myself as a poet."

"But not a serious writer."

"What's a serious writer?"

"You don't embrace issues, you don't tell how the world really is."

"Hold on a minute, Maria. And, besides, how is the world, really? You're jumping to conclusions. You haven't read my poetry."

"I don't read poetry."

"Now, that's a shame. I was just published in German. First time, too. In *Rote Fahne.*"

He'd got her that time. He had to hold back a smile. Bull's-eye.

They walked in silence for a block or so. The girl clutched her arms to herself, just under her breasts. The nights were growing cold, her sweater wasn't enough. Thorne was just fine in his jacket, with a ghost of wine in him. He sympathized with the girl. He'd been cold. It was incredible how cold the torrid regions of the earth could become at night.

Finally she said, "So. You're an American poet who is published in *Rote Fahne,* who rescues strangers from the German police. I find this somewhat unusual, Mr. Thorne." She pronounced it "Torn," hopelessly German when it came to enunciating *th.*

"Call me Jack. Please."

"What are you doing in Bad Sickingen?"

"Oh," Thorne said, strolling out his answer, "I've been here before."

"Yes?"

"I've been here before, that's all. I was here years ago, when I was younger and different, and I wanted to come back now."

"And why is that?"

"You ask a lot of questions, Maria. Maybe I'll tell you the answer to that one if and when I get to know you a little better. For now, let's just say I'm building the New Jerusalem, and let it go at that."

"I don't understand that."

"Probably doesn't translate. It's sort of from a poem. From a time when our lives were poems."

"I don't read poetry."

Thorne smiled, genuinely amused at her strictness. "You told me that. What do you do?"

"I study. Medicine."

"The textbook." Thorne thought for a moment. "But there's nowhere to study here."

"I study in Mainz. At the university. I take the train in the mornings."

"Long way to go every day."

"Not really. And it's not every day. Besides, Uwe's job is here."

"Medicine. That sounds fine. More useful than poetry."

"Mr. Thorne—"

"Jack. Please call me Jack. I really will feel like an old shit."

She let the reference pass, there was something more important to say.

"Jack, you seem like a very nice man, and I want to say something to you very honestly. You should not go back to the Soonwalder Hof. Perhaps you shouldn't even stay in Bad Sickingen—have you been here long?"

"A few weeks. Several, actually. I have a room in the Kirnergasse."

"Oh? I have a friend who lives there."

"Kirnergasse twenty-two?"

"No, a different building. But I know number twenty-two. You mustn't be making very much money writing your poetry."

"People don't do everything for money."

"Germans do."

"That doesn't sound very patriotic."

"I'm not patriotic. I hate this country. When I become a doctor, I'm going to leave. I'm going to go where doctors are needed. I *hate* it here." For a moment she was, again, the crusader of the sloshed beer. "The people are terrible, and the government's worse. A herd of fascist pigs. *Bas*tards."

She had fury. And yet. He couldn't find murder in her voice. She sounded brilliantly angry, sincere, and a little bratty. A medical student. Going to go where doctors were needed. And her warning to him not to go back to the Soonwalder Hof. Underneath her temper she seemed all youth and decency.

But he didn't know her, and he realized it. He didn't know her devils. And the old bloodthirst slept in everyone, didn't it?

"Why did you say I shouldn't stay in Bad Sickingen?"

She stopped. She turned to face him in the bad light, searching him out. "Because you helped me. And I don't want it to turn out badly for you. You don't know what's going on here."

"I know your police lack a certain charm."

"It's not a joke. They're ruthless. And Krull's the worst. He's the big one with the orange hair. He's a madman." They began walking again. Some of the strictness, and all of the fury, passed out of her, there was sorrow, even despair in her voice now, she was no longer guarded before a stranger. "Oh, God," she said. "I tell myself that I live in a civilized nation, where the police protect the people and there is some justice, however harsh. I tell myself this, and can't believe it anymore. Do you know that the American Army commissary here in Bad Sickingen was bombed?"

"No," Thorne said.

"Perhaps it was before you arrived. It must've been. You would've known. It happened over a month ago, in August. That was the beginning."

She fell silent again, walking out her thoughts. Thorne was excited now, struggling to keep his outward cool. The scent was finally in the wind.

"The beginning?" he said, awkwardly late, prodding.

"The beginning," she said, "of the craziness. This town is crazy now. The police have all gone mad. It's been terror. And tonight . . . tonight I behaved so foolishly. They'll make it bad for Uwe."

"Terror," Thorne said, "is a strong word."

They drifted along in another of her tantalizing silences. She was full of private visions now. Thorne knew that the smart thing to do would be to beg off now, not to push any further tonight, to plead diverging paths and go home to his room and think. But it was nearly impossible to do.

"Terror," she said suddenly, "is exactly the word. How I wish, even now, that I could believe in a government as beneficent as the God they teach to children. I had a friend. *We* had a friend. The police questioned him, just as they've questioned all of us. About the bombing. They're desperate over it. They questioned our friend. He isn't—wasn't even so far left, really. DKP, but only out of loneliness, I think. The police questioned him, and they let him go. Two days later—last week—he was found dead from an overdose of heroin."

"Junkies die," Thorne said.

"Yes," the girl said, "but this friend of ours never used drugs at all."

Believe no one, Thorne reminded himself. Trust no one. But check it all out. And, if it was true, why hadn't it made the local paper? He didn't remember reading about it. Of course, he hadn't been looking for it, either. One more smack-freak gone.

Tomorrow he would go through the back papers in the library.

Christ, wouldn't they be some kind of cops. Not unbelievable, though. Then he caught himself. Why, all of a sudden, did his hacked, hammered and imperfect instincts want to trust this girl? Because she seemed so big and plain and sincere? Because he hadn't had any pussy in a month? Or was it a reaction to the big cop's loutish behavior, the result of his own dislike for bully boys? And what about the girl's nasty, temperamental lover? Little old Uwe. He'd been plenty scared when the shit seemed to be coming down around him, but Thorne could picture him doing the job with a bomb. One with a long time delay. And the cops were, after all, on Thorne's general side, until proven otherwise. No big deal, either. There were plenty of shits riding with the good guys.

When the girl spoke again, her guard had gone back up. "If you live in the Kirnergasse, you've already come far out of your way. I'll be all right, I live in the next street."

He was being dismissed. And it was time to go. You never crowded. You had to give the illusion of room to move and air.

"Are you sure everything's okay?"

"Oh, yes. Uwe'll be coming along. Thank you for your help."

She held out her hand, the European shake. Thorne stuck out his own, found her warm. The cold girl in the old sweater. Was she a killer? Did she know killers?

"Good night," she said.

"Auf Wiedersehen," Thorne called in her trail.

6

The next morning was gusty and gray, the autumn offensive was in full swing now. Thorne had a late breakfast of coffee and rolls in a downtown café, feeling tired and half hung over, even though he'd slept a full night and hadn't had an unusual amount to drink. He sat in a heart-backed chair with an embroidered seat, at a tiny, linen-covered table, surrounded by tables of chatty, upper-middle-class wives. Feeling like an old shit.

He tried to read the morning paper, but the words made only slow, shallow sense. He thought of the girl, worrying that he'd been a little taken in by her the night before. He hadn't had a conversation with anyone in so long. He cringed at the memory of the trust that had all but gushed out of him, and, at the end of a jam-covered roll, he had a sudden sense that men grew old and abilities withered. It struck him hard, the way the obvious always does when you drop your guard.

The newspaper was impossible now, an alphabet

gone mad. He let it go, ordered more coffee from the reluctant waitress. He'd have to get it together, in a little while. He would have to clear his head before he went back to the library. He knew he'd manage it. He always did his duty. He would plow alertly through the weeks of newspapers, investigating the girl's tale of heroin death. Or murder, though that definitely would not be in the papers.

He listened to the women bitch and brag on all sides of him. But their voices, like the newspaper, blurred, their language was newly foreign to him. He'd always loved travel, been glad to wake to the exotic jabber of new cities. But there was a point, it occurred to him, when travel became exile.

But hadn't it been exile all along for him? A self-inflicted wound? It seemed to him now that he'd never really enjoyed it, the constant need to move, readjust, reload the psyche. But he knew that was as much a lie as anything else. Often, very often, he'd loved it. He'd entered new lands with the same excitement he'd felt while entering fresh women. Even in Nam, there had been days . . . when he'd loved it.

Excitement? Thrills? The helpless belief that the Answer to Life waited just over the next hill?

One day, one thing—next day, another. Most likely that. But this much was certain: he was tired now.

He longed to go home. That very minute. Not only back across the miles, but back in time as well. To his family, all dead or drifted now, and to the coal banks and derelict collieries, to the brave white birches that climbed the steep heaps of black waste. To the broken towns and the plain kindness of the familiar.

Why had he always been so willing?

And why had he said that to the girl? About building the New Jerusalem? What had brought that to mind? The old password among his poli-sci classmates at the university, in the days of the Great Society, with the Asian war just a summer thunderstorm off behind the hills. How sweetly they'd all believed. They were going to go forward, in the spirit of a martyred President, to build the New Jerusalem. They'd discussed, with tremendous seriousness, the difficulty of achieving a balance between effective socialization and unrestricted personal freedom, all dreamy hows and whos, the smart girls in Shetland sweaters, their blooming tits deliciously lonesome across the chianti bottle, and he and his male friends —hadn't they been classic?—all books and beer and weekend sports, a year later with lengthening hair and the rare furtive joint and the new music. Not one of them had had uniforms and jungle firefights in mind. Then it all went crazy. And, on R & R in Bangkok, he'd met an old classmate on a hotel terrace. Larry had been ice-cold at first, outraged at Thorne for going the officer route, not wanting to even hear any explanations. He nastily called Thorne "sir." Thorne hadn't had any good explanations at that point, anyway. They'd all died. Once upon a time he'd honestly believed it his responsibility to lead, because he knew he was capable and mustn't let another do his work or die for him. But they'd died for him anyway. He'd done his best, and still the street-corner punks and the farm boys had died because of his miscalculations, and even when he did everything right they still died. He'd never believed in the war, only in obligation. Now all beliefs were chaos. And Larry stood cursing him, with tears in his eyes. He was a medic. It was, he said, his job to clean up the mess Thorne—all the Thornes—made. Thorne let him ramble. Larry was obviously stoned. He damned Thorne, but couldn't tear himself away, just as Thorne couldn't turn his back and go, wouldn't turn from anything now. Finally they sat down and drank, and, somewhere in the gin, they eased halfway together again before either of them realized it. They drunkenly joked about building the New Jerusalem, they were going to build it in Chu Lai this time. It was good for half an hour after that. But they ended by making themselves sorry, and they were both relieved when it was time to go to their separate hotels.

Thorne finished the chill, gruesome bottom of his coffee. The waitress would be glad to see him go. He remembered how, in the university, he'd been starved to know how the world really worked, what went on behind the scenes.

Now he knew.

Bravo Tree One, this is Romeo Six Niner. Going in to shut this one down. Over.

Lieutenant Thorne's last broadcast. He remembered the words exactly, he remembered the fire in the elephant grass and the way its heat fractured the air. The smoke dropping off. The entire world was silent except for the lazy flame-crackle and the decisive click of a fresh magazine going in. They were all so sure they had the little fuckers, no one surer than Thorne himself. Going in to shut this one down. Battle jacket hanging open like John Wayne's vest.

They'd got the shit shot out of themselves, walking

right into it, with by then goof-proof Lieutenant Thorne one of the first men down.

Going in to shut this one down. Mr. Macho. Then the incredible way pain hurts. His exclusive agony in a bursting world. *Not me, not me.*

The new kid whimpered over him, "He's dead, he's dead," answered by that furious scream of McCallister's:

"Shut *up. Pick him up.*"

SSG McCallister, who'd never liked him, who hated every officer, who called Thorne the great white collegeboy, had dragged him out in a poncho. Under big-time fire. He'd scooped up the bits and pieces Thorne had become and dragged him out, when he'd deserved to be left out for the wild pigs.

Over.

Thorne paid his bill and went out into the sprinkling gloom. He walked down streets as vividly foreign to him as India now, while the sky hacked and drooled. He made his slow way to the library.

The overdose had made page two. There was even a picture, Thorne half remembered it now. He hadn't been interested in the local drug scene before. The article was half death notice, half sermon.

It still didn't prove anything. The girl had as much as said police-murder. She was probably full of shit. For all he knew, this dead kid had been at the black-veined end of a longtime jones.

But he was troubled by it all. Why would she have lied to him about it? Out of doctrinaire hatred of the police? Or to scare him away? And why would she want to do that?

He realized now what he'd believed about her: her fear.

As Thorne left the library, the male librarian watched him closely to make sure he wasn't stealing anything.

Thorne went, inevitably, out past the slummy rows of barracks, to the blasted and abandoned commissary. He watched it for a while, wanting to be moved by it again, to be spurred to energetic action. But this time when he wished that this thing had never happened, it was for selfish reasons. He'd wanted this job so badly. Now it was costing him. And he could not understand exactly why.

"The mills of the gods," his father had been fond of repeating, "grind slowly—but they grind exceedingly fine."

Thorne wondered what fine point was being made to him now.

On his way back past the *Kaserne*, he stopped for a beer at a street-front sausage bar across from the main gate. He watched the tired boys in their green janitor uniforms and baseball caps slump out under the guns of the big wooden cowboys. They looked terribly young to him today. Like children. With all the playfulness punished out of them.

Two enlisted men stopped at the stand and bought bratwurst, carrying on a conversation about stereo systems. Twice they used slang terms Thorne didn't recognize. It worried him. You couldn't write poetry when you lost the living feel of your language.

It really was time to go home. Before it was too late.

He went back toward his room, with the poor day

winding down around him. In this uncontrollable torrent of memories, he felt as helpless as he'd been that day in the elephant grass. Waiting for big hands to pick him up. And he found the girl, Maria, sitting in the brown twilight at the top of his stairs, snoozing against the wall.

A textbook lay in her lap, a pile of books sat on the landing beside her. Her mouth hung slightly open, as though she'd fallen asleep while pronouncing a word.

He stood quietly below her, watching the steady lifting of her big breasts, the peacefulness of her plain face. She certainly didn't look as though she'd been born to much luck. Neither did she look like a murderess, with her chubby chin tucked into the collar of the same bulky gold sweater she'd had on the night before.

Long after he'd stopped climbing stairs, in the hush of his watching her, she sensed him. She startled, then mastered herself. When she made out positively that it was Thorne, she shut her book and stood up.

"I read your poems today," she told him.

They went together through the wet streets, darkness drooping around them like baggy pants. She'd invited him to share the evening meal with her and her lover. She walked bent forward against the fine rinse of rain, hands crammed into the pockets of her jeans. But she smiled a little now.

"You'll see that he's not a bad person," she said. "He was frightened last night. Not only for himself. I know he worries about me."

Thorne made no reply, careful of feeling now.

When he didn't make the appropriate noise, the girl carried the conversation on alone.

"We've had a very bad time lately," she picked up. "I explained to you. About the bombing . . . and our friend. It's been terrible. Houses and apartments have been searched—destroyed, really. People have been taken into police custody, questioned, let go, then picked up again. It's against the law—*their* law—the way they do it. They stretch the law, and twist it, and finally ignore it. No one complains but the victims—and no one listens to us. There's a panic in Germany. The police have only to mention the word 'terrorism,' and the law is swept away. And the law was bad enough."

"They questioned you personally?" Thorne asked.

"Yes. All of us."

"Us?"

"Everyone they even imagine to be a leftist." The holy anger was rich in her voice again. "They asked me everything, stupid things that have no bearing. Krull, the big cop, was in charge. He wouldn't let them stop. Again and again and again, they asked the same questions. What films do I see, what music do I listen to, what am I studying, who are my friends? Was I a happy child? And always: was I involved in bombing the Americans?"

"Were you? A happy child?"

She didn't answer immediately. The concentration in her face looked physically painful now. She tried to shake it away with a toss of her rain-heavy hair, and said angrily, "Why shouldn't I tell you? It's nothing for me to be ashamed of." But she wouldn't look at him. She watched the pavement up ahead. "Krull did something to me. He made me do something. After they were finished questioning me, after all the others were gone." She crumpled slightly, as though something hurt deep down in her belly. Her hands left the pockets of her jeans and she wrapped her arms around herself. "It really wasn't such a terrible thing. He made me give him oral sex. He told me he'd knock my teeth out, he said that it would feel better for him anyway, if I had no teeth. He made me get down on my knees." She shut her eyes tightly for an instant, then opened them wide, forcing herself to wake up. "I did what he wanted. It wasn't so bad. It didn't mark me. And I still have my teeth."

She suddenly jabbed her hands down into her pockets again, bracing herself up straight. She fixed a determined look on her chubby face and picked up her stride. When she spoke again the anger in her voice was all directed against herself. "I don't know why I make such a big deal out of it, telling you like this. When it doesn't even matter to me. I could do it again, if I had to. Human beings have gone through far worse. I'm only afraid I'll be forced out of the university. The police can do it, it's easy for them. At the very least, I'll lose my stipend. *That* matters."

A sudden blast rattled windows. It echoed swiftly down the valley and disappeared.

"The damned jets," Maria said. "They fly too low. They break windows and think it's a great joke. The military have a free hand in Germany. Did you know that Bundeswehr cadets in Munich had a drunken party and sang Nazi songs and threw pieces of paper marked 'Jew' into a bonfire?"

"Who do you think was responsible?" Thorne asked quietly. "For the bombing?"

"Oh, who knows. Everyone hates the Amis."

"It's all the rage," Thorne said. Then, "You believe it was a good thing? The bombing?"

In the distance, sirens began to rise. The girl looked at him curiously, her face shimmering in the rain. He wondered if he'd been too heavy-handed, too anxious. But she only said:

"I'm a medical student. I want to *save* lives."

"And the revolution?"

On the far side of the street, a board fence surrounding a construction site was scabbed with shredding posters. The wet, bubbled faces of rock stars flanked a death's head that warned the world of the viciousness of the neutron bomb.

"Oh, the revolution," she said wistfully.

"It's all the rage," Thorne said. But his voice was more delicate with her now, almost against his will.

"Do you really believe there could be a revolution in Germany, today? I don't. Revolutions need the support of the people, and the people here have too much. They want to protect it, not risk it. No, no revolution in Germany. But that doesn't mean you can give up. It means only that you have to settle for small victories, or even for slowing the triumph of evil just a little bit, diminishing it slightly." Textbook shit, Thorne told himself, leaflet slogans. And yet her voice was rending as she continued. "I talk revolution sometimes, with the others. But only because it's so important to them to believe. It's all many of them have. Can you understand that?"

"Yes," Thorne said. "I think so."

In an abruptly mundane voice, she said, "I hope Uwe hasn't run off. I told you, didn't I, that Uwe lost his job because of all this? Because of last night? They told him this morning. They said only that they didn't need him anymore. The bastards. When he does the work of three men. He's a tremendous, true worker." The true worker. And the politically conscious college girl. Thorne thought he caught a glimpse of something sad. And the girl left off worrying and complaining for a moment, running her private, indignant film clips of her lover's troubles. Then she said, bitterly, "I'll be glad to leave here."

"You're leaving?"

"Oh, yes. We'll move to Mainz. We stayed here only because of Uwe's job. And it'll save me the train ride. Besides, Mainz is very good. Do you know it?"

Golden Mainz, with the wine pubs clustered behind the cathedral, packed with girls from the university and the lively bitches from the ZDF TV. Mainz, with the lived-in dirt of a big working class and the exciting health of good business and the casinos and clubs across the river with the richies in Wiesbaden.

"No," Thorne told her.

"It's a good city," she said, stopping in front of a doorway. She lived on a too-narrow, too-busy street. "We'll be happier there."

Across the river, sirens raced.

"Must be one hell of a fire," Thorne remarked.

"Will you please hold these?" Her books. He took them from her, surprised at the weight, standing behind her as she fumbled in her bag for the key.

Door open, she took back her books and poked a

light switch, leading the way up a dusty flight of stairs. Someone in the building was cooking cabbage, and the day's nostalgia blazed back up in him. Pennsylvania blues. Cabbage was the damned state flower.

"It's at the top," she called back down over her shoulder, "like yours."

He watched her big-boned rump swagger gracelessly up the stairs in front of his face. Pale worn half-moons in the seat of her jeans. It was not a very inspiring sight. Why was it, he wondered, that the beauties never wanted to doctor the foul babies of central Africa? But it was a bad question, he knew. It was one of the easy ones to answer. And, even so, you had to leave out the word "never." He'd known beauties who'd wanted to go, or at least said they wanted to go. They just hadn't gone. But then few of the homely ones went, either. There was always another degree, or practical experience to get first. Or some dude possessed of a bit more animal magnetism than the foul babies of central Africa.

You're getting old and nasty, Thorne told himself. You had to at least give them credit for dreaming the dream. Old shit.

The girl had the key ready when they got to the top of the stairs, but before she could fit it to the lock the light went out.

"Damn," she said. "This always happens. It's automatic, you know, and our landlady keeps cutting the time shorter and shorter. As if she's training us."

She didn't bother switching the light back on, preferring to probe around the lock until the key slid in. It took her a while, there was no more grace in her fingers than in her big ass, and Thorne hoped that of all the kinds of doctors in the world she was not planning to become a surgeon.

It gave her a childish pleasure, though, to manage in the dark, and as she pushed open the door the light poured out onto her smiling face. She called her lover's name.

Then she froze, hardly a step inside the doorway. Thorne nearly walked over her. Just as the start of the scream came, Thorne shut a quick, lifesaving hand over her mouth, steadying her with his other arm.

But she was heavy, and powerful. She tumbled to the floor, shutting her eyes tightly, a kid at the horror matinee, pulling Thorne down with her, hard onto his knees, shaking her head slightly, then shaking it wildly, biting Thorne's hand. Krull, the big cop was surprised again, this time by Thorne, who was an unexpected guest. The big meaty face with the orange-red whiskers had the same bewildered look it had worn the night before, when the wave of beer swept over it. The Ingram machine pistol lay dead in the cop's huge paws. For the moment. And Thorne had time to admire the professional choice of the Ingram for a job like this. Superb noise suppressor on the Ingram.

The girl had folded herself down like a praying Moslem, face pressed into her knees, Thorne resting his hands on her back now.

He was thinking clearly now, it was beautiful how clearly he could suddenly think. His head was clearer than it had been for weeks, months. He looked over the incredible arsenal that had been arranged all over the carpet. U.S. M-60 machine gun, disassembled as if someone had been cleaning it. M-16s, good-old-antique-goddamned M-1911 forty-fives. And 9mm. Brownings from the Brits, Fabrique Nationale 7.62 NATO rifles. And, from the other side, a Dragunov sniper's rifle and a salad of the airborne-variant Kalashnikovs with folding stocks. Claymores, frag grenades, fuses, crates of ammo. All of it displayed ridiculously and falsely, brilliantly and picturesquely around the sofa where Uwe lay twisted and open-eyed and dead, assault rifle in hand. There was a good, tight shot-group in the kid's chest. The whole spectacle was marred only by the fact that the weapon in the kid's hand didn't have a magazine in it.

"Stand up," the big cop said. He was over his surprise now.

"Maria," Thorne said softly. He lifted her with all his gentleness. But the weight resisted. She sobbed and quivered and hid from the light.

Thorne was a miracle of calm inside. The Zen of war. He was able to think clearly and pityingly of the girl's sorrow and of the terrible fear she must have, watching her from a cloud.

Police vehicles *beepburp-beepburp*ed in the distance, rushing toward them. The operation was clearly being run on a tight timetable.

"Get her up," the cop said, "or I'll kill the both of you there."

Thorne knew that the girl wasn't going to die—at least that this man wasn't going to kill her. There were several easy approaches to Krull, all of which killed two at most.

"Maria," Thorne coaxed, "get up now."

The girl cowered and wept. The heavy sweater had

slipped a small way up her back, a few inches of downy skin showed between denim and wool.

"Don't shoot," Thorne said, trying to load the sound of fear into his voice. "Just don't shoot." He got to his feet, lifting the girl by the armpits. He made sure he was firm-footed between her and the cop. "That's right," he told her soothingly.

Outside, the hoot of police vans filled the night. A few blocks, maybe.

"There," Krull said, "in the doorway." He gestured briefly, slightly with his gun. To where he wanted their bodies.

But it was enough. Thorne leaped hard-bellied onto the wrist, at the side of the machine pistol, breaking the elbow back over his knee. It took all of his weight in a forward fall to snap the thick arm back. The weapon zipped a short burst into the carpet and fell.

Instead of going over backward, the big cop only dropped sideways, into the classic pose of a mermaid. Thorne hammered his own elbow again and again into the bridge of Krull's nose, the eyes.

Outside in the street a police wagon braked to a stop and doors opened.

Krull was stunned, but he'd got a mindless grip on Thorne's hair and he wouldn't let go. Thorne felt as though his scalp would tear off, he hammered the pulping face over and over again, straining to reach the Ingram with his other hand.

But Krull's crazed grip held him out of range.

"Maria," Thorne begged.

The light went on in the stairwell and a staccato of boots drummed up the steps.

The girl suddenly picked up an M-16 by the barrel end and smashed it furiously over Krull's head. The stock broke off, drooling spring. But the cop was finished.

Thorne scooped up the Ingram and dived through the doorway onto the landing, spilling his firing position over the top of the stairs.

Three cops, half a flight down, bunched stupidly in their hurry. They didn't even have their weapons drawn, one lugged a press camera. It was all supposed to be over with.

This was big. Jesus. He hadn't even begun to think about it yet, but he knew it was big.

"Halt," Thorne screamed. "Hold it."

The hall light went out.

Thorne rolled instantly out of the path of doorlight from the apartment, firing low into the remembered frieze.

A voice howled, one pistol boomed in reply, the noise outrageous in the enclosed stairwell, rounds punching the wall above him. Thorne put his last burst on the flash, then launched himself back into the apartment.

Maria was sitting on the sofa, mothering dead Uwe, removed from time. Her face had the sexless beauty of a madonna in a backwater chapel, modeled after a peasant girl dead half a dozen centuries. She cradled the dead boy gently and lovingly, unconcerned that she made a perfectly framed target for anyone coming up the stairs.

Thorne kicked the door shut behind him and yelled, "Get on the floor."

But the girl didn't pay any attention to him. He scrambled over to the sprawled, bloody-headed cop and tore at the buttoned pockets. Precious seconds deserted him, time became hostile. Krull was still breathing, unkillable as the devil himself.

Finally, after perhaps three seconds, he found two beautifully heavy magazines in a jacket pocket.

He released the empty mag and fitted a full one, chambering a round. Then he lay still for a moment.

The girl's low-cadenced crying, groans from the stairwell. And still another *beepburp-beepburp* rising in the distance.

Go. Thorne lifted himself and dashed to the wall by the door. He made eye contact with the girl, waved her mean-faced to the carpet. This time she obeyed with unexpected promptness, watching him in terrified fascination as she moved.

Moans from the stairwell.

Beepburp.

Thorne switched off the light in the room and silently grasped the door handle with his left hand. He gave himself another second of perfect inner and outer stillness, then threw back the door and jumped onto the landing in a deep firing crouch.

Nothing. A pained grunting, gagging.

Weapon fixed against his hip, Thorne sent his left exploring along the wall for the light switch. He stubbed his fingers against it.

He tapped the switch and dropped low again.

The three cops lay sprawled over the stairs, half a flight down. Two of them were moving slightly, errati-cally, shying around the big hurt. The other lay recognizably dead, a sack of useless crap now. In death, he still clutched the shattered camera.

Thorne turned back to the apartment and the girl. She lay in the stream of light that flowed in from the hallway, hiding her face, covering her ears with her hands.

Beepburp.

"Come on," he ordered.

She didn't move. Fiery-nerved, Thorne felt a blast of fury at not being instantly obeyed. Didn't she realize that to survive you had to learn to obey instantly? It crossed his mind to leave her.

But he couldn't. He grabbed her by the sweater, he stretch-tore it lifting her, dragging her up in quick clumsy stages.

"Uwe," she said.

"He's dead. We're alive."

He rushed the door, determined to beat the light this time, giving himself this small goal because it was important always to have a goal and he sure as hell had not received a warning order on this one, had not had time to plan, didn't know the rules or even who all was playing. The big goal, as always, was keeping one's ass alive. But that was strategic. You had to have tactical goals along the way. He dragged the girl behind him.

She was with him now, though. It was only that she wasn't used to moving out sharply. Battle speed. She was with him, committed, only not yet fully effective in her movements.

He hurried her down through the slaughtered tangle of cops. One of them was rolling tenderly back and forth now, mewing and trying to hold his belly together. Thorne thought the girl would lose it again. But she followed obediently.

The scene outside resembled a bizarre killer disco, with the pulsing blue light of the curbed police van, the confusion of headlights and the terrifyingly loud sound of the next backup van. Thorne dragged the girl into the middle of the street and stood facing the oncoming traffic, weapon pointed theatrically at the chest of the lead driver.

White Peugeot, a bald man. He braked hard and raised his hands from the wheel. Thorne covered him and side-stepped quickly to the passenger's side.

"Get in," he told the girl. She scrambled into the rear seat, alive with fear now.

Thorne could see the blue light of the backup racing over the hump of a bridge a few blocks behind them. But there was a good pack of cars jammed back along the narrow street.

"Drive," Thorne said.

"Where to?" the driver begged. He was balding and plump, a prosperous insurance salesman. "Where to?"

Thorne had no idea. Away.

Thorne nosed the weapon against the man's cheek. The man winced and pulled his face away. The barrel was still hot.

The car began to move.

Thorne turned to the girl. Her sweater was all blood-smeared. For a moment, he went cold. Then he realized the blood was from the dead boy.

"Awake," he commanded. "Alive. In control."

The car stabbed recklessly through a brilliantly lit crossroads, leaving behind a riot of brakes and horns. The driver was a brave man in his terror.

"My God," the girl said. "Uwe."

"Forget him," Thorne said irritably. He was getting the first slivers of afteraction nerves now. "He's dead. Gone west. And we've got problems." Then he spoke to himself, in Army English. "Beaucoup big-time problems, lady."

The girl's eyes looked ahead. She screamed:

"No."

Just in time for Thorne to sense what was coming and tuck himself down.

The crash threw him hard against the dashboard, hurt his shoulder. And the spin-off spread him back onto the seat.

He looked at the wide-eyed, bloody-faced driver. The man was weeping. He began hammering at Thorne with his fists, dropping the blows down like a woman.

"My car," he complained, "my *car,* you bastard."

Thorne backed out the door. The girl was already standing in the street waiting, staring childishly at the bright bouquet of traffic. They'd smashed into a line of cars at a red light.

Thorne took her firmly by the arm.

"Come on."

He ran for the undisturbed front of the line, headline for the lead car, a pale Mercedes.

This time he shoved the girl into the back seat, forcing her over a load of packages. As soon as her rump had cleared the pile he followed her.

An old woman sat up behind the wheel, watching their antics in disapproving amazement.

"Drive," Thorne told her. *"Go."*

"I can't go," she said, in a reasonable voice. "The light's red."

Thorne didn't put on a drama with the Ingram this time. He just climbed over the seat in a chauvinistic rage, cursing all Germans. He reached across the woman's lap to the door handle, threw it open and shoved her out into the street. She landed with a bounce, on her ass, and sat there looking up at him.

"The light's red," she insisted.

Thorne squealed the Mercedes hot into the flow of traffic, heading out of town.

"Where are we going?" the girl asked from the back seat. Thorne was glad to hear a return of some life to her voice. He was glad he hadn't left her behind. There had been a point at which his strict desire to keep her alive had changed in fury to an unwillingness to let any of these incredible sons of bitches kill him. The police, yet. The damned police. He was not going to die in Germany, not at their hands, and he was not going to die until he had sorted things out. And there was plenty to sort out.

He was *angry,* wonderfully angry, on an adrenalin glory high. It was like sex after light years of abstinence. He felt *fine,* and he refused to question it just yet. He went with it.

He slashed the powerful car in and out of the lines of headlights, confident of some head start over institutional confusion. Even the Germans wouldn't be immune to institutional confusion. For the moment, he was just another obnoxiously aggressive driver.

"Where are we going?" the girl repeated. A child's voice.

"You tell me," Thorne said.

7

The girl sat beside him in the front seat now. She was functioning better, but her faculties were still scattered from the emotional blast. The villages of Rheinhessen glimmered by. Thorne's shoulder was sore and slow, but he could tell there was no serious damage. He realized how incredibly lucky he'd been to walk away—untouched—from the OK Corral. Even with the best training in the world and years of experience, you needed luck out the ass to play it one-on-one against the world like that. Luck, training and dependable weapons. The Ingram lay on the floor, a duck and a grasp away.

"You have to think," Thorne told the girl. "There must be someplace, somebody."

But the girl was thinking back, not forward.

"I don't know," she said, "I don't know."

"Think, dammit." Then he caught himself. "Please, Maria. Try to think. Out of all your friends, the people you know, the people you talk politics with, there must be somebody you think might be able to help us out. Somebody with connections."

A blue-and-white autobahn sign flashed by. Mainz or Koblenz.

"Somebody from the university, maybe?" Thorne went on. "Listen, we have a little time. But not much. We need direction."

And it was all for her sake now. He had enough time for himself. All he'd have to do would be to put a call through and sit tight. They'd pull him out. They wouldn't like it, they'd bitch, it was messy. But they'd pull him out. At least, he thought they would. But that would leave the girl.

Local national, in high-profile trouble. Thorne knew the limits. No way would they pull her out with him. And he couldn't just leave her. Not now. He'd committed himself.

He had another commitment, too. The commissary. The basic mission had not changed. But it had grown a little more complicated.

The first thing to do was to get the girl out of range. He didn't know how he'd do it yet. He couldn't use any part of the U.S. net. But he had an idea or two to play with. What he needed now was a base camp, a place where he could catch his breath, plan and make connections.

He thought of the cops again, the absolute filth of the setup they'd tried to pull off, and he smashed his fist into the dashboard in uncontrollable outrage.

The really shitty thing was that they were still on his side in the overall mission. As near as he could figure it, their convictions about law, order and justice had cracked under pressure to produce culprits responsible for the commissary bombing. He could picture it clearly. A yokel police department in the international limelight, an anxious mayor and cops worried about careers. Then throw in one crazy mean sonofabitch like Krull and give him a little authority. It sure as hell was not excusable. But it was, almost, understandable.

The ugliest part was the coldness with which they'd done it all. There had obviously been a great deal of prior planning. The incredible weapons cache had had to be assembled. And a whole scenario had been laid out. In the meantime, they had had time to reconsider their actions. But they had gone ahead.

And it would've worked. It would've been a beauty, with high-quality photos for the press. The world would've accepted the story on visible evidence. Case closed, careers saved, even furthered.

But he'd made a mess of it on them. And raised the stakes.

What had he wanted? An easy one? A black and white one?

"For Christ's sake," he told the girl, "think."

They streaked by another autobahn sign.

"Mainz," she said.

Mainz. The autobahn wasn't far now. The Mercedes would kick ass on a good highway.

"Anywhere particular in Mainz?" Thorne asked.

"Yes. I do know somebody. I think he might be able to help us."

"Tell me about him."

The girl didn't answer immediately. Thorne could see the autobahn in the distance now, a river of light.

"He changed," the girl said. Her voice was slow, discovering thoughts along the way. "I knew him in my first year of study. He was always at the center of things, he led the rallies—factions of them. He was a good speaker, he had a lot of anger. I remember being afraid of him because he spoke so intelligently about justified destruction . . . even killing. He was intelligent and merciless. Then he changed."

Thorne turned onto the autobahn entrance ramp, gunning the Mercedes up into the flow. If they were better than he was giving them credit for, they'd have the choppers out spotting already. And the autobahn exits were not all that frequent. He was opting for speed and he realized that he might've made a Big Mistake. But no guts, no glory.

"He dropped out of sight," the girl continued, "and when he began attending classes again he was a different person. He wore suits and ties—good suits —and he became a model student. But all very quietly. He never showed up at protest meetings anymore. He dropped most of his old friends."

"Maybe he just grew up," Thorne said.

"No. Not him. There was always something wrong with it, I could always feel it. Then, a few weeks ago, a friend took me by to visit him. And there, in this beautiful apartment he has, he was the same old Kurt. No. He was worse."

Thorne sighed. It sounded more promising than ringing doorbells at random, but not by much.

"What the hell," he said. "Let's give it a shot."

"Please speak German to me."

"We'll try it, Maria. See if we made the radio yet."

The girl bent obediently toward the dial, tried, found only some vile German disco music.

"Radio Hessen," she said. "News every hour."

"You all right now?"

She didn't answer.

"I mean," Thorne explained, "I . . . don't know what the hell I mean. Of course you're not all right. But are you okay? How do you feel?"

"Afraid."

"Well, don't be. I'm going to take care of you. I'm going to get you out of this."

Boy, Thorne thought, you talk a good fight. He slashed and stabbed the Mercedes from lane to lane. But the German drivers held their own. Once it had been weapons, now automobiles brought out all the savagery in the German soul.

Still no hovering searchlights.

The girl began to cry again. "I'm afraid. How can I not be afraid?" She wiped at her nose with her fingers. "Aren't you afraid?"

"No." And it was the truth. His nerves were tuned tight, and he was in a symphony of rage, but he wasn't afraid. "Everything's going to be all right."

"You can say that. You're used to this. You're used to killing."

"Wait a minute, lady."

"You're *used* to killing." She was crying and half shouting. "But Uwe's dead. Uwe's dead and I'll never be a doctor. I hate you. I hate you all." She wept down at the radio, to a stupid come-on tune sung in heavily accented English. "All those beautiful poems. All lies. You talk about changing the world. But all you do is kill. Do you really think you'll change the world with terror?"

"What?"

"You won't ever make the world a better place with

100

guns and bombs. All you ever do is hurt innocent people."

"Maria, I'm no terrorist. Holy Christ."

She wept furiously into her cupped hands, as a series of bleeps led the radio into the hour and the news.

"What are you, then?" she demanded.

Thorne shook his head. Good question. "Think what you want," he said, anxious to hear the news report. And, sure enough, they were headliners.

Bad Sickingen . . . Following the bombing of the police station—

The girl sat up with a jerk. "The sirens," she said, "that—"

—in which two police officers lost their lives, the police raided a terrorist hideout . . . In the ensuing gun battle, one terrorist was killed, while another police officer lost his life. Three other members of the police security force were wounded, two of them critically . . .

"Those sirens," the girl said again. "The jet blast . . ."

Thorne was doing arithmetic.

A second terrorist, a female, escaped. . . . The woman is known to be armed and dangerous. . . . Anyone having information regarding the whereabouts of Maria Burckhardt, age twenty-one, brown hair, weight . . .

"They don't even mention you," the girl said, unbelievingly.

"Wait. Listen."

But that was all. Iran on the verge of civil war.

"They didn't say anything about you. And you were the one. You shot them."

"And I suppose I planted the bomb in the police

station, too. While we were walking from my place to yours."

"You could've done that earlier. You were gone all afternoon. I waited a long time for you."

"Make sense."

"Nothing makes sense."

"I'm not a terrorist."

"Neither am *I*," the girl wailed.

"Listen," Thorne said. "Please. Listen to me. It's going to be all right, Maria. I'm going to get you out of this. I promise."

But he didn't know how. Right now everything depended on somebody she thought *might* be able to help. And if it was a letdown? Then what? And now this new business about bombing the police station. That made no sense at all to him yet. The police, as a rule, did not anywhere in the world blow themselves up. But the timing was just too, too slick.

Things were going too fast, as soon as he thought he had a grip on it all it turned out to be far more complicated than he'd thought. He needed a place where he could sit down and think. This was like trying to concentrate on the psychology of the Sultan while you were dancing barefoot in his snakepit.

But the girl was wrong. Everything made sense. You just had to sort it out. Down underneath the bombs and bodies, there was an answer to every question. A flesh-and-blood human being had planted the bomb in the police station, just as a flesh-and-blood human being had put the bomb in the commissary. But it hadn't been the girl. And he certainly hadn't done it himself. He didn't believe that the dead kid, Uwe, had done it, either. That was a start. And in the end it would all make sense, and Thorne had every intention of living to see the last piece fall into place. It looked like it was going to be a hard road, but his confidence was growing now.

They hadn't mentioned him in the news report. There were several possible reasons, but each of them gave him room to move. Maybe it wouldn't even be he alone against the world.

But then, if the secret was out, did that mean they expected him to come in? And what would they do when he didn't show?

The girl sat curled over herself, still crying. Thorne let her be. The autobahn was flanked with the reassuring dazzle of nighttime Mainz now, and he was grateful for the safe passage.

8

Downtown Mainz was bright and empty. A few couples were arranged over the steps of the theater, a pack of teenagers nursed motorbikes by the fountain in front of the floodlit cathedral. But the streets were clear. Maria tried giving him directions.

"Hold on," he told her. "We have to dump the car."

The car hadn't made the news broadcast. But that might only mean that the authorities didn't want the public looking for it. It didn't mean the cops weren't hunting. Instinct said get rid of the car.

He drove down to the boulevard that ran along the Rhine, by the convention hall and the Mainz Hilton, and parked. He didn't think the cops would initiate their search in the neighborhood of the Hilton, and, anyway, it was the most inconspicuous place in town to dump a Mercedes.

He shut off the lights and the engine, then waited in his seat, scanning the lot for interested bodies.

"Check the bags in the back seat," he told the girl. "See what we've got."

The girl jumped encouragingly into action, heaving herself up around in the seat. Thorne kept his eyes moving along the rows of cars, listening to the girl rustle and putter.

"Groceries," she said, "bolts of flannel."

Okay.

Thorne twisted around in the seat himself and dumped everything from the plastic shopping bags, then quickly threw all the ready-eats back into one of the bags and wrapped the Ingram in a length of flannel, making a glove he could slip his hand into if the need for the weapon arose. He tucked the dressed Ingram neatly into the top of the bag of food, then took off his jacket and gave it to the girl.

"Here," he said. "You look like the butcher's boy."

"You'll be cold," the girl said, with absurd politeness.

Fuck it, Thorne wanted to say. Fuck manners. Fuck all civilization. None of it counts anymore. We are operating on a very simple level, and you had goddamned well better get with it.

"I've been cold before," he said. "Let's go." And he opened the car door.

A footbridge led them up out of the parking lot and back toward the center of town. From atop the elevated walkway, Thorne scanned the bridge that led across the big river to Mainz-Kastel. The taillights were backed up halfway across the Rhine.

They were searching now.

He rolled his denim shirtsleeves down against the evening chill, then started off at a brisk pace, shopping bag in one hand, the girl clinging to the other. The downtown streets and alleys were deserted, as though a plague had shut them down. It was eerie but not unusual, and it had nothing to do with them. German cities, with a few exceptions, shut down early and everyone went dutifully home.

The girl trotted heavy-breathed to keep up with him. At first he was the hard, determined soldier, thrifty with his kindness. But, when the girl didn't complain, he slackened off slightly. He would have to be careful, he thought, not to take his anger out on her. The human animal, when enraged, had a tendency to want to kill everything in sight. He'd seen that first-hand.

At the same time, it was important not to let her feel any pity. He needed her whole and functioning, and pity crippled the frightened. Some curled up and let you do their fighting for them, others lost their wits and died.

They waited at a curb for a lonely car to wander by, and the girl rested warm against him, gasping for breath. And Thorne felt his hard-ass determination dwindle. She was trying, she'd been trying, and he was halfway killing her. Why in the hell did she have to be such a cow? Why couldn't he have gotten into this mess with some skinny number he could throw over his shoulder? Or with a female athlete, for that matter?

They went on at a pace that seemed excruciatingly slow to him. But it let the girl survive, even pant out a few words.

"You lied to me earlier," she said. "You know Mainz."

But she didn't sound angry, or even annoyed. It was just an observation.

"I was a soldier here," Thorne said. "Once upon a time, before they sent me to Nam. That was several lives ago and it's a subject I'd just as soon skip. Okay?"

The pace was impossible. There was no way he was going to crawl across the city like this and let some cop earn a cheap promotion. But the girl was at her limit. It was decision time again.

Again, he decided to opt for speed over caution. He led the girl out of the alleyways to the bus stop in front of the theater.

It was all in the hands of the gods.

Thorne checked the posted schedule, pleased to see he'd remembered the line numbers after a decade. He remembered the *feel* of this place, too. The theater was dark tonight, and there were new glass doors. But he remembered it with the clarity of detail that fills the memory with special sorrow. He remembered women he'd brought here, and how he'd swaggered so childishly for some of them. He'd seen *Macbeth* here, done in clunking German, accompanied by an educated woman whose name he couldn't remember now. He'd made cheerful love to her later, untouched by the mortal agony of the play. The blood on the hands had been mere literature in those days.

The schedule promised a bus in a few minutes, and Thorne led the girl to a bench in the shadows. She sat down gratefully, but made no comment about it. Thorne barely sat, leaning forward off the bench like an anxious coach, ready to leap into action. That was when she surprised him.

"You can leave me, if you want," she said. "They're not even looking for you. You don't have to die for me."

She was speaking to his back. But he didn't have to see her face, he didn't have to look into her eyes. Her tone was unmistakably simple and honest. She wasn't acting, or speaking the mandatory lines so that he could manfully insist. He could tell clearly from her tone that she would not have been surprised if he stood up and walked away from her. He wondered then how many men had walked away from her. And then he knew that it didn't matter, because now, when it truly counted, the man wasn't going to walk away. He was ashamed of all the nervous bitching he'd done to himself, and he was free of it now, and he realized, finally, without rhetoric, how serious it all was and that he was committed to her irrevocably. Her few sentences had freed him from obligation, then reobligated the part of himself that he wanted most to believe in. She was no beauty, no man was ever going to slay dragons for a piece of her ass. But she had her moments. When she threw the beer in Krull's face, and when she talked about the sexual viciousness the cop had put her through, swearing that it didn't matter. And now, frightened and tired and still so brave, on a bench at a bus stop. He knew her courage wouldn't last, that she'd cry again and be a burden. But it didn't matter. He could handle it.

"Here comes the bus," he said.

They took a seat toward the rear of the bus, near the exit door. The bus was lonely with the last evening travelers, all of them tired, none curious. The girl leaned her head exhaustedly on Thorne's shoulder. Schillerplatz fell behind them, the *Bahnhof.*

"I'm so tired," the girl said. Her brown hair lay in wild splashes over the shoulders of the too-big jacket, it spilled around his arm, over his chest.

"Watch now," he told her. He bossed more gently now. "We don't want to miss our stop."

The bus wound up around the flank of the university. There was more of a pulse here. The longhairs in their fatigue jackets were a throwback to the scene in his own country a decade before. According to the magazines and films Thorne tried to keep up with, the States had gone slick these days, disco dudes and their prancing Cleopatras. It was a long way, curiously downhill, from Kent State to Allan Bakke. But it was far worse here. This was death. Here the youth were caught in a time lag, imitating a culture of which they had only a superficial grasp, still shrieking about a war that was over, still pointing fingers and flashing on Bertolucci, forgetting who the classic fascists had actually been. Young Germans had no indigenous culture, and what they stole they misunderstood, wearing their hipness with the idiotic strut of a native chieftain with a pair of jockey shorts on his head.

What was it like back home on the streets of the college towns? As safe and dull and diminished as it sounded? What would it be like now if he'd taken the other road? A junior professor in designer glasses, telling tweedy tall tales to earnest little girls with hungry space between their legs? Jogging about the campus to keep a willful belly under control, critically reviewing other men's actions?

Thorne caught himself, annoyed at his own closed-mindedness. If it was safe and dull back home, what did he have against it? What was wrong with being safely dull? Or dully safe? Had he grown to love the struggle so much?

If so, he was on the satisfaction express.

They got off the bus in front of a row of apartment buildings, Thorne cradling the shopping bag in his arms like a baby. The bottom was tearing out.

He had his mind back on practical matters again. He'd chosen Strasbourg as an interim destination. He knew people in Strasbourg, people he'd crossed paths with in Lebanon. Their primary business was gunrunning, but they'd traffic in anything for a price. They were fine Protestant businessmen, capable of delivering light tanks built to spec. Scooting a girl off to a new life would be well within their capabilities. But the price would be high, and he would have to pay in information. He hadn't fully accepted the idea yet, but it at least gave them a goal to run for.

The girl was extremely nervous again, her fingers locked onto his arm with remarkable strength.

"I don't even belong to the Communist Party," she said suddenly.

"Calm down, Maria. There's nothing to worry about now."

She gave him a wondering sideways glance, doubting something seriously.

"But I'm known here," she said. "I might be recognized. Someone might've heard the news."

Shit. He hadn't even considered that. He went furious at himself, unable to accept an oversight of this magnitude. He was tired, of course. But there was

110

no allowance for being tired. You had to think clearly and constantly and comprehensively. You had to take charge. He could see how it was going to be. Like going through those fucking swamps.

"Everything's going to be all right," he said for the hundredth time.

But the few blocks to her friend's building seemed like a very long way, there was no route sufficiently dark, and it seemed to him as though the entire student body was out strolling.

The worst of it was the foyer. They had to wait in a brightly lit glass cage, on display for anyone passing by, while the girl buzzed her friend's apartment. It was like going through the jungle in the dark now. Waiting for the magical talking wall to come to life. More nerves in the soles of your feet than a normal being had in its entire body. He was about to put it back in the street when the intercom suddenly crackled and spoke:

"Kunkel."

"It's Maria Burckhardt, Kurt."

Break. *"Please?"*

"Maria. *Burck*hardt. Weber brought me over the other week."

Another wait. Through the jungle. In the dark.

A gang of students stumbled noisily, colorfully by the building.

"We argued about the Chinese," Maria pleaded with the wall.

Finally, reluctantly, the door release buzzed.

Thorne, flooded with caution now, led the girl up the stairs. The thick carpeting ate noise, huge-leafed plants guarded each landing. He let the girl go first

111

down the long, hushed hallway, and leaned casually against the wall as she took up her position in front of the peephole.

The door opened, but only a few inches. It was still held by a safety chain.

Through the opening Thorne saw a narrow face framed by dark, styled hair. High, knobby cheekbones jutted out under gloomy eyeshafts, jutting out so far under taut skin that it seemed they might burst out into tusks. The lips were starved and purple-pale. It was not one of the most congenial faces.

"Kurt," Maria said, greeting.

But Kurt clearly wasn't ready for Thorne. He made no move to open the door.

"Who's your friend, Maria?"

The girl turned to Thorne, as though she expected him to supply her with words. How to describe the man you've just been to a massacre with.

"You haven't heard the news?" she begged the face. "You haven't heard yet?"

"Who's your friend?"

Thorne nudged the girl out of the way. He held the Ingram, still draped in fabric but unmistakably a weapon, off his hip.

"I'm the man with the gun," he said. John Wayne, Audie Murphy. "I want you to shut that door and undo that chain, pal. If, when you shut the door, I don't hear the chain immediately, I'm going to put a long, low burst through your door. *Do it.*"

The door shut, chain clattered.

The apartment was not the postered, romantic mess that was so becoming to students. Gleaming Scandinavian wood and glass supported thick arrangements of plants and dried and fresh flowers, a state-of-the-art stereo rack climbed a wall between fine, boring decorator prints. Kurt stood on a rug that was a soft, seemingly random swirl of colors, a small man with a bad face, in a black turtleneck and gray wool slacks. The apartment was a moneyed, inhospitable place, their host snake-sullen.

Thorne was content to be the armed man of the two. "Sorry about the cowboy shit," he said. "But the hallway was not the place for the conversation we're going to have."

Kurt decided to ignore Thorne now. "What's this all about?" he asked Maria.

"We need your help, Kurt."

"Turn on your radio," Thorne said. "I think they said two—or maybe it was three—dead cops. Anyway, that was only the bomb in the police station. I'm not sure how we did in the gunfight."

"And you came here?"

Thorne had to lock his face not to smile. He had the definite feeling that Kurt was not all on the up and up. Something in the air. But Kurt was one surprised dude right now, and Thorne enjoyed keeping him off balance.

"She thought you could help us," Thorne said coolly. "We are definitely in need of help."

"I can't help you. Why should *I* be able to help you?" Kurt attacked his stereo system, hunting for a suitable radio station. "You were crazy to come here," he went on.

She's right about him, Thorne thought. She's a smart girl.

But she was crying again now. He felt the sourness

rise in him for a moment, he'd hoped she was all cried out. Then he pictured again what it must be like for her, remembering, too, how grand she'd been the night before and then on the bench. Hell, it was confusing for him, and he was a veteran of the great confusion.

"Sit down," Thorne told her. And she obeyed, taking a place at a dining-room table just inside the door. Kurt was still frantic at the stereo. No news. The radio danced over opera and top ten, flashing bits of Yankee English from the Armed Forces Network.

"Trust me on the information, friend," Thorne said.

Kurt turned his face from the tuner. He'd regrouped, he was cold and demanding again now.

"Why did you come here? What could you possibly expect from me?"

"Maria thought you might have connections."

"With whom? Did she tell you I'm a law student?"

"I'm unimpressed." Thorne looked theatrically around the room. "Fancy living for a student. But, you know, if I were planning to operate as a terrorist, I'd set myself up in a place just like this. Great cover."

"I don't understand you, you're talking nonsense." But he didn't meet Thorne's eyes now, instead he fiddled with the stereo tuner. "I can't help you," he said stingily. "And I don't even know who you are."

"I told you who I am. Don't like that, try an American poet on the run. I don't know you, either. Maria just thought you might be able to help us. She couldn't think of anyone else. Got good instincts, though, the girl does. I picked up an immediate gut feeling about you myself."

"Is this a joke? Are you from the police?"

Thorne grinned. He couldn't help it. It was like a play that revolved around repeated instances of mistaken identity. Maria had a notion that he himself was a terrorist, and now this joker, who had terror written all over him, thought he was from the police. And here he was, just a poor goddamned soldier, looking for a foxhole big enough for two.

"No, brother," Thorne said. "Just take it easy for a minute. Let me tell you how it was. Maria and I were heading up to her room. To meet Uwe—you know Uwe?"

Kurt nodded grudgingly.

"Well, Uwe's dead. The cops put him away. We walked in on a beauty. Uwe with neat little holes in his chest and his back all gone, a staged arms cache. All of it very well done, except that I wasn't supposed to be there. Good thing I was, though, or your friend Maria would be one cold piece of meat right now. But she's alive. And the two of us are deep in the shit."

Thorne knew he'd gone too fast, but he wanted to kick his host off balance again, to keep him wobbling until he fell into line on the right side of things.

"Who are you?" Kurt asked, a trace of desperation in his voice again.

"A traveler with a problem. How to get myself and your friend out of the country. To Strasbourg, I think."

"I couldn't even begin to help you."

The news came on. Same as earlier, dead cops and the fleeing girl. Maria Burckhardt. Armed and dangerous.

When it was over the two men stood in a thoughtful

quiet. Thorne even began to doubt. What if this sorry sucker really was nothing but a law student?

Then Kurt said, noncommittally, "They didn't mention anything about a man."

Thorne shrugged. "Bureaucratic botch-up. So much the better. But I can tell you this much: they're already checking the bridges over the Rhine. It's a good thing we don't have to cross the Rhine to get to Strasbourg from here, don't you think? All we have is one little border. And you know how easy borders are."

"I'm sorry for your troubles. I even sympathize. But I can't help you. And waving your gun at me won't help."

"No more gun-waving. That was just a foot in the door." Maria's head lay on the table in the classic pose of a passed-out drunk. "She's afraid they're going to kill her. And they will, if we don't get a little help. And she doesn't particularly deserve to die. You and I both know she's not the stuff hardened terrorists are made of. Don't we?"

Kurt stared obstinately over Thorne's shoulder. Thorne hated the little man now, hated his power over them. If he didn't help them, Thorne thought, it would probably be best to kill him. It would almost be necessary. Thorne wondered what it would be like to kill someone for the pleasure of it, wondering if he could. He wasn't sure how much conscience was left in his fingers.

It occurred to him how rare and various life was. He had been many things and had come a long way. I am supped full of horrors, he thought-remembered. I have chowed down at the cosmic scumtrough. And yet, so much beauty remained. Even the conscience survived, though it changed. It grew unpredictably selective.

"Tell you what we're going to do," Thorne said. "Maria and I are just going to move in here and spend our last few hours in comfort. You can leave, if you want. I believe in keeping casualties to a minimum."

"You can't do that."

"Maria?" Thorne called. "Are you hungry?"

She didn't answer. She'd cried herself into a deep sleep.

Thorne watched her breathing against the rhythm of the radio. The raising and lowering of the big shoulders. All your educated life, you were taught what a great tragedy it was when beauty faded. But they didn't tell you what a bitch it was never to have any beauty at all.

"There's no reason for her to die," Thorne said softly now. "I think I can help her, if I can just get her out of the country."

"To Strasbourg? Who are you? You're asking a tremendous amount, and I don't even know who you are."

Finally there was possibility in Kurt's voice.

"It's all for her, friend," Thorne said. "As for me, I think it's safe to accept that we're both on the same side at the moment. Dead cops and all."

"An American poet," Kurt said sarcastically.

"Help us. Help the girl."

Kurt was thinking now. With no fanfare, a mask had been torn away.

"I honestly don't know if anything can be done."

"Try."

The hard little man turned abruptly away and

picked an all-weather coat from a rack near the door. It was all very simple now, and Thorne felt exhausted. Kurt looked back once.

"If the door buzzes, don't answer it. Don't answer the phone." He stared at Thorne for a last moment with his wretched face, still offering no display of comradeship or even humanity. He held their lives now, and both men knew it. "I don't know how long I'll be gone."

"We'll be here," Thorne said.

When the footsteps were gone, Thorne switched off the radio. The program had changed to good North American folk music, heavy on bluegrass, but he wanted quiet now. He was glad the girl had nodded off. He listened to the masculine heaviness of her breathing. It was out of his hands now.

He went noiselessly into the kitchen and helped himself to a bottle of beer. Pilsner Urquell, the left lived high. Then he settled himself down across the table from the girl, facing the door, shopping bag at his side.

The part in the girl's hair had gone awry, she had the stubby fingers of an overgrown child. She was a born victim of this and that. If Kurt called the cops or, perhaps, some deadly friends of his own, her end wouldn't draw much sympathy. The citizenry would pass over her newspaper photo with a self-satisfied nod. He would, he knew, have done the same thing himself.

What prisoners men were of woman's beauty. Worse, what prisoners the girls themselves were. For them, it was solitary confinement. The boys could piss and moan to each other, making beery poetry of their tragic sense of life. But only the most beautiful women could make jokes about their own unattractiveness. Tough duty, when the state of your soul didn't matter as much as the condition of your tits.

Even now, drinking a beer at the edge of death, he shuddered with desire to think of the lean, sun-lavished women on the islands. To lay a hand on a warm flat belly, then tease north or south amidst the quiet of a hidden beach. He loved their hot wild embarrassment under the watching sky, the way their legs opened and the inside of their thighs quivered half insane at the water's edge. The universe focused in their bellies, they were goddesses, the beauties, and men danced around them in the exalting ritual of Romance. The girls who were not beauties were nothing. It didn't seem very fair.

Maria woke suddenly, as if from a bad dream. She sat up, looking at Thorne, and all possible hope died from her face. She drew back a confused spill of hair.

"Where's Kurt?"

"Gone," Thorne said. "He's going to help us."

"Thank God." Then she thought about it. "Are you sure?"

Thorne was tired of lying. It seemed to him that there'd always been a tale to tell, even to those who were most intimate with him—and what could be more intimate than dying together? He longed to tell the whole truth, just one time.

"It looks good," he said. "Go back to sleep, if you want."

"No."

"It's all right."

"How long have I been asleep?"

"An hour or so."

"I don't want to sleep anymore. I don't want to waste any more time. Not now."

"Want a beer?"

"Please. I'm so thirsty."

"Hungry?"

She shook her head no. Thorne went into the kitchen to grab two beers, and while he was bent over the refrigerator a key stabbed the doorlock.

The Ingram was a long way, too far, away. If it was Kurt, he'd been very efficient to return so soon. Or unsuccessful. If it was the cops, it was all over.

It was Kurt. Alone. He came in quickly and silently and laid a black overnight bag on the table. His face was bland, even the knobby cheekbones were subdued now. He pulled out a starched white uniform—the sort a cook might wear—and threw it to Thorne.

"Put it on," he said. "Hurry."

9

Thorne was not particularly at ease as he crouched in the back of the ambulance van. He did not feel he was doing a very efficient job at this point. He was, damn near helplessly, dependent upon people he couldn't trust. He was headed toward Frankfurt, where he didn't want to go. And, in a few minutes, they were going to try to bluff their way through a police roadblock. It was not exactly an ideal state of affairs.

Kurt. Good old Kurt. A sweet guy.

The van went over a stretch of cobblestones and the IV bottles rattled and chimed. The girl lay quietly on the stretcher, covered to the neck with sheets and strapped in. Her face, one eye, was patched with bandages. Maybe, Thorne realized, it was easier for her to be strapped down like that. But it took a particular, trusting brand of courage he didn't think he'd personally be capable of. Even if he was a prisoner in the back of this van, he was armed and he had freedom of movement within its restricted area.

Within certain parameters, he could act. He knew the van was a death trap, but it still allowed him the illusion that he could bust out and muscle his way through. If Kurt was dicking them, it would all be over in a torrent of bullets. He knew that. Yet, with hands and feet still entirely his own, the part of him that dreamed beyond reason, the part that both made poetry and let him justify his continued soldiering in terms of goodness, imagined counterattacks, great good luck, and even survival.

The Ingram had a new home now. It rested securely between Thorne's right foot and the wall of the van in the black medical bag Kurt had given him. Kurt had been very efficient, he'd organized a thorough plan of action and mobilized the necessary equipment in a startlingly small amount of time. Then he'd just as efficiently left himself out of the plan's execution. The ambulance had been waiting in the basement parking garage of the apartment building, complete with a speechless young thug in a costume like Thorne's to play kamikaze pilot. Unless the whole thing was a police setup, the German terrs were far better organized than anyone thought—and the experts already had a high opinion of them. It was an explorer's glimpse of a new continent, and Thorne wondered whether he'd ever come back to tell the tale. All he had going for him was an enemy's promise, the unknown factor up in the driver's seat, and a couple of clips for the Ingram.

They turned onto a boulevard, closing toward the bridge over the Rhine and the roadblock. Quick regular waves of light slapped through the van as they passed under high roadlamps. Most of the time, the girl's one visible eye was shut from one flood of light through the next. Not in sleepiness, though. He could feel that the eye was prayer-shut.

He wondered whether she believed in God or not. Not that that was any requirement for prayer. It had been his experience that, when the thunder got too close, even the loudest nonbelievers begged the universe they were so reluctant to personify. Christian, heathen or chemistry fan, the girl was praying, and he didn't bother her.

But he wondered what she really believed in. On a day-to-day, life-shaping basis. Beyond the professed, mandatory leftism. In being a doctor, she'd said. The good doctor. Well, that was gone now.

Even if he got her to Strasbourg, even if he could do business, she was dead in this incarnation. The best he could hope to give her would be a brand-new life. And he'd had some limited experience with brand-new lives, on a temporary basis. He knew that when men and women thoughtlessly wished they could make a new start they had no idea what they were asking for. First of all, the death of the past. In moments of despondency, people imagined that they wanted to shut out their histories. But even the harshest life had its cherished moments that, sooner or later, the new man would long to describe to a new friend. Human beings longed to speak meaningfully to one another, to identify themselves and see themselves admirably or at least decently reflected. And for this girl the hardship would probably be compounded by a new language as well. Thorne knew what it was like to tell careful lies to honest lovers in a stranger's tongue.

But you lived with it—and that was the positive

side. The beast was magnificently adaptable. A new language might even suit her better than the tongue she'd been born to. And the best lovers didn't need to ask a lot of questions. New and bolder dreams might emerge from the wreckage of the old.

Maybe. Maybes stretched from here to the roadblock and perhaps right on to a jovial senility. But there would be no going back to class after a holiday weekend.

If she couldn't be a doctor, could she be a nurse? Was she glad to be alive, in any case? He figured that probably hadn't hit her yet. In the apartment, she hadn't wanted to go back to sleep. But he didn't think it had really hit her. It might be months or even years before it did. And she might be dead before it struck her. Now she would have only the confusion and the fear, maybe an astonished sense of the injustice of life. Why me?

Because you happened to get in the way, young lady. Like the Palestinian kids in the camps when the rockets came down, like the Israeli kids in the border settlements when the rockets came down. Because during the great long moan of history men generally wanted very little: enough to eat, shelter, security for their loved ones. But the soldiers came, or the rain didn't. If the human race had a motto, it should be just that: Why me?

They were running along the river now, by factories and floodlit barges. Thorne could see the bridge about a click away, lit up like a carnival. The relentlessness of the journey chilled him, and he thought again of Kurt in the underground lot. He'd waited carefully, until the girl was strapped down and Thorne was huddled in beside her, to break the news. Hand on the rear door, ready to slam it, he'd told Thorne:

"You said you wanted to go to Strasbourg. That's impossible tonight, from here. You're going to Frankfurt. There are facilities there."

Kurt had beat him. It was only a question of how badly. And Thorne, crouched in his white uniform that was too short in the legs, hadn't had much choice at that point. He'd had to go along and trust a man who'd just proved that he wasn't trustable.

Thorne had instantly grasped the futility of complaining. All he could do was hope this man had come up with some reason of his own to actually help them. When he reached out a hand to stop Kurt from shutting the door, it was only so he could ask a practical question:

"What about the bridges over the Rhine? I told you they're blocked."

Kurt stood there in the concrete gloom, smiling his first tiny smile. Whether it was a smile of pride in a hard task cleverly mastered or a sneer, Thorne couldn't tell.

"Don't worry," Kurt said. "The police are expecting you. An emergency transfer from the university clinic. You're cleared to cross the Schierstein Bridge." He gave Thorne a last opaque stare. "Good luck." And he slammed the door.

The van sped up around the access ramp to the autobahn and the bridge now, flashing and beeping. Cars pulled off to the side to let it pass. The ambulance was a daring idea, Thorne realized, and, if they hadn't been betrayed from the outset, it might even work. It wouldn't be the first miracle he'd seen. But it sure as hell wasn't the way he'd been trained to do things.

He was one of the nightwalkers, the paint-faced do-it-in-the-dark creepers.

This was like going in with flags and bugles.

The van hurtled. Thorne could see down the autobahn and across the long flat bridge to where the distant lights flashed warning. As if they'd shared a thought, the driver glanced back over his shoulder at Thorne. But if he'd had anything to say, he thought better of it. He turned back to his job, and the van raced down a lane cleared by scooting motorists.

Who was this man? The short look Thorne had got had shown a tall tough with the standard German mustache running down into the standard little German beard. There hadn't been time to register individuality, to imagine character. And, in a pair of minutes, they might die together. At the cop-crowded end of this long red V of taillights. It was, Thorne considered, just like real life.

To hell with the driver. There wasn't time to care about him. That was just like real life, too. Maybe he'd worry about the driver after he'd taken care of himself and the girl.

Her eyes were open now, she'd sensed the increasing, exploding tension. Sudden ranks of bridge lights lit the night haze yellow and she looked to Thorne. Thorne was afraid she was going to speak now, when there was no more time to be understanding and decent or even human with words.

But the girl didn't say a word. She only watched him with a look either too dumb or too complex to be categorized. Thorne thought again about the straps holding her down, sickened at the idea. He tried to make a face that would be classically reassuring. But her look was too difficult, too intense, to respond to. Up ahead, the blue dazzle of the police barricade grew more and more distinct, insisting on his full attention.

Thorne reached down into the black bag. The Ingram felt very firm and strict and clutchable. The driver was on the same wavelength, because Thorne heard the unmistakable sound of a weapon being cocked in the front seat. It was always a wonderfully reassuring sound when it came from one of your own positions. Even when it meant that hell itself was coming, it promised you that you were not alone.

The driver turned his face back toward Thorne just long enough to ask, "All right?"

"All right," Thorne guaranteed him.

"Everything should go smoothly," the driver said.

"But if it doesn't . . ." Thorne said coolly, anticipating the words.

"Stay in the vehicle. The police weapons aren't accurate at any significant range," the driver explained, "and we can probably outrun them. Are you capable of using the gun you have?"

"Yes."

"Then fire through the rear window. You don't have to hit anything. By the time they get behind their vehicles, we'll be out of range."

"And if they're already behind their vehicles?" Thorne asked, smiling an old Nam smile at the probabilities. "Or if they're set up in depth? Or if they have birds up?"

The driver shrugged. "Then . . . we're in the shit."

The bright, stilled lines of traffic seemed to be pulling them toward the blinking blue lights. Thorne could make out the large white letters on the broadsides of the Volkswagen vans now. POLIZEI.

"Is it now?" the girl whispered.

Thorne nodded his head honestly, eyes locked on the scene up ahead. The lanes of red lights funneled into the flashing blue cluster. And beyond the barrier the diamond spread of Wiesbaden lay as cool and magnificent as Paradise itself. He'd known a girl from Wiesbaden once, a sly, fun girl. He'd bought her blue jeans at the PX. Her politics were nonexistent and tiny black hairs climbed her belly like a line of ants.

"Please," the here-and-now girl said. Only that. Please. She never finished it, or maybe she wasn't speaking to him at all. Thorne recklessly broke discipline and glanced down at her. The eye was shut.

Up ahead, uniformed men seemed to leap out of the slow blue strobe effect. But they were only standing at the ready, weapons across their chests or braced off their hips.

Police vans had been backed across the broad lines so that there was barely room for one car to pass through the roadblock at a time. And a car was in the gap now.

"I don't know," the driver said.

There was a brand-new nervousness in the voice. The bravado was draining fast.

"Listen," Thorne said quickly and firmly, "give it a chance. Don't charge it or start any fireworks until you're positive that we're in trouble. *Give it a chance.*"

There was no reply.

Red lights, blue lights, white lights. The world had become a giant pinball machine.

I'm going to finish this one, Thorne swore to himself. First the business with the girl, then all the rest of it. You won't kill me, you bastards. Slicker suckers have tried and died.

Double-time combat boots in the Georgia sun and the bloody bits of small-timers all over the commissary floor. This unlucky girl and a thousand ghosts and the sad, lost New Jerusalem.

Not here, you shits. Not yet.

The ambulance slowed toward the roadblock, cruising in behind the clogging car. The police watched them come, stone-faced, hands on their weapons.

"Give it a *chance,*" Thorne whispered furiously.

There were too many cops. In front of the vehicles and behind the vehicles. Cops and more cops.

The car that was blocking the narrow passageway suddenly pulled out, freeing the way.

Another cop stationed in the rear waved them on through. Go.

Go.

The ambulance was gaining speed again even as it entered the inspection lane.

Thorne bent his face down toward the stretcher, left hand playing at medical expertise.

Once he'd watched a boy trying to load his dead buddy's brains back into his head. Crying and shoveling in the raw brains.

They passed abruptly from the inferno of lights, and Thorne waited for the shots. And waited. But they didn't come.

After they were out of the range of the machine

pistols, he waited for the pursuit cars. Or the huge throb of choppers. Waiting with his battle nerves, the combat energy.

This stretch of the autobahn was lonely as a winter prairie. They went swiftly, half madly now.

The driver slapped the dashboard. He slapped it repeatedly, drumming joy. "Done," he sang. "Done."

Thorne let go his grip on the Ingram and reached instead for the outline of the girl's arm. Her muscles were stony as old death.

"Maria," he said. "We made it."

═══ 10 ═══

For two days, Thorne and the girl remained shut in an apartment in Frankfurt. The pair of austere rooms in a postwar block of flats reminded Thorne of transient billets. He and the girl slept on separate mattresses on the floor and ate canned food delivered by a businesslike young woman who said her name was Luise.

Luise was their sole flesh-and-blood link with the outside. She'd been waiting for the ambulance in the labyrinth of forested paths and roads just south of the city, and, after a no-nonsense transfer to an old Opel, she delivered them to the apartment. Then the questions began. She was very intelligent, very thorough and devious. Really quite a good interrogator. But Thorne had had plenty of practice with the masters. And, at the moment of truth, she always backed down. Thorne figured she'd been warned about him.

The whole business was very chancy. He could only hope the underground would be willing to risk blowing part of their setup for the sake of the girl. It was a goodness-of-your-hearts sort of deal, and he could only be skeptical about the people he was dealing with. Maybe they were better than their publicity.

There were a few good signs. Luise took their measurements and brought them new clothes. Then she took photos that might be used for passports or identity cards and asked what languages they spoke well. She made no promises, and Thorne was sure plenty of minds were at work wondering just what in the hell to do with the two of them, how to either turn the situation to advantage or at least minimize any damage. Which might mean two bodies dropped in the Main River, or, maybe, a shuffle across the border. Or God knew what other options. But Luise did bring them a portable television so they could follow the biggest manhunt in the history of the Federal Republic of Germany.

Anyway, there were enough positive indicators to convince Thorne to give it three days. If things weren't on the move by then, he'd contact his own people and try to tough out a deal for the girl. He wasn't even remotely hopeful about that particular course of action, but, if the underground types weren't going to help them, there was no other choice. There was no way they could go it alone. The scope and intensity of the television reports had convinced him of that.

There was still no trace of Thorne in the media reports, but Maria was famous. An overnight sensation. No press agent could ever have etched a starlet's face so swiftly into a national consciousness. The girl's flat, graceless features filled the screen once every half hour or forty-five minutes. Armed and dangerous.

ARD even ran a hastily assembled half-hour biography. The title was "A Child of Prosperity," even though it was stretching the truth to describe her background as lower middle-class. They interviewed her mother at the bakery where she worked. She spoke unintelligently, although that might've been from confusion. She said that Maria had been an intelligent girl, but rebellious. She'd lacked a father's strong hand. The woman cried. She was so dull in every respect that it required a healthy imagination to find a resemblance between her and her far more vivid daughter. Only their husky builds were alike. And the father who'd been so sorely missed—he was never interviewed, his absence was never explained. Instead, they cut to unflattering school photos and to serious-faced teachers who remembered Maria as either bright or hard-working. But they also added that she was a willful loner, stubborn, ungrateful and quick to criticize her classmates. She had not been popular, not with anyone. The narrator/host played at a bit of cheap psychoanalysis, then the program switched to a montage of Germany climbing out of the postwar rubble, building and building and building. It was an extremely well-done bit of flag-waving, though not terribly pertinent. Followed by a brief, cautionary history of left-wing terrorism in the Federal Republic, which led, in turn, back to the mother. She was asked if she believed her daughter was capable of committing crimes such as these. The big woman said she didn't know. It was really a very sensible, almost wise response. Anyway, it had become apparent that the woman had long since lost the thread of her daughter's life. When Maria had left her home in Bochum for the university in Mainz, she'd left her home for good. Something had gone intentionally unexplored there, just like the bit with the father. Finally, there was an interview with a professor of anatomy. The girl, Maria Burckhardt, was one of his students at the university. She was a somber, one could almost say a secretive girl . . .

It was pigshit. It told you nothing, but left you with the feeling that the girl was not a team player, that she was rather a nasty case, unlike the viewer. Blatant media manipulation of a cowed common denominator. The goodly State had given her so much, yet she'd turned her rabid disregard for human life on its noble representatives, etc. It was all aimed at the audience that read the Springer papers, whose theoretically free votes theoretically controlled the Federal Republic of Germany.

Maria cried and cried and didn't talk much the first day. She remained overwhelmed by it all, she was drowning in it. The girl who came home at dinnertime and found her lover butchered amidst a crazy arsenal. Gunfire serenade.

Thorne sat calmly with her, keeping her quiet company, cleaning the Ingram. He made an efficient show out of stripping the weapon, then reassembling it. He wanted her to associate it with him, to blur and confuse him with this deadly puzzle of steel. He'd decided to become a machine to her, a trusty killing machine that she could depend on the way you could never depend on flesh and blood. He wanted her to have confidence in his effectiveness, to associate him with the shootout, not with the worried poetry she'd read. He hoped she'd forgotten that completely now. There was no time for the polite anxieties.

They were making patriotic martyrs out of the dead policemen, latter-day Horst Wessels. The final count between the blasted stationhouse and the shootout was five dead. The TV stations did biographies of them too. It seemed that all five had been good scouts who had studied hard in school when they weren't playing merry pranks. They had grown up, of course, to be responsible family men. Their saintliness, and even the very real suffering of their relatives, was overdrawn with a gruesome sentimentality that seemed peculiarly German to Thorne. The footage of the bomb-gutted police station and the bullet-swept stairwell of Maria's apartment played again and again, the cameras lingered over the weapons in the arms cache.

Thorne had real difficulty accepting it all. He'd had a left-field hope that some tough-ass reporter would catch a whiff of something rotten. But no. The media had fallen one hundred percent in with the crusade.

Thorne tried to put together a plausible scenario from his big wild thoughts and the handful of facts. The police—elements of the police—had set Maria and her boyfriend up. Fact. Probable reasons: the pressure was on to nail somebody for the commissary building, and Maria and her lover looked right for the part. He doubted that it had anything to do with the beer in the cop's face. That would be too incredibly extreme and, besides, the affair had been too well coordinated, you couldn't put a package like that together overnight. But the whole business was so crazy that he wouldn't rule even this beer-faced motive out completely.

The next hard fact was the bombed police station. It had not been merely coincidental timing. He was convinced that the police themselves had done that too, to excite the world's fury beyond reason against the "terrorists." If so, were the lives lost in the stationhouse random victims? Were their deaths even unplanned and accidental? Or had the victims been selected because they weren't playing along satisfactorily? Was there, perhaps, an ultra-right-wing organization involved, some of whose members happened to be policemen? At what level did complicity end?

If it had begun as a strictly local affair, he'd changed that but fast. He'd been a giant X factor. The shit had hit the fan, and at least some of the truth had buzzed immediately to the highest levels of the government, where he'd been identified and they'd decided to leave him out of the case. That decision had certainly been made at a fairly high level. The local cops would've wanted his balls, no matter who he was. And did it mean that elements of two governments were now involved?

He wondered just how much of the truth had filtered up through the various echelons. If the people at the top had any grasp of the police plot, it meant that the entire Maria Burckhardt affair was being cynically stage-managed, that the government, or elements thereof, had decided to lay it all on the girl, anyway. That would be big-time.

The possibility still existed, however, that the police had managed a quick local cover-up of the worst of the mess, and that the boys at the top sincerely believed in the girl's guilt.

Either way, they were going to do their best to kill her.

It was the afternoon of the second day, while he was slicking his weapon together one more time, that Thorne got the mighty ice in his stomach. He realized, shocked by his nearsightedness now, that he'd forgotten to ask the most fundamental question of all:

Who had really bombed the commissary?

That evening, the girl screwed everything up. There'd been no resupply of groceries all day, and they split the last can of goulash and drank the last of the beer. The girl washed up the few dishes as though it mattered, drying them carefully before putting them away. And it seemed to calm her. Really, she was improving noticeably. Over the foul soup she'd talked. About Uwe. She didn't cry, but spoke vividly and sadly, with a biographer's eye for the conjuring details. It was a small, rough-draft answer to the slick television tributes to the dead cops. Thorne listened, but said nothing.

Then they watched the television again. Thorne felt as though all reality were breaking down. There were clips from the police funerals, with politicians highly visible in their quietly histrionic dignity. One of the dour businessmen from Bonn gave a brief speech explaining that there could be no freedom without the order these men had dedicated their lives to maintain. Then there was a news flash. The police had raided a suspected hideout up north, in Bremen. They believed the girl had been there but had left earlier in the day.

Maria seemed to be managing now, though. There was a growing strength about her. It reminded Thorne of the way he'd felt as a boy, a week or so after his father died. That sudden ability to continue after the world's end.

In a way, he was the shaky one at this point. The thought that it might have been the police who'd blown up the commissary, even the one-in-a-thousand chance of it, disarranged his universe. He realized the superficiality of his cynicism about men and institutions. Even after Nam. He'd secretly cherished his lifelong faith in certain things. His own kind, the guardian officials of his own culture, might occasionally turn out to be genteelly corrupt, but they did not murder their charges in cold blood. For all his conscience-soothing sympathy for the left, he'd still automatically assumed that it had been left-wing terrorists who'd done the bombing. Everyone had assumed that. Now he at least was no longer sure.

But, if it had been the police, what about the Greek captain in Athens? All that couldn't have been coincidence. Thorne tried to remember exactly what the man had said. It was difficult. So much of it was atmosphere, it was hard to sort out exact words from intonations and his own goddamned preconceptions. He wondered how many times he'd blown it over the years because of his previously invisible set of basic assumptions. Had men died because of it? Had people recognized the failing in him and used it? And the Greek captain. Katsovakis. Was *he* really what he let on to be?

There were so many questions. But, after the initial stab of despair, they weren't paralyzing. Not at all. On the contrary, there were suddenly dozens of things to do. He had to go south, to talk to Leedom, to see what he'd found out. Once he was back in the system, on his own ground, he could work it all out. Hammer the guilty bastards.

For a sweet moment, he was full of half a dozen plans of action. But, inevitably, his thoughts tumbled back to the girl. And the excitement died. She was the chain, the stumbling block. Without her to care for, he could kick ass and take names. Solve the world. She sat beside him on the rug, watching the fluid gray screen. Even in the near-darkness, the sloppy pouch of fat was evident where it welled up over the waist of her jeans. And she had one of her worst, least intelligent expressions on her face. She sat placidly, letting the TV light splash over her. She looked as though she had all the soul of a cow.

Thorne leaned back onto his elbows and smirked bitterly. He watched the girl's shoulders. Fucking halfback. And she was the greatest, maybe even the final, responsibility of his life. There wasn't a hell of a lot of glamour in it this time. An old shit and a fat girl.

Sometimes it was hard to be a good soldier.

Thorne got up and went into the bedroom. He didn't turn on the light. He stepped between the litter of mattresses and bunched blankets, where they'd slept primly and mercifully apart. He went skillfully, prowling down a jungle trail, to the window. He opened the heavy drapes a little way and let the diamond city night into the room.

He often wished there were a god to believe in. A tremendous being to whom you could abdicate your responsibilities. But there wasn't. There was only a dreadful world full of zapped villages and bomb-gutted grocery stores and the methodical heartless-ness of Mohammed's Law.

He admired the abundant lights of Frankfurt, the exuberant wastefulness, the tall, steady brilliance, with splendor rushing through the streets below. It was a hard, a terribly hard and beautiful world, and it was unacceptable that there was no peace at the end of it. He had waded in blood, he was covered in blood, it was incredible that the earth wasn't a crimson slop by now. And he'd done it all to make a better world, because he *was* his brother's keeper. Some of the blood had even been his own, he'd given his youth and he'd endured unarguable physical pain and had to relearn life. His eyes closed at the memory of how it hurt. You could never really remember, but even the faint ghost of it flickering by was enough to contract his stomach muscles. And he couldn't see that the world was any better for any of it. This visually overwhelming mass of rock and steel, glass and bone. Dear God who isn't there, he thought, I'm not old enough to be this tired, I don't deserve to be this tired.

He heard movement behind him and crouched swiftly out of the deadly windowlight, always ready now.

It was only the girl, of course. He was embarrassed at his nervousness, ashamed of the insane efficiency of his response.

"You surprised me," he said, watching her dark figure come slowly toward him, faintly silhouetted by television glow from the other room. Then he turned back to the window, exposing his outline to her, a sheepish gift of vulnerability.

She said nothing, her bare feet hushed over rug and strewn blanket. She stopped just behind him, half beside him.

He opened the drape a few more inches and made room for her. She brushed against him, drew back, closed slightly again. They watched the near and far of the city together, listening to its life with a sudden unexpected intimacy. In the building across the street, a sprinkling of windows presented golden scenes from strange lives. The street below shimmered and dashed.

When the girl finally spoke, it was in a hushed, museum voice.

"Why are you helping me?"

Thorne suddenly remembered that the Ingram was in the other room, that they were defenseless here. But he stayed with the window and the girl. He didn't know what to say. He said: "Because I choose to. No. That's not exactly right. Because I *have* to."

Surprisingly, she seemed to accept that. No further questions. Until he'd relaxed his guard again and she asked abruptly, "Are you with the police somehow? Are you using me? Who are you?"

Thorne was amazed and sick at heart that she could still ask such questions. They were still so far apart it was chilling. Despite all they'd been through.

Thorne caught himself. These were reasonable questions, after all.

The girl's forehead and cheekbones shone like porcelain in the windowlight, her eyes gleamed.

"No," Thorne said. "I'm not using you." He met her eyes, sharing the stray light between them. And he figured to hell with it. At this point she deserved the truth, or at least what shreds of the truth he could sort out of it all. "I'm a soldier," he said. "I am an officer in the United States Army. I was working undercover in Bad Sickingen, trying to find out who'd bombed the U.S. commissary." He took hold of her upper arm, firmly gripping the warmth under the cotton blouse she'd been given, afraid she wouldn't allow him time to really explain. "I was in the Soonwalder Hof on a tip—probably a bad one, as it turns out. And you gave me a chance to break into the circle. I *was* going to use you."

"But I didn't know anything . . . anyone. . . ."

"I know that. Now. At the time, nobody knew anything, we all collided in the dark. The German police had no idea I was there. It was just dumb luck, the way things went. And me being there with you when everything happened."

"If I hadn't read your poems," she said to the window. Then she looked back to Thorne. "Are they really your poems?"

Thorne nodded. "Anyway, they weren't expecting me. Just you. I screwed everything up on the buggers."

"And now you're taking care of me. Because you have to, you say."

"It's my duty."

"As a soldier," she said. Thorne thought he heard more than a little cynicism in that, and cynicism was the wrong way for her to be heading now.

"*Yes,* goddammit. As a soldier. And maybe it's more complicated than that, too. But it doesn't matter. I'm *going* to take care of you."

"And your government? Your Army? You killed German policemen . . ." It wasn't cynicism at all, now. She was just mixed up. Like every other poor bastard on earth.

"They would've killed me."

"So all this is why you're not on the television."

Thorne wrinkled his mouth, amused at the graveside. "Yeah. It looks like they want to keep it national."

"Are your people waiting for you? Out there?"

"Probably. I'm not sure what they think of all this, how much they know." He shrugged. "They've waited before. But listen. Please, Maria. There are three things you must believe. One, I'm *not* using you. Two, I'm going to take care of you. I'm going to get you out of this shit-eating country, for a start. And, third, I'm going to come back here and fucking well crucify the sonsofbitches responsible for all this. Maybe I'll be able to do it through the governments, maybe they don't know the whole story. But if I can't, if they're in on it, I'll do it some other way. I'll do it with my bare goddamned hands. But I'm going to finish this."

She leaned her body against the window, pressing her forehead against the glass like a child. Her thick arm had no strength in Thorne's hand anymore.

"I don't know," she whispered. "I don't know." She was exhausted from too much thinking. When nothing made sense. "You saved my life, I know that. And I'm grateful to you. I even trust you, though it's probably foolish of me. I have no choice, you see. Anyway, as soon as I was able to think—to feel—I knew I trusted you. I only wanted to know why I'm going to die."

Thorne yanked her furiously away from the window, made her face him. This sloppy, weary child.

"You're *not* going to die, goddammit. If you trust me at all, trust that."

"They'll kill you too," she said calmly. "The police kill everything. I don't want you to die, though. It's not necessary, I think. And you've already given me two days."

Thorne almost slapped her face. He just wanted her to believe. It was vital that at least one of them believe.

"You're not going to die," he said, pleading now.

"They kill everything," she insisted. Suddenly, before he could prevent it, she was clutching to him. There was strength in her arms again now. She held her body, her belly and breasts, shut against him. And he was staggered by the incredible softness of her, the sad big-girl smells. He gave up on the machine man and laid his arms gently around her.

"It doesn't matter," she said. "It doesn't even matter. People die all the time. . . ."

They lay calming on a mattress on the floor, with a light blanket drawn haphazardly over them. Thorne had one hand slipped back beneath his head, while the other comforted the girl. His feet were sticking out of the blanket, sweat-chilled in the cool air. He drew one leg up into the warm and kicked the covering lower, a little too low. The artificial starlight of the city shone in blue on the girl's pooling breasts.

She was lovely to look at like that, just then, in the bad light. Thorne didn't readjust the blanket immediately.

"Cold like that?" he asked.

She smoothed her cheek and hair against him: no.

In the other room the television groaned Bavarian music. Horrible noise, far better than the news.

"Maria," Thorne whispered.

"Yes?"

"Nothing. Just 'Maria.' "

Live to be a hundred. Have a dozen babies with some up-front dude. And grin a lot.

"Just rest."

At first, she'd been a shy and clumsy lover—then abruptly exuberant, overwhelmed, drained. With no levels of accelerating joy in between. But it didn't matter. It wasn't a hungry seduction, he'd had no urgent need of her, he would never have elected to be her lover. He was too responsible. Yet, now, he was suddenly glad to make love to her. To give her pleasure, give her anything. Even as they had lain adjusting their bodies, familiarizing toward first rhythms, he'd felt that it wasn't really him she was making love to. But it didn't matter at all. He'd cheated that way, too, in his day.

The slaphappy racket on the television ended in midbeat. News bulletin. The Minister for Internal Affairs has requested the extension of special emergency powers to the police . . .

"Have you ever traveled?" Thorne demanded. He didn't wait for a reply. "Do you know how wonderful and beautiful the world is? Every single place has its spectacle and glory, for those who are willing to see it. Sometimes you only have to open your eyes. Sometimes you have to look around you pretty hard. Sometimes you have to be patient because it's a special time of day or night or year. But it's always there. The magnificence is always, always there, the beauty, the wonder . . ."

"You're beautiful and wonderful."

"Oh, no. That's wrong. You mustn't say that. Don't say anything. Just listen to me now. Once, an incredibly long time ago, in a war, *my* war, I was leading a platoon of scared kids through the jungle. This was a new place, spooky as hell, and I was up there leading with maps that only showed blank expanses of green because nobody'd ever been there—at least nobody who was making maps for the U.S. Army—and this jungle was so thick overhead photography couldn't begin to penetrate it. I tried to act like I knew where the hell we were going, but really we were just following a compass azimuth. They all knew the maps were bad. But they'd decided to trust me, to make me responsible. It was my job, after all. And I was so afraid. All those lives and a useless map in my hand and fucking jungle that reached out and grabbed you no matter how carefully you moved. And hot. God, it was hot. The jungle really stinks when it gets that hot. Grabbing and grabbing at you. We went through so slow. Just waiting for the shit to come down all around us. And—suddenly—I pushed through a curtain of vines and found myself on the edge of a goddamned cliff. I mean it must've been over a hundred meters straight down. And not even a bump on the map. Everybody bunched up around me and we just stood there. Amazed. Shit, words don't do it. A bunch of burned-out grunts looking out over miles and miles of the richest, ripest, sun-happy green greenness any man ever saw. There was even a breeze.

It was like turning a streetcorner and meeting God face to face. Nobody said a word. We just sat down and rested. It was so beautiful I almost broke down in tears. But I couldn't let my men see me crying. It was important for them to think I was tough. Anyway, it was a good day. A great day. Nobody died. They were always good days when nobody died. Later, of course, we fought in that valley. Didn't go particularly well, either. In the end, the flyboys had to strip it with chemicals. It's on the maps now, though."

The girl petted him, being kind and understanding in the best tradition of a long list of lovers and top-shelf whores. The story really *had* been for her, he swore it to himself. In the beginning, at least, it had honestly been for her.

The TV played more bad music in the other room.

"You must be a good soldier," the girl said, tracing the line of a scar. They always found the scars, in every darkness. It wasn't difficult.

═══ 11 ═══

In the morning, Thorne went to call his people. He left the Ingram with the girl. He'd shown her, painstakingly, how simple it was to operate. And she'd nodded dutifully. But he didn't really believe she'd even try to use it. It was only that leaving the weapon seemed the gallant thing to do, he'd been conditioned by a thousand films. He realized his folly, and even—amusedly—its motivation, and still went unarmed down the stairs.

The normalcy of the streets came as a shock. Shut away with the relentless distortions of the television and the girl's fear, he'd begun to imagine that the world outside was in a state of siege. But, out on the pavement, the wives with their net shopping bags were far more concerned about the quality of the tomatoes than they were with dead cops and hunted girls. Traffic lurched, idled and nudged, shops swarmed with mathematics-bothered women while in raw lots workmen built. Thorne's course took him past two utterly unconcerned policemen.

He made the call from a booth in a café that was vivid with morning-coffee smells.

Ferry answered immediately. "Trans-Atlantic Vehicles." Thorne figured his hard-luck colleague had even slept in the office, waiting for this call.

"How's the war?" Thorne asked.

"Jack—Christ, where are you?"

"I'm here."

"Here *where?"*

"In the European theater. Do the Germans monitor your line?"

"Jack, we've got a problem."

"And I'm it."

Ferry hesitated for just a second. "You could say that. We need to see you, you have to leave Germany. As soon as possible."

"Maybe I've already left."

"The connection's too good."

"All right."

"The locals are pissing fire."

"I know. I figured."

"What actually hap—no, save it. You can tell me everything in person."

"No. I can't. Not just yet."

"Why?" Ferry was becoming a bit exasperated now. Days of sitting and coffee and cigarettes.

"I've got a problem, too."

There was a pause, all complicated by their near-friendship and their separate duties. Then Ferry said, "We shouldn't be talking about any of this on an open line."

"Sorry. You'll have to convince me from now on."

Ferry hesitated again, then apparently decided to hell with the rules. "I'm afraid for you. The Germans say they're reconciled to letting you walk away from it—God knows, they should be. But they won't rule out chance accidents. If you get in the way. And the Chief's done all he's about to do on your behalf, he flew in from Brussels to deal personally with the Germans on this. He wants this case closed fast. Can you imagine what the headlines would've been if the Germans hadn't clamped a lid on the whole affair? 'U.S. Agent in Gunbattle with German Police.' Have you ever been around a four-star when he's sweating something?" Ferry snorted. "Lucky thing for you he's so pissed at the Germans. He has a gut feeling they haven't come completely clean yet. There've been a lot of disconnects on this one. Personally, I think they're up to something, too. You've got to come in where we can help you." Ferry broke off for a few seconds, but he hadn't yet passed the conversation back to Thorne.

Thorne pictured the older man sucking in life through his cigarette. When they'd first worked together, in Berlin, Ferry had smoked constantly while bureaucratic paranoia had degenerated into silliness around two sensible men.

"The Germans could have big trouble with this one," Ferry went on. "They want that girl, Jack."

"I know. Can we help her? No, let me rephrase that: are there any circumstances under which we would help her? I mean, she's innocent on every goddamned charge—they know that, don't they?"

Ferry was thoughtfully slow in answering. Fueling himself up with his Marlboro. "To the last question:

yes. It's pretty well sorted out. God, they've got a bad one on their hands."

"And they're handling it badly," Thorne said calmly. It was vital, and exhausting, to remain calm. "They're doing a terrible thing. An inexcusable thing. And you haven't answered the other question."

"They don't see where they have much of a choice. It's a mess, the present government could even fall. I agree the business with the girl stinks, but they're cleaning up the other end too." Ferry's voice seemed to come closer to the phone, to hush. "I'm telling you as a friend: everybody's rushing to cover their asses. And you're standing in the middle."

"Answer my question. Fuck friendship. You're absolved of your responsibility. You're speaking for my government now. You're an official representative, and I want an official answer. Is there any way we'll help the girl?"

"Please, Jack. Come on in."

*"An*swer me."

"All right. The answer's no. You know that. She's theirs."

Thorne had known what to expect. He'd known, with absolute certainty, what the answer would be.

He punched the phone booth wall with his fist.

"They have no *right.*"

He didn't understand this. He felt his guts go all out of control. There was an actual physical pain that bent him at the waist, dropping him weakly against the wall of the booth.

Then it was all gone. Except for a tiny ache in his hand. He peered out of the booth, making sure he hadn't attracted too much attention to himself.

The café-sitters were reading papers or spreading butter.

Ferry was speaking to him. "Don't. For everybody's sake. You know how the world works, buddy. You give it your best shot, then cut your losses. And you've given it your best shot. Come on in. For your own sake."

"What about the girl's sake?"

"Is she really so important? Come on, Jack. Is one girl as important as the survival of the closest thing to a rational, decent, functioning democratic government the Germans have ever had? What do you want—the Cold War back? Don't pretend you're naïve. If you've done any thinking at all the last few days, you know they're going to have to wrap this one up fast. They don't like it, either. They're not monsters."

"Bullshit. Did you see the Chancellor on TV?"

"Where are you?"

"I'm with the girl. And I'm staying with her."

"It won't do any good. You're only going to do more harm to more people. And possibly get your own ass dead into the bargain."

"I won't stand for it. I can't. Shit. How can you?"

It was finally too much for Ferry. It was a lot for any man. Thorne knew.

"Goddamn it, Major. I'm *or*dering you to get your ass into my office."

Thorne let the sad echo of it die away. Then he said gently, "I regard that as an unlawful order, sir."

"What are you, cuntstruck over the little bitch?"

Thorne smiled. It was a ridiculous thought, unthinkable. "We have one last item of business, sir. You said both you and the Chief think the Germans are holding something back. Well, maybe I can help you out on that one. I finally got a few things sorted out last night. Couldn't believe I'd been so dumb. Did the Germans tell you who actually bombed the commissary? Do you have any idea how big this really is?"

"What're you talking about?"

"You must have all the technical afteractions on your desk by now. Go back and read them again, and think about what I'm going to tell you. Two bombs, set by pros with access to the facility. Think about everything that's happened since." Thorne laughed bitterly. "Hell, the Germans aren't just involved in a cover-up. They're involved in the cover-up of a cover-up. The commissary was bombed by the police themselves. Our good buddies, the German *Polizei*. Did the Germans brief you on that?"

"That's crazy," Ferry said. "That's the craziest goddamned thing I've ever heard. Who's telling you this? Who's helping you? Where are you?" But the man was only talking, he'd lost the weave of the conversation, lost Thorne.

"I'm going to hang up now," Thorne interrupted. "In case the electronic wizards are out."

But he didn't want to hang up. He felt there was more, somehow, far more to say. He looked out through the glass at the neat tables of customers munching sweet rolls. A waitress rushed by with a steaming metal coffeepot. It was a terrible way to end it, Ferry deserved better. Ferry and he could've been —should've been, almost were, friends. And Ferry'd gone out on a limb for him on this one—hell, the hardluck bastard was probably on a damn thin branch right now. Ferry was one of the good ones. Thorne shut his eyes, trying to get everything to come clear. It was important to come up with just a few decent, accurate words. Precious opportunities were being thrown away forever.

Thorne hung the receiver back on its gallows.

Luise, their link with the underground, opened the door of the apartment for Thorne. She hadn't come alone this time. A fashionably dressed young man stooped around the kitchen table, laying out barber's tools. The chairs were draped with a choice of men's suits, elegant flannels and respectable tweeds. Thorne put down the bag with the pastries he'd bought.

"Where's Maria?" he demanded.

The young man went on with his task.

Luise said, "In the bathroom. Being prepared. Where have you been?"

Thorne gestured nonchalantly toward the bag he'd set down. "Hunting up some breakfast."

"You were told not to leave this apartment." She was quite stern, a no-nonsense character if there ever was one.

Thorne was not in the best of moods. But he kept his discipline now.

"Lady, you didn't bring any supplies yesterday, and for all I knew you weren't coming today."

Luise considered for a moment. Thorne expected her to start making threats and laying down additional conditions. But she abruptly changed her tone.

"It doesn't matter," she said. "Sit down and we'll

get started. Your journey's all arranged. To Strasbourg, as you requested."

Thorne could hardly believe he'd heard her correctly. The beautiful simplicity. Sit down. Strasbourg. All arranged. After the phone conversation, with its strenuous fury and despair, this was nearly unbelievable. Strasbourg. Maybe they had a chance, after all.

He'd known something was up when he saw the young man with the barber's kit. But he'd assumed it would be just another move, or only a precautionary make-over. He hadn't dared to hope. But the harsh little woman had said it. Out loud.

Thorne did as he'd been told. He sat down. Reeling gleefully behind his stone face. And the young man took up scissors and a comb from his neat row of gear.

"This is Georg," Luise said. "He'll be your driver. He's good."

A tuft of severed hair dropped past Thorne's eye. He was going to make a crack about a man of many talents, but he let it go. There was no point in antagonizing these people in any way, not now, not if there was a chance in ten thousand.

"We're going to put you across at Wissembourg," Luise went on. "One of the customs officials is sympathetic to us. Many people are, you know. You would be surprised."

"On which side do you wish your hair to be parted?" Georg asked. He had a calm, reassuringly manly voice.

Thorne had to think for a moment. It had been years since he'd parted his hair. He always wore his hair spilling in loose curls and waves, even in the heat of the Mideast. He hadn't worn a part since his uniformed days.

"The left," he said. Clearly, these people had been hard at work, putting a package together. With the police gone rabid all around them. Thorne was impressed. He was almost happy. He had to restrain himself now so as not to begin thanking them prematurely.

Strasbourg, City of Wonder.

Two more women came in from the other room. It was a long moment before Thorne recognized Maria.

First of all, it was the other woman who caught the eye. Blond, affluently sexy type. Much leg. The hot young exec's wife, with an adventurous approach to fidelity. The other girl looked like a secretary who'd made the big connection and stopped watching her figure. The poor goddamned girl, Thorne thought. He already remembered her jeans and tumbling hair nostalgically.

Her hair was cut short now, curled and hennaed. Her broad face was heavily made up and she wore a dark flowered skirt with matching vest over a soft turtleneck. As a transformation, it was incredibly effective. This was not the same girl. But it made Thorne sad.

The worst of it was that Thorne sensed a newly awakened pride in her now, she was modeling for him.

"I didn't recognize you," Thorne said.

"Neither will anyone else," Luise cut in. Her voice, at all times, had a special sourness. "It'll be the same with you."

The tufts had stopped falling and now tiny snippets dusted off his nose and made him wince.

"You know," he said to Luise, Georg and the meat-quickening blonde, "I wasn't sure you were going to help us." He leaned forward, away from Georg's touch, and slid the bag of pastries across the table toward Maria. It was hard for him to look at her now. They'd made her look insensitive, in addition to her normal bigness, like some nasty steno bitch. And she wasn't insensitive, he knew. "Breakfast," he said, "they're good," and he sat back under Georg's hands.

"We weren't sure," Luise told him. "We still don't understand your peculiar relationship to all this. *I* don't trust you. But Maria does. And we would do anything for Maria." She smiled—her first smile—at Maria. It was a bad smile, given by an indifferent aunt to a child. An unnatural, constructed thing. "Maria is a heroine."

Thorne looked quickly to Maria. And he met the old intelligence in her eyes again. She, at least, had no illusions about being a heroine. Her wise eyes pleaded with Thorne to let it pass, to take advantage of this foolishness.

Of course. That was the whole point. Thorne realized he was too jumpy, too touchy.

"My concern," Thorne said, "is that she remain a living heroine." He turned his winter-eyes, Zen-of-killing look on Luise for the first time, just to bring home his point. And it startled her, he could tell. "That's all you need to trust about me."

The woman backed down, and dug deep into her handbag. Georg brushed off Thorne's ears and neck, then offered him a mirror.

It was funny. He looked like a soldier.

He put down the mirror and looked up at Maria.

She was going hungrily at one of the pastries, leaning over the table so as not to get any crumbs on her new clothes.

"You look different," she said through a munch.

Thorne nodded. He smiled a little.

Luise produced two passports, both Swiss. "At the border, if you should be stopped, speak French to the German police and German to the French."

Thorne took his passport and opened it to the photo. It was incredible. The picture the woman had taken two days back looked more like him now, with disciplined hair. The whole passport was good. Thorne had never seen a better job.

"This is good," he said.

"We have the best of everything," Luise told him with cold pride. "People, talent, resources. They have no idea. They see only the tip of the iceberg."

Thorne's professional interest was aroused, and he decided to tease a little, probingly. "And the right? Don't they have anything?"

Luise looked at him fiercely. Eye to eye. There was no "Maria's a heroine" bullshit in this look.

"They," she said, "have Germany."

=== 12 ===

They had good tourist weather. They left Frankfurt in the last glistening mists, riding in a fast BMW sedan with Swiss plates. Georg was an excellent driver, he flashed through the confused traffic by the airport and got maximum benefit out of the autobahn. Along the tough highway the leaves were changing, and a huge, inspiring blue sky spread itself over the industry-choked cities and towns. They turned south, and on their left the long sudden ridge of the Odenwald seemed to curl like an autumn-colored wave above the productive, ignorant towns. At Mannheim, they crossed the wide, gray Rhine, heading west now. The factories thinned and the car turned to flirt with a line of hills. Men and women worked slowly in yellowing vineyards, and the light had a thoughtful clarity on the land. Side windows lowered a few inches flooded the car with cidery air. In the back seat, the girl slept with surprising ease, and Thorne wasn't badly worried.

In the imagination and the Army, borders were crossed on miserable nights, with rain to cover your noise, or at dawn, in force. But this would be a passage in early afternoon, in fine weather. Wissembourg was another one of many, many places he'd been, a French border town that prospered by feeding visiting barbarians well. If it all went neatly, they could cry a few happy tears and chow down.

And if it didn't go neatly? Georg had an automatic pistol, and he had the Ingram, and it wouldn't be the worst imaginable day for it. Good weather, good terrain. And an enemy who needed combating.

If only he could get the girl through, though. To sneak her away and find her another name and wave her off on a boat or a plane to another chance at a life. He'd almost given up on her. He would never have abandoned her, but he'd come very close to the sin of despair. In the minutes after his phone booth argument with Ferry, he'd gone through the healthy streets like a man addled with plague. Now, once again, there was hope.

They left the wine villages and drove over the golden crests of the Palatine Forest, dodging main roads. Thorne could feel France looming up ahead, he could visualize the sudden lowering of the terrain and the big French radar stations perched back in the Vosges.

Driving through a village in the hills, Georg decided he wanted to stop. For a beer. Thorne looked him over for the first time in an hour and saw a different man. The confident driver looked nervous as hell. With the border coming.

Yes, it was a frightening thing after all. Thorne hated to stop when they were so close, but Georg was obviously in genuine need of a beer, and maybe of more than just one.

They pulled into the dirt parking lot of the next *Gasthaus*. Nothing special, not even touristy. A bar for the locals, with shingle siding. The girl was still asleep, Thorne thought that she must've been a dozen kinds of tired and he was tempted to leave her in the car. But he was afraid she'd panic if she woke up alone.

He reached back over the seat, touched the nearness of her thigh, full flesh under the new skirt.

"Maria," Thorne whispered, as though it were now only dawn, "Maria . . ."

She came gently to herself, with no sudden fear of bullets and borders. "Where are we?"

"Beer stop. Georg's thirsty."

Georg smiled weakly at the two of them. Thorne hoped this stranger wouldn't lose it completely at the border. It was hard enough fighting alongside men you knew and trusted.

Maria made a motion to brush hair out of her eyes as she sat up, a habit from the years of long, full hair. But there was no long hair now, and she remembered, smiling at herself.

"So many new things to remember," she said with a smile that was not at all clear.

Thorne opened the car door to the crisp air.

"Come on, lady," he said. "Let's get a beer."

It was good to stretch for a moment, to look up at the overripe hills. The colors and scale reminded him bittersweetly of northern Pennsylvania. All it needed was the sooty-plaid jackets of old hunters and the pop of a Remington pump down the valley.

Ringnecks rising from brown grass, then, later, in silent whiteness, deer elegant against black tree trunks. Tracking. And the old man liquor-breathed and wild in his pride at his son's first kill. The carcass on the car hood, the family fuss. My Jackie's a born hunter.

Thorne slung the carryall with the Ingram over his shoulder like a kid's bookbag and reached a hand back to steady the girl.

Georg led the way in. There was no light on, the taproom was amber in the cast of the windows. It was empty, maybe closed for an after-lunch pause.

"Anybody here?" Georg called back over the bar, at an open archway.

No answer.

"Hello?"

They stood waiting in the rich shadows. It seemed somehow silly for the place, the one place they'd picked, under these circumstances, to be closed.

"A man could help himself," Georg said. He already seemed calmer. Sometimes it only took fresh air to rinse the sudden fear off you.

At last they heard footsteps. A mustached antique of a man, one of the Kaiser's finest, with a ball belly that sagged like an old tit, shuffled in from the back room.

He smiled at the business, bowed his head respectfully to the girl.

"Three big beers," Thorne told him. Relieved, the three travelers loosened from each other and circled round a table, Thorne guiding Maria casually so that her back would be to the old man. You had to pay attention to detail.

The beer was cold and pleasantly bitter, Maria drank lazily. She looked as though her head were still full of dreams. Georg, by contrast, drank swiftly beside Thorne, heading determinedly for the bottom of the glass. Thorne suddenly felt a pitying comradeship for the younger man. It was okay to be a little nervous. It was hard to be a good soldier, and today the two of them were being good soldiers, fighting the good fight.

"Tonight," Thorne announced to his comrades, "we are going to dine like lords in France. Wine for Mademoiselle, and only the best Alsatian beer for the gentlemen."

But his companions' thoughts were on other things. Georg paid attention only to his glass, and the girl smiled blankly at him. Still, this little disappointment only filled Thorne more fully with feelings of comradeship, of shared justness and danger, almost-love. There had to be a way to wake the decency that slept in all men. The right philosopher just hadn't come along.

"I have to go to the toilet," Georg said, and he was up and gone. The old man was off somewhere, too, leaving Thorne and Maria alone.

He reached for her forearm, taking hold of it tenderly, asking her attention.

"It's simply amazing—"

The world exploded in Thorne's ear and the girl tore away from him, her face bursting out with a white and crimson gush. But she wasn't dead, she was screaming and falling, rolling off the table onto the floor. In a pulse, Thorne's trained hand reached down for the bag with the Ingram, even as he was rolling out of his chair, the gunman's position already computed and his own best cover selected.

But the Ingram wasn't there. The bag was gone. A second thunderclap put an end to the girl's screams, and everything fell into place. Georg's nerves, the beer stop so close to the border, the trip to the john. Thorne scrambled between the tables, in heartsick fury at giving up the girl's life and his own so stupidly.

He was looking toward the windows, the door, getting ready to break, still not willing to give up but at the same time waiting for the wasteful end of it all, when a voice said, "You can get up now, Major Thorne. Nobody's going to harm you."

There were plenty of men, with plenty of guns, and other men with cameras. The photographers were careful to get only the dead girl in their frames. Thorne sat obediently at a corner table, staring down at the brand-new U.S. passport, at the plane tickets and the money, listening.

"You will be escorted across the border. We will drive you to the airport at Strasbourg. You will fly from Strasbourg to Paris, where you will make a timely connection to your own country. Obviously, you will not be welcome to visit the Federal Republic of Germany at any future date."

Everyone had wanted the girl dead. Everybody but him. And he'd lost.

He was waiting to feel it.

The man across the table from him had on a truly beautiful suit. It was the gray of October mornings when rich women rode horses. It was a wonderful suit, and it fit the man perfectly. Clearly, it took an official of some importance to wear such a suit and to speak with such incontestable authority, oblivious to the punctuating flashbulbs.

Of course, there were countries where the Prime Minister did not have such an estimable suit, countries where the women worked like horses and only machine guns spoke with incontestable authority. But those savage nations were remote and not pertinent. This was a matter between civilized men, in a land full of well-dressed officials.

"You understand that we would have been perfectly justified in killing you, Major Thorne. The only reason we didn't was the gratitude our government continues to feel toward yours for favors long past. Personally, I can tell you that we are not flattered by this sort of meddling in our internal affairs. The Federal Republic is not a third-world nation."

The man in the glorious suit stood up and went away. He had a very important walk, and the men with the guns and the men with the cameras moved quickly out of the way to let him pass. When the suit disappeared, Thorne watched the photographers. He had no interest in the men with the guns, he'd seen plenty of men with guns. But the photographers were fascinating to watch as they fluttered and perched over the dead girl. They took close-ups, full-length shots, even pictures of the blood-spattered wall. They didn't watch their step. They watched only for good angles and tramped unconcerned over bits of bloody garbage. *Der Spiegel* would get small crisp black-and-whites, *Stern* would be able to run full-page shots in color. The Springer papers would get a chance to do a truly sensational front-page, with a faceless corpse artfully wedged between the overheadlined columns of non-news. Everything would be in order. The editorial writers would continue to wonder smugly what had gone wrong with the overprivileged young. . . .

The man in the marvelous suit came back into the room. All the gunslingers and photographers crowded each other to clear the way again. As he passed the girl's body, a brief smile spooked over his strict official lips. It was the smile of a victor.

Thorne looked at the girl one last time. Dead meat in a fine new dress.

The man in the suit stood over Thorne. There were two other, younger men behind him now in suits that were very impressive, though not so bluntly wonderful. But you sensed from these men that the wonderful suits would come. Just as you could sense all three of these men struggling not to break discipline and smile in satisfied glee.

The girl's legs were askew, her carcass sagged. She was as graceless in death as she'd been in life. She made an ideal corpse for them to close the case with. All the newspaper and magazine readers, all the millions of television watchers would get a thrill undiluted by guilt. No one would have to feel sorry for this sloppy dead thing.

"It's not over," Thorne promised, in English. He didn't even consider speaking German now. He raised his face slowly, until his eyes met the eyes of the man in the hateful, enraging suit.

"It's not over, cocksucker."

The man in the suit didn't understand, or simply wasn't impressed. Even his eyes were professionally superior and aloof.

"Come along, Major. It's time we started you on your way."

PART
TWO

=== 13 ===

Thorne waited in the darkness of a doorway for Leedom to come out. It was almost restful to wait now, after the days in motion. It hadn't been difficult at all to get back to Athens, but it seemed as though the trip had taken a very long time. Two nights and parts of three days from Paris. Time enough to review a lifetime.

No one had even been waiting to meet him in Paris. They'd all assumed it was over and, apparently, that he'd do what was expected of him at this point. Out of gratitude for being allowed to walk away from the mess. It was only common sense.

But it wasn't over. And he wasn't feeling particularly grateful. And common sense had no place in any of it.

In Paris he'd simply cashed in his transatlantic ticket and jumped on a bus. In the city where he'd always liked to sit and drink while the sidewalks painted themselves with women, there'd been just enough time to buy a sweater, jeans and a train ticket to Bologna. In the morning, in Italy, he'd had several good coffees and a bad sandwich, fighting his way through a hangover of whirling thoughts. Then there was the long day's ride on down to Bari and the slow local on to Brindisi. All that stretch of the journey had been devoted to sorting things out one more time, learning again how stupid intelligent men could be. What had been unthinkable a few days before was now infuriatingly obvious. Perhaps there was still more, but he believed he was getting the thing into focus at last. The hard part now was to overcome his anger.

A little bit of anger provided energy. But he was engulfed by it, and he had to regain operational control. The first step was to clearly identify his objectives. It wasn't viable to just start wasting everyone who seemed to deserve it like the avenging angel of the Lord. The pig in the elegant suit would have to be written off. And it would be a waste to go after the underground types who'd sold them out. Sooner or later, the German government would take care of them.

Ruling out the bureaucrats and the underground left Thorne with a clear target: *the bastards who'd started the whole business* by blasting the commissary, who'd killed Maria's lover and sent her on her way to her death. Krull, the big orange-haired cop, and his pals. It seemed outrageous now that he hadn't killed the sonofabitch when he'd had the chance.

Thorne still didn't believe in revenge for its own sake. Or at least he didn't think he did. But he still, in his way, believed in duty. And he'd been given a mission, which he still hadn't completed. He'd been very strict and clearheaded about everything when he got off the train at Brindisi and bought his ticket for the ship to Patras. Then, getting on board, the painful business with the new girl had begun.

But he refused to think of her now. He was too tired and it was too hard. He had troubles enough in this changed city, and if a goddamned heartbreaking young woman had stumbled in at the worst, the most insane, of all possible times to insistently remind him that *he* wasn't dead, it would not do to think about her now. He had a mission, the one he'd wanted for so long, the one that had already destroyed so much of what he'd believed in.

It was just like Nam, really. So many terrible things done by men of high ideals.

Thorne was cold in his doorway, the sweater wasn't enough against the autumn night. Athens was a sad city now. The summer plumage was all gone. What the August light made dramatic was shabby in the off-season pale. The tourists gave the Greeks identity. But now there were only a few hardy wanderers and disappointed retired couples who'd mistakenly assumed this was a constantly sunburned land; and the Athenians were identical crows. The popular excuses disappeared with the swarms of tourists, leaving the city embarrassed by its lack of planning, terrible air and the inability to serve its own needs. On the fabled hill, the ruins had cancer. Below, in the government buildings, dogmatic men wasted their energies blaming each other for every screw-up, then united to blame other governments. They were all waiting faithfully for membership in the European Economic Community as though it were the new Messiah.

Why couldn't men govern themselves effectively? For thousands of years they'd written so beautifully about it, they routinely made speeches full of hope and saintliness. But they never pulled it off.

And this city. Its dead, dead past was a plague on it. When all else failed the incompetent Greek politician, he invoked the inaccurate popular notion of that brief semidemocracy. *We* shaped Western civilization, they cried, as though Western civilization were still something to be proud of. While modern Athens strangled itself. No fucking wonder people dove headfirst for the myths of Atlantis and Shambala. Reality hadn't shit on them yet.

Thorne waited, a bit less patient now. He was so tired, and it was so damned hard to keep going, and the girl on the ship had nearly wrecked it all. But it would only be a little longer now, and Leedom would have to come out. Old Lee was the only one left. The woman, Julie, was hours gone. The young college-type was gone, too. Thorne wondered if the kid had dropped Mary Renault yet. You read that pretty crap at the risk of missing the history that was sweating itself out all around you. It made Thorne think of the maze of markets, an Oriental side of Athens, one that genuinely deserved touring. In the markets of Athens you could buy peacocks and all spices. But the main attraction was the cruciform meat hall. Strong, fat, shirtless men grasped the raw sides in their arms, bathing in blood, engaged in useful labor, hurling carcasses and laughing with their companions. In summer, the place reeked unforgettably from old scraps that had found their way into cracks and corners.

God, he was tired of all the killing. He was sick of man-wrought death of Europe, of travel and the hundred too many lovers who'd finally just been fucks because they had no frame of reference from which to truly love him, not even the right language, and he himself hadn't had the time. He could hardly believe the mess he'd made of his life, and he thought he understood now how men on death row felt. There had always seemed to be good enough reasons at the time of the deed. . . .

This was the last one. Definitely. He was shutting it down after this and going home. To hell with them all.

He hadn't even noticed the girl standing in front of him in line until the ship's officer started giving her a hard time. She hadn't gone to the harbor police to have her ticket stamped. The officer explained the problem to her in Greek, Italian and German, while she told him she didn't understand, first in American English, then in pretty schoolgirl French. Thorne was anxious to get through control and put another border behind him, and, on impulse, he interrupted and explained everything to the girl in English. Then the ship's officer started beseeching him, in German, to tell the girl to hurry, the ship was leaving in ten minutes. Unreasonably nervous of using German, Thorne answered the man in ungrammatical, halting Greek. Several escalating confusions later, Thorne was leading the girl hurriedly along the dockside, then up a flight of stairs to the harbor police.

They rushed back to the ship, only to find that, as usual, there would be a half hour's delay before sailing. For a kind moment, Thorne was just amused at being back in the Med again. And the girl smiled happily, setting her small backpack down by his flight bag, and insisted on buying him a cup of coffee. She was unarguably pretty, with very dark brown hair and smart eyes, and never doubted that her offer would be accepted. She didn't even give him time to reply.

Thorne watched her as she went to fetch their Nescafés, only now beginning to wake up to her. Her jeans didn't have the European death-grip on every fold of her ass, but they fit her nicely. She went confidently on long legs, an old herringbone blazer trailing off her squared shoulders. Now that he was really letting himself look at her, he felt an ache of recognition. He didn't know the particular girl. But he knew the type. It was amazing how some things didn't change. As she came back toward him with the steaming plastic cups and one of the finest smiles American dentistry could secure, he felt belly-haunted. She was even wearing a Shetland sweater with a neat plaid shirt collar dressed out.

He was suddenly afraid to talk to her. He had no time for the self-indulgent pain of nostalgia now. He had to focus everything on the mission, it had to be his sole reason for living. Especially since he didn't really want it anymore, since he was sick at heart and just wanted to run from the whole thing. He had no energy to spare on dreaming about old girlfriends and getting stiff-dicked over some young college piece. So many people had *died* and he had so much to carry on alone and there was such a long way to go. It didn't even seem decent to chat, somehow it wasn't acceptable to even be civil. He had Maria's blood all over him.

But he *wanted* to talk to this smart-eyed girl. Just to speak pleasantly with her for half an hour. He was even boy-afraid that she was only doing her duty by buying him a cup of coffee in thanks, that she'd dance away before he could use her to rest his soul just a little.

She stood before him, holding out his Nescafé.

"Shall we drink it out on deck?" she asked. "I've never actually 'set sail' before, and this *is* the Mediterranean."

Thorne followed her obligingly. They went up on the top deck, behind the wheelhouse. There was a night wind off the water, and it was cold. But the girl said she didn't mind. She sipped her coffee and turned her face into the eye-narrowing gusts and seemed to bask in it. She had unbothered girlish lips and a small nose of marble exactness. The big engines growled power, and the horn, blasting from its perch above their heads, made the horizon jump. The girl looked up, white-faced. The sky was a black velvet river of clouds flowing in from the sea, with moon-burned gray shallows. Then she turned her speechless enthusiasm to the jewelry of the shoreline. It was important, and difficult, not to watch her too much. Thorne leaned on the railing and watched the sea.

Pushing fifteen years. Since he'd gripped the earnest girls as they braved their first whole nights of grown-up sex. He'd been as serious and silly as any of them, and they'd had wonderful times which they'd dreamed through and taken for granted. Girls in classrooms and coffeehouses, in touchingly bohemian apartments and in hunting cabins on weekends that got beyond sex by Sunday, for better or worse. Later on, after the war, when he'd tried to go back, it hadn't worked. Those had been bad years for the girls, or maybe just bad years for himself. But there was no doubt in his mind that the earlier years, his true college years, had been the sweetest of his life. And the girls had been only a small part of it. He'd had tremendous faith in the future then, with none of the pain of reality.

Her name was Kate, and she'd gone to Penn, of all places. She'd studied the summer away at the Sorbonne and now she was roaming through the autumn. She was going to begin grad school—French lit—winter term, and she wanted to write. This trip was to acquire experience, she said. And Thorne smiled. She didn't seem pretentious to him, she didn't have that kind of voice. Only wonderfully unscarred, emotions lagging years behind her fine education. She spoke excitedly and intimately about books, mostly read, some to be written, with a stunning memory, heart half wild with too much intelligence. Thorne leaned steadily over the railing, a lonely, comprehending sponge, close enough to smell her coffee breath and be dusted now and then by a windy billow of her hair. At times he listened to her as he might've listened to Homer himself, at other times he half listened in a rich daze, slowly crumpling his empty plastic cup. It was cowardice, he realized. He was desperate for a place to hide, an excuse for stopping this unreasonable, vital pursuit of blood-diluted justice. But he was tired. And he remembered that he was a being who could order chaos into manageable beauty with words. He seemed to himself at the moment to have regained sight of something that had almost been lost. He'd slipped into a life foreign to all his real values over the years, something almost like madness. And this rare, typical girl seemed like the offer of one last chance. A final reminder that there was a world open to him even now where men could love and marry and have beautiful children and worry about things as trivial as differences in punctuation between editions. How long had it been since he'd made love to the same woman until he'd bored her? Even that seemed a great privilege to him now.

She confessed suddenly that she'd been watching him earlier, in a café in Brindisi. She'd found him interesting-looking, it was almost as if she'd known him from somewhere, and she wondered what nationality he was. He *was* American, wasn't he?

Oh, yes.

And what, she asked now, after more than an hour of talk, did he do?

"I'm a poet," Thorne said, for once in his life without calculation or embarrassment.

The girl was surprised, excited. "Really? What university do you teach at?"

"I'm afraid I don't teach. I just sort of write poetry. I do some travel writing and a bit of feature writing to pay the bills."

"Jack Thorne—or do you go by John? I feel terrible admitting it, but I'm afraid I haven't . . ."

Thorne smiled, in love with her tremendous seriousness, her diligence. "Oh, I had my brief vogue. But it would've been before your prime, Kate. We're different generations, you and I."

"I'm twenty-three," she said.

"I didn't mean that insultingly. It's only that when I was twenty-three we had a war going on, and—"

"Wait," the girl cried, almost shouted. She backed

away just an inch, turning fully to face him, to look at him without slant or obstruction. Her eyes were wide. "Wait. I *saw* you. I *have* seen you." And she thrust out a hand and before he could react she was touching at his hair, his cheek with breathtaking gentleness. "A long time ago," she said, speaking softly now. "I was only—you were on television, on PBS. It was a round-table with young writers and painters and photographers who'd been in Vietnam. I remember you, I really do, because you didn't say very much and you were so handsome—you had longer hair then— and you looked so sad. You were the saddest-looking man I'd ever seen. I remember waiting for it to be your turn to read a poem. But you never did. I was disappointed, and angry too. I remember I even tried to buy a book of your poems. Jack Thorne, I *do* remember now. But the bookstore didn't have any in stock . . . and I suppose . . . well, I suppose I just forgot about it after a while." She dropped her hand away and Thorne cringed at the loss of it. Something fine had exploded inside him, but it was already dying away. She looked at him with a faint gleam and shadow of eyes. "That must be why I thought you were so interesting-looking. An unconscious remembrance. Oh, I can't *speak,*" she said, suddenly angry at herself for not having an infallible command of her language at all times.

Thorne just looked at her without speaking. It seemed unfair that he should be hurt like this for no reason, with such a peculiar hurt. Unfair to be regaled so lovingly with one's botched life.

The girl was pensive now. Perhaps some difficult remembrance had been conjured in her too. She was truly lovely and bright, and he knew without question that he could even marry her, if he chose to. And it would be bliss to grow dull with her.

But it would've been vampirism. Things had gone too far in his life, and hate it and dread it and struggle against it though he might, he recognized that the only acceptable course was to follow the black karma to the end. You couldn't abruptly embrace sweetness and light when you'd joined the dance of the dead in the pit of demons. Could you?

In the deep night, the girl slept by him on the big lounge chairs ranked inside. The next day they ate together and sat on deck all day, talking under gray skies as the stony western coast of Greece wandered by. Thorne indulged himself. He thought of it as the prisoner's last meal. And when she finally asked him, with a pitiable attempt at nonchalance, what he was going to do after they arrived in Athens, he told her he was meeting his lover.

Alone now in an Athenian doorway, Thorne sensed that there was going to be movement across the street. A second later the side door to the antique shop opened and Leedom, sparse white hair gathering vagabond light, came out, hunching back over a jingle of keys. Leedom of Kinshasa, Leedom of Saigon, Leedom of Teheran and Phnom Penh.

Leedom of Athens.

Thorne stepped into the street to meet him, revealing himself in the little light there was.

"Christ," Leedom said, startled. "Thorne."

"Call me Jack, Lee. You always did."

Leedom looked older than Thorne remembered

him. Dying malarial skin, the sorry effect of spending year after year in countries for which you were not genetically programmed.

"Jack," Leedom said, "I . . . we weren't expecting you."

"I'm not here in an official capacity. Not exactly."

"We . . . heard there was trouble."

"There was. There is."

"We heard you'd been called in."

"We have to talk."

"You know the rules. Unless it's official . . ."

"Cut the shit. I'm onto it. I was a fool not to pick up on it right away. But I was excited. Christ, was I ever excited. You really suckered me. And I paid for it. I'm not the only one who paid, either. Now it's your turn to pay some back."

"I'm afraid you've lost me completely, Jack. And you know better than to threaten me."

Thorne shook his head, pissed off, with just a half-inch left on his fuse. "Lee, old buddy, I know a place a couple blocks away. Stays open late, enough light to keep a card game honest, strictly native clientele—your typical homeless brothers. Suppose we go there and have a couple quick ones and talk as though we were both honest men? For half an hour?"

"The only place I'm going," Leedom said sharply, "is home. And you'd better be on the next flight out."

"The alternative," Thorne said, "is for me to kill you here. I'd be doing my country a favor, wouldn't I, taking out a traitor in a sensitive position like yours?"

"What gave it away?"

They sat at a wooden table in a bright, boisterous

room. The younger customers accompanied their rapid conversations with a semaphore of handthrusts, while old men in cloth caps played clacking backgammon and sipped thin cloudy glasses of ouzo. An unshaven few snoozed over near-empty drinks. The radio jabbered. Between Thorne and Leedom sat two ouzos with two glasses of water. The liquor was still clear and undisturbed.

"Everything did. If I hadn't been playing with my dick, I would've picked up on it immediately. First of all, I know how good you are. You know their military inside out, it's your job. And any captain who drives a Mercedes, picks up foreign intel folks and treats them to a fascist spectacular in this political climate would tend to stick out just a little. And he found me too easily." Thorne shook his head over his memories of the scene with the captain. "Even after the business in Cairo, the Greek intel boys had no fucking idea who I was. Yet this dude knows my biography inside out. I pegged him for a phony, you realize that? I *had* his damned number. But I was nervous about trusting my instincts. After Cairo. And then the phone call to Ferry shot my gut feelings down. The bombing seemed to verify everything the captain said."

"Stroke of luck there," Leedom said. "Surprised us too."

"It wasn't very lucky if you were inside that commissary."

"We didn't know about that, Jack. Honestly. We only knew the U.S. Forces were going to get hit. Exactly when and in what way, we had no idea. It was supposed to be your job to find out."

"Perfect man for it, too."

"We thought so."

"The only operative who might've been open-minded enough or just goofy enough to see the situation for what it was once he was on the ground. Right?"

There was still caution in Leedom. But he was loosening now, even without the liquor. The look of sorrowful relief on his face was genuine.

"Yes."

"Then why didn't this captain—is he really a captain?"

"Oh, yes."

"Then why didn't he just put it to me straight? As a right-wing number? Why go to all the theater and trouble of painting a picture full of left-wing tangos when it would only confuse me and slow me down?"

Leedom sighed. He finally took a drink of his ouzo, a serious drink, without diluting it. "We weren't *that* sure about you. I thought I knew you. But who really knows anybody else in this business? That poetry of yours, for instance. For all I knew, some little secretary back in the Department of Defense churned that out for you. Part of the role. A role within a role. And, even so, wasn't it mentally easier for you to accept it when you thought it involved the left? It's conditioning."

Leedom was right, and the realization startled Thorne. He took an undiluted drink of his ouzo, too, and smiled close-lipped at himself.

"Yeah. Yes. I'm not proud of that."

"And, even if," Leedom drove on, "even if you had accepted the possibility, would anybody else have bought it? Would it have been politically convenient?"

"If it involved American lives," Thorne said.

"Jack," Leedom said, "it *did* involve American lives. What came of it?"

Right again. So far the old bastard was right on target. But it was still not an acceptable excuse.

"Something's going to come of it. That's why I'm here."

Leedom's face cleared, drawing back toward self-control. Thorne knew him well enough to sense the mind at work now.

"There's more," Thorne said, "isn't there?"

"Yes," Leedom said quietly, as if the volume level suddenly mattered.

"Want to make a deal?"

Leedom grew a far sorrier look than the one he'd just mastered. He took another self-indulgent swig of the liquor. "I'm not in a position to make a deal."

"Who is? Katsovakis? Our mystery captain?"

Leedom considered things one last time, then nodded slowly. "Yes."

"You know, goddammit, one thing that gave me an especially bad time was trying to figure out how a right-wing cowboy like that survived the fall of the military government. Of course he survived the crash. He helped engineer it, didn't he?"

"You'd have to ask him."

"Shit, they're better than us. Aren't they?"

"Us who?" Leedom said dryly. His voice was sour, but when Thorne looked at the face there was no more discipline left in it.

"Yeah," Thorne said. "Us who."

"I know he'd like to talk to you now," Leedom said. "Let me call him."

"About a job?" Thorne said, with instantly regretted cruelty. Leedom was bleeding. He'd probably been longing for this situation for years, just as he'd been dreading it.

Still, Thorne caught himself, the man was a traitor to his country. Something he himself was not. He was only disobedient. There was a world of difference. At least in the conscience.

Leedom overlooked Thorne's nastiness, anyway. When you'd gone through it all yourself, it was just a flea bite coming from somebody else.

"I can tell you this much," Leedom said, "the West Germans haven't solved their problem. They think they have. But we have reason to believe that this problem may soon be far worse than before." Leedom stopped. "That's all I can tell you. I shouldn't even have told you that much. You'll have to talk to Katsovakis."

"If Katsovakis' people are so interested in this, why don't they do something about it themselves?"

"Not in a position to. Listen, Jack, I'm not in a very good position myself. It would be better if you heard it from Katsovakis."

"Lee?" Thorne said, in a sudden, helpless burst of sympathy. "How'd it happen to you? I'd just like to know. For myself."

Leedom dropped his eyes toward his drink and looked it over as though the answer were reflected there. Then he smiled a little. "Got your devils, too. Haven't you? All the better men do. Although I'm not sure that applies in my case. How'd it happen? Easily. Through cowardice. Way back in Leopoldville—you remember when we called it Leopoldville?"

Thorne nodded. He remembered it from the newspapers. He'd been in high school.

"I was kidnapped. Or captured, if you will. Six of one, half dozen of the other. And I turned out to be a coward. I knew what they did to their enemies—oh, we did it, too. Not personally, so much, but we had local hire—and as soon as the gag was off my mouth I started talking. I told the other side everything. I've been telling them everything for years. I don't really think they're all that much worse than us—than you—than *them*. But it doesn't always sit well on the conscience." Leedom had kept his eyes on his glass. But now he looked Thorne directly in the eyes. And he didn't say anything further, only stared. Or let Thorne stare.

The view chilled Thorne. There was an emptiness in Leedom's eyes that earth and moon could've tumbled through. And Thorne realized he was talking with a dead man. Or, more exactly, with a man whose entire world had died around him. And this inhabitant of a dead world was decently, generously letting him have a free look at what his own future might hold.

"Go home," Leedom said abruptly, adamantly. "I won't call Katsovakis."

An old man at the next table cackled and choked over a backgammon victory. The sound was peculiarly horrid and unhealthy and it broke the stare between Leedom and Thorne.

"No," Thorne said. "I'm going to finish this."

═══ 14 ═══

They drove down familiar boulevards in Leedom's battered Fiat. With the summer dead, Glyfada had a widow's scent about it. The beaches that had so recently been dynamically overcrowded wore scarves of garbage in the moonlight. The lights of a big jet disappeared behind last season's failed discos, and the late traffic straggled off until the Fiat went through sleeping Vouliagmeni quite alone.

The highway wound around juts of rock, tamed into small resorts and hugged mountainside again. Lights blinked offshore and the dark bulk of islets interrupted the sheen of the sea. It was a ghostly drive, though not haunted by the romantic spirits of history or myth. The eeriness was right inside the car, behind the glow of the instrument panel, in the unsettling kinship Thorne was reluctantly beginning to feel with Leedom. He had no intention of signing his soul away in blood as Leedom had done, he was confidently strong about that. Yet he *had* defied his own people, and he was on his way to deal with the devil.

They were nearly to Sounion when Leedom pulled off the road and stopped by a closed gate. Through the bars Thorne could see a driveway winding up to a small partially floodlit villa edged over the sea. They had to wait only a few seconds, engine idling, before two men in dark workman's clothing materialized from a blur of scrub pines. One of them, submachine gun slung over his back, opened the gate, while the other stood at the ready with his own weapon.

The captain was waiting, alone and unarmed, by a well-lit garage. He wore bell-bottom jeans and a windbreaker and he looked as relaxed as his clothing now. A different man from the theatrical neofascist bully.

The captain didn't test anything with the offer of a handshake, but took Thorne by the arm instead, guiding him toward the house as though he were an old friend.

"Major Thorne," he said, as though he still couldn't quite believe he'd been so honored, "how fine to see you again." And he called pleasantly over his shoulder, "I'm so glad you took the initiative and arranged this meeting, Leedom."

"Captain," Thorne said, "I don't want you to misunderstand why I came here—"

"Oh, don't worry," the captain said firmly, "I have no intention of trying to enlist you on behalf of the World Socialist Order. We have more important things to discuss, I hope."

"I hope," Thorne said.

The villa had not been furnished on a Greek captain's pay. Elegant modern comforts and select antiquities blended together in one of the most congenial applications of wealth Thorne had ever seen. The captain led them into a study hung with icons all gilt and gloom and columned with leatherbound books titled in an orgy of alphabets. It was not your stereotypical Marxist reading room.

"Sit down. Please. Brandy? Perhaps for you, then, Leedom?"

Leedom was definitely drinking now. Thorne sat down in a firm chair that was covered in patterned rug cloth from the mountains. The captain handed Leedom his drink without looking at him and dropped into a chair adjacent to Thorne's.

"No doubt you're angry with me?"

"No," Thorne said. "I was. I can't afford it now."

"Leedom told me on the phone that you had everything figured out."

"Not everything. Enough. Ninety percent of what I was coming back to Athens to find out I figured out on the way. Now, it seems, there's more."

The captain dropped the last tone of sociable playfulness from his voice and got real. "Yes. There's more. It's very nearly out of control now."

"What 'it'? I want to be sure we're on the same sheet of music this time."

"The conspiracy," the captain said. "The right-wing plot to bring down the present German government and clear the way for the fascists."

"By fascists you mean the conservatives?"

"Initially."

Thorne sat back, discouraged. "No. We're not on the same sheet. I see a small plot—right-wing—to bring down the wrath of God and the German fetish for order on the radical left. To force tougher antiterrorist measures through the present government, perhaps with some faint hope of eventually bringing the conservatives back into power. But, basically, it's just the local yokels taking it into their own hands to clean up the streets of Dodge. And it looks as though they've succeeded, to a large extent. The measures have been taken, the government stands, the case is closed. Except for my end of it."

The captain shook his head, indulgently, as with a slow child.

"Yes, the government stands. The government of the Federal Republic of Germany performed magnificently, a balancing act only the most astute bureaucrats could have brought off. A threat that would have polarized the citizenry, perhaps alienated the most important Allied nation and horrified the world, has been neutralized. At the total cost of one girl. The aberration has been swept under the rug. And the present government, which is, for all its faults and willingness to play rough, the most amenable and decent the West Germans have ever had, stands."

"That's what I said, more or less." Thorne was growing impatient. It was the fate of this Greek captain to keep him eternally on edge.

"Yes," the captain said, "so far. The problem is that the success of this band of fascist terrorists, which came as rather a surprise to them, considering the casualties they took from you and the way you nearly spoiled everything—this success has only encouraged them. There's only a pair of them left—they were never more than a handful. But it takes only one man with a revolver to alter the course of history. And, you see, the government, for all its apparent success, has actually painted itself into a terribly vulnerable corner. Think about it, Major Thorne. Before all the world, they've committed themselves to the line that this entire chain of events was the doing of leftist radicals and of leftists alone. It seemed the safest thing to do. But they can't go back now. This Maria Burckhardt's body blocks the way. If the world ever learned the truth, the Chancellor and his government would certainly go tumbling. Thus, they are irrevocably committed to further punishing the left for any additional incidents that might occur. And there *will be* further incidents. The man you beat so badly, his name is Krull—"

"I know," Thorne said.

"He's been the ringleader, the prime mover in all this. A low-level official, obsessed with an idea that I would call crazy, had it not worked so well. With the aid of a few comrades he either persuaded or bullied into joining him, he caught a government by surprise and managed to steer it from below, along a pre-planned course, for a time. He must be a clever man, in his way. Certainly he understands the psychology of his countrymen. Of course, his case is not completely without precedent in Germany. At any rate, our source tells us that Krull has something new in the works right now, an operation even bigger than the others. Unfortunately, we're in the same position we were in before—our man isn't a member of Krull's inner circle, and he hasn't been able to learn the details. He's trying, but there are, of course, significant risks."

The captain kept his eyes locked with Thorne's for a moment of emphasis, then he reached for a cigarette case on the desk. He held the opened case first toward Thorne.

"I remember that you don't smoke," the captain said. "But allow me the politeness of offering."

The captain next made a perfunctory wave of the cigarette case in Leedom's direction. Leedom nodded the offer down from his seat in the shadows. But he soon drew his own crumpled pack from his suit jacket. He looked worried. Leedom always looked worried, but tonight was special. He looked like a sinner about to hear the judgment of God. He lit his cigarette with his malaria-palsied fingers, and each quiet twitch conveyed the pain of an animal that needed to be shot.

The captain lit himself a cigarette, then leaned back through its first haze toward Thorne.

"Do you know what sort of punitive action was taken against Krull? The man who bombed your commissary and later his own comrades at the police station? Do you have any idea? None. The government did their best to keep his name completely out of it. They lied and lied and lied. They have no real sympathy for the man, but it did take them a little while to grasp what was going on, and by then they were content just to keep the media from making a hero out of Krull as they did with the policemen who died."

The captain offered to share an unhappy smile with Thorne, holding his cigarette a few inches from his mouth. "No, the only price paid was the one you exacted. There was a chain reaction of panic as the truth slithered up through the various echelons of government. Everyone got their hands dirty rushing to cover things up, the guilt was no longer contained at a manageable level. So a blind eye was turned from top to bottom. It's unfortunate, actually, that the Germans have so little imagination. You beat Krull badly, so badly that he was briefly hospitalized for his elbow and a slight concussion. And there's no place where death can be so neatly arranged as in a hospital. In the end, though, there wasn't even a verbal reprimand." The captain chuckled. "What could they have said? Anyway, our source claims that Krull has only one dependable co-conspirator left, and that he's even more afraid of Krull than he is dedicated to any sort of right-wing cause. Apparently, the government feels that the two of them will be grateful to escape with their lives and even their careers relatively intact. They're supposed to settle down and be good Germans. But the psychology is all wrong. Krull has only been encouraged by all this. Now he has the government where he wants it, rather than vice versa, and he knows it. A highly visible terrorist operation now would be proof positive that the accusations of the rightist opposition parties are valid, that the government, as presently constituted, cannot contain the terrorist threat. On the other hand, if the government tries, at this point, to backtrack and put the blame where it truly belongs, they can only make themselves odious in the eyes of the world. And the German electorate is rightfully sensitive on that count."

"Tell him," Leedom said from the shadows, "about the Americans." Leedom had been drinking steadily during the conversation, but Thorne was still surprised at the boldness in his voice. "He deserves that."

Katsovakis looked at Leedom with a face that had been stripped bare of expression, as though awaiting the selection of a mask. Then he ground a smile into the tautness of one cheek and shifted his attention back to Thorne.

"Yes," the captain said, "I'm sure you're interested in exactly where your people stand in all this. Quite simply, they're furious. At the Germans. Americans always have such faith in their allies of the moment that disappointments are inevitable. At first, your people were . . . irate . . . but understanding." Katsovakis looked sharply at Thorne, clearly gauging him. "That was before you made your phone call to Colonel Ferry."

Thorne didn't have the captain's discipline in the face of surprise. His lips parted, ready to speak, though he hadn't begun to formulate the words. Initially, he was only startled at the evidence of just how good the other side's intelligence actually was. Then his belly tightened to cold cement as he realized that the captain either wanted his cooperation very badly or, most likely, didn't think he was going to make it to the end of the operation alive. There was no other explanation why such a professional would compromise the reach of his own intelligence network.

Katsovakis continued as though he hadn't even noticed Thorne's reaction. "That phone call from Frankfurt stunned your organization. Even with follow-up reports available and clear inconsistencies in the Germans' story, not one of your people had

connected Krull and the police back to the commissary bombing. It's interesting, don't you think, that all
the while the Americans saw how cynically the Germans lied to their own media and people not one
American had more than a faint suspicion that the
Germans might also be lying to them? You really are a
people of boundless faith. That phone call was really
very fortunate, you know. For you personally. Your
bit of news rather electrified Colonel Ferry. It didn't
take him long to realize that what you were saying
made absolute sense. On his own initiative, he got on
every possible line to his German counterparts and
warned them that if you were killed the Americans
would publicize everything. It never would have happened, of course, but it terrified the Germans.
Otherwise, you undoubtedly would have been shot
with the girl."

"So they know about it now," Thorne said. The
words swam clumsily against a torrent of information.
"They finally realize who bombed the commissary."

"Yes. They know. Unfortunately, it doesn't really
change anything. Oh, there've been a few painful
realizations. But what can the Americans do? With-
draw their troops from NATO? Turn their backs on
their most important European ally? You see, for all
your trouble, you delivered only useless knowledge.
Oh, you sparked a few high-level shouting matches.
But make no mistake—the governments of the
United States and the Federal Republic of Germany
will continue to present a united front to the world.
The Americans will be less trusting behind the scenes.
But even that will change with the next staff turnover.

Really, everyone will do their best to forget this whole affair."

"Not everyone," Thorne said.

The captain hooked his smile back into a cheek. "You know, you are a lucky man. You've made friends along the way who believe in you, who've been willing to stand up for you. And you've walked away from mortal danger. But I will not lie to you. If you continue to involve yourself in this affair, your friends will not be able to help you. If you give up, I suspect that your slight defiance will be forgiven and you will, at worst, find yourself forced into an early retirement. But if you go on you will find that you are interfering with decisions made at a level where twenty-two bombing victims are of little importance and where your single life will have no importance at all. No one will love you for your efforts."

"Do they have any idea where I am?" Thorne asked.

This time the captain's amusement seemed genuine. He even flashed a brief grin at Leedom. "Major Thorne, until you scared Leedom half to death, *we* didn't even know where you were. And if we didn't know, you can be sure that American Intelligence doesn't. Pardon me if I sound a bit haughty. But, you see, your people seem to have lost all interest in you for the moment. As nearly as we can tell, they're just assuming you've gone to ground somewhere, that you're a bit worried and confused. They're confident that you'll surface once you get a grip on yourself."

The little twist of amusement nagged at the captain's lips. With his pertinent knowledge and his lean horseman's body, he was a genuinely confident man.

Thorne felt erratic and unshaven beside him. He had nothing incisive or even sensible to say in reply to these better-informed revelations. He brooded in the moment's silence.

Katsovakis turned one of his beautifully managed smiles toward Leedom. "Well," he said, "have I dealt fairly with him, do you think? Are you satisfied?"

Thorne's patience tore. The notion that he might be even imagined to be in Leedom's debt was too much for his strained nerves. He wanted to tear at the room and the men in it.

"Listen," he said, "I've been fucked with by everybody in the goddamned hemisphere. And *you*—you say you've got a source on the fringes of Krull's little operation. What the hell's he been doing, waiting to read about things in the goddamned newspapers? You sit there and smirk and tell me you know every move American Intelligence makes. Well, that's just great. But you don't know shit about what matters. What's Krull going to *do?*"

The captain didn't rush to answer. He looked at Thorne with open curiosity, perhaps wondering about the wisdom of trusting this nerve-wracked man so much. Then he lit himself another cigarette and tossed the match into a brass ashtray.

"You know, Major Thorne, you've always been a mystery to us. We've kept tabs on you for years, of course. But we never could understand you. Your motivations were never clear. In our line of work, it's usually one thing or the other and that's that. But you're a strange character. At times I'm almost tempted to believe that your primary considerations are truth, justice and the hope of a better world." The captain grinned. "Of course, I know you're not so simple-minded as all that."

All the violence had splashed out of Thorne's anger. When he spoke again it was almost pleadingly. "Is there anything else at all you can tell me about what Krull has in the works? Possible time frame, type target, anything?"

The captain shrugged. "I wish there were. As you see, our system is very thorough—but not always satisfactorily responsive to unexpected developments. We all have our weaknesses, Major Thorne. We . . . are incomparable planners. But operational flexibility —the quick fix—is more of an American specialty."

"Tell me about your source."

"Yes, I suppose I'll have to. His name is Becker. He's a judge, a fairly important man in Bad Sickingen. He wouldn't have met you at the Soonwalder Hof, by the way. We steered you there just to put you in touch with how harmless the local left was, and so that we'd have had a place to get in touch with you, had the need arisen. But we had, quite honestly, no plans to compromise Becker then. He was too important to us in the long run, and we had no idea how big this matter was going to become. At any rate, Becker's largely his own man, what he does for us is strictly voluntary, ideology-based—perhaps the two of you will hit it off. One difference between you, though, is that he's not so accustomed to violence. In fact, he's a bit fearful of it, and that's the primary reason he's not a better source of information. He only picks up what he does because he poses as an ultraconservative and he's helped

Krull and his followers out of a few jams. But he's terrified of arousing Krull's suspicions, and he works slowly. We've tried to get him moving a bit faster on this one since it all blew up, but he sets his own pace.

"Could you—would you arrange a meet for me?"

"You *have* decided to go back to Germany?"

Thorne nodded. "There's never been any question about it."

The captain slowly stubbed out his cigarette. It felt to Thorne as though the man needed to think. Perhaps things weren't going exactly as planned. Or perhaps they were just going too fast for him too.

"All right," the captain said. "I believe I can arrange it. Becker won't like it, from what little I've come to know about him. Bluntly, he's a bit of a coward, and you'll definitely be an unwanted element in his life. But I think we can appeal to his ideological beliefs."

"And what do your people get out of all this? Just for the record? Why should you concern yourselves in any of this?"

"Perhaps," the captain said, "you and I should join Leedom for a drink after all. Would you do the honors, Leedom?"

Leedom came obediently out of the shadows with the decanter. But he'd lost his tormented-hound look. He appeared newly confident, as though he'd made a difficult decision with firm resolve, and the quickness of his response was only the enthusiasm of friendship. Thorne could make no sense of the change, and when Leedom held out his glass he took it and set it down with only a glance at the old man's puzzling face. He had no time for Leedom now, he had to keep his focus on the important things. He watched the lamplight explode off the decanter.

As he was being served, the captain began his explanation. "What do we get out of it? More than you will, personally. You want revenge—or justice, call it what you will. But it'll be a trade-off for you. If you can head off Krull before he can do any more damage, the side effect will be the rescue of a government you have every reason to despise. And your chances for personal survival may not be good. You're stepping far out of line—but you know that. Frankly, we never expected you to turn up here, we'd already painted you out of the picture. We were wracking our brains for a viable means to deal with this situation. Naturally, I was overjoyed when you turned up. You represent a low-risk—almost no-risk—means of dealing with the situation. Minimal compromise of our own network, and, to put it as pleasantly as possible, we have no long-term investment in you. In the short term, of course, you'll have our complete support."

They were all becoming the same, it occurred to Thorne. Systems men, talking like businessmen and bankers. Nobody rode to the sound of the bugles anymore. In times of crisis, they rallied around the computer and the Telex. They'd never understand if you told them that the image that stayed with you most strongly from all this was of a bully humiliating a girl.

"We want, essentially, two things in Germany," the captain continued. "The same two things any other European nation with common sense and a memory desires. We want to lay to rest forever any notions of German reunification—that is an absolute, which doesn't directly concern us here—and to prevent the apparently indestructible West German right from regaining its stranglehold on the government. The present Chancellor may not be ideally suited to our purposes, or to yours, for that matter, but he's far preferable to the opposition leaders. He's a reasonable man, for a German, and his party wants continued peace, prosperity and social calm. They're not about to precipitate a European conflict over a misunderstanding or some minor matter. But the right—to them it might not be unthinkable, under certain circumstances. We don't want a repeat of 1914."

Thorne almost laughed out loud. They were talking around the same issue NATO had been concerned about for years. "The First World War," he said, "started in what's now Yugoslavia."

The captain didn't answer, and Thorne didn't force him to. "Tell me," Thorne said, "what are you and Leedom going to do? You'll have to assume that I'm going to report all this."

That released the captain's tiny smile again. "Oh, we'll have adequate time to worry about that. You won't contact your people until you've finished with the matters at hand. And even then it won't be a major problem. Leedom's earned himself a safe and comfortable retirement under our protection. As for me, I don't really have any desire to leave my present situation. I suspect I'll just stay where I am. I have friends within the government here who are quite capable of taking care of me. Besides, open accusations would just be regarded as more American inaccuracy and paranoia. It would be quite easy, I think, to put the affair in the light of an unacceptable insult to Greece."

"Suppose I just came after you myself?"

"You won't. You couldn't quite justify it, I don't think."

Thorne turned suddenly to Leedom, who was sipping his brandy in the shadows. "You mind taking a walk, Lee? The captain and I have some private business to settle."

Leedom got up without protest and shuffled out of the room, bad posture and bad skin. He closed the door behind himself as casually as if he had no further interest or involvement in any of the matters under discussion.

Thorne finally took a sip of the sweet, thick brandy that had been poured for him. Then he leaned close to the captain and put on his best little Buddha smile.

"There is one way I could justify coming after you," he said. "That's if I find out that Leedom's turned up dead in a ditch somewhere. Don't let it happen."

The captain straightened. "Such a thing would be unthinkable. Our operational codes are the same as yours. Stalin's been dead for a quarter century, you know. This is a different world."

"Like I said. Don't let it happen."

"Why should it matter to you, anyway? The man betrayed your country. Why should you be sentimental about him?"

"Oh, I'm not so simple-minded as all that. We could say that he was the closest thing to a friend I had for a little while. Or it could be that I'm a real bastard for wanting him to live as long as possible."

The captain clearly found this an unproductive line of conversation, and Thorne had said all he wanted to say on the subject. It was time to wrap things up.

"That's lame shit anyway," Thorne said. "You just set things up with your man Becker and lay on some transportation for me."

═══ 15 ═══

The men who came for Thorne were very efficient. He didn't hear them entering his hotel room. He slept on until the hand slapped down hard over his mouth and yanked his head around so that his confused eyes opened to a hovering black silhouette. The barrel of a pistol jammed into the space between his eyebrows, then scraped down until it pressed between an eyeball and the bridge of his nose. He had been dreaming of blue water, sunlit miles of it. Now he smelled the stale breath of the man who would kill him.

He thought he sensed the finger tightening on the trigger. He expected the end to come at each next instant. And all he could feel was a sickening disappointment, thinking: this is how animals die.

But the punch of the bullet never came. Instead, the light flashed on, making him wince. The hand left his mouth and the pistol pulled away from his face. But the weapon continued to point at him as it withdrew.

The pistol belonged to a short broad-shouldered Greek in a business suit. Behind him, by the light switch, stood another Greek, this one younger, in a pea jacket, with the blue eyes and tawny blond hair of the classical heroes. The blond held a sawed-off automatic shotgun pointed at the middle of Thorne's body.

The short Greek barked a command, too fast and broken for Thorne to understand. The blond crouched down over his shotgun into a tense firing position.

The short man pulled at the muddle of sweater and jeans Thorne had left on a chair, feeling for weapons. He threw the sweater. It landed over Thorne's face, a terrible blindfold. Thorne fought down the instinct to remove it. He made no movement at all, waiting for clear orders.

The jeans slapped across his chest, splashing a few coins off onto the tile floor.

"Get dressed," the command came in English. "Hurry up, asshole."

It was the short Greek. By the accent it sounded as though he'd done a few years in New York. Thorne obeyed promptly, but without any abrupt movements. He sat up and right-sided the sweater, then pulled it over his head and worked his arms through. Then he swung his legs out of the bed and drew on his jeans.

The Greeks watched him intently, keeping a careful distance and following his movements with their weapons. He could sense that these men weren't going to make any exploitable mistakes, and he wondered whom they belonged to. It was possible that his own people had caught up with him, discovering him in what they considered an act of betrayal. Or very likely, he realized, all this was totally unconnected with his current mission. The odds were good that it was a grudge hit from one of his earlier jobs in the Mideast, two paid assassins who'd been waiting patiently for him to turn up in one of his known bases. Offhand, he could think of Libyans, Syrians and Lebanese who would probably pay well to have him killed. Over matters in which he no longer had the slightest interest. His mouth tightened at the irony, and he wondered if he'd be tortured.

As soon as Thorne had his shoes on, the shorter Greek yanked open the door and the blond backed out into the hallway. Then the shorter man stepped aside and waved Thorne through the doorway. Every movement was executed with military finesse, as though they'd repeated this as a team many times.

"No crap," the shorter man said. "Get moving."

Thorne went. Down the hall, down the stairs. The lobby was empty, the door open. Outside, a car waited with the engine running.

Thorne recognized the car even before he spotted the man in the back seat. It was the two-door Mercedes sedan in which Katsovakis had picked him up the day it all began.

The blond with the shotgun opened the door on the passenger's side and then stood away, gun barrel trained just below Thorne's waist. The other Greek jabbed his pistol into Thorne's back and nudged him along.

Captain Katsovakis sat in the backseat, huddled under a dark overcoat. He didn't look at Thorne. He faced forward, and the upper portion of his fine profile stood out clearly, quite pale, against the darkness. Thorne crawled in and took his seat without a word, too furious and confused to say anything worthwhile.

The blond covered Thorne while his partner jumped into the driver's side. Then the shorter man held his pistol on Thorne while the blond got in. As soon as the blond had slammed his door, he twisted around in his seat and aimed the shotgun at Thorne while the car took off.

Katsovakis waved a gloved hand at the blond. "It's all right now," he said. "Lower your gun, it's all right." He spoke clear, beautiful Greek in a soft voice that rescued the language from the chatter of wives and waiters.

The blond, a bit hesitantly, took his weapon off Thorne's chest and turned around in his seat. He was a true professional, despite his youth, and didn't much like turning his back on the man he'd just kidnapped.

The driver took them through the streets at a swift, smooth pace. The city looked so deserted that Thorne knew it had to be about five in the morning. He struggled to make sense of events. But couldn't. He didn't even understand their direction of travel. At first they'd seemed to be heading northward, out of the city. But then the driver had taken the car through a series of turns that canceled each other out.

Begin practically, Thorne told himself. Establish what you can.

"Where are we going?" he asked Katsovakis.

The captain didn't answer immediately. He leaned slightly forward, lifting his chin out of the deep collar of his coat. He still didn't look at Thorne, but for a moment he seemed about to speak. Then he sat back again, and Thorne realized that the man was having some sort of difficulties of his own.

At last Katsovakis spoke, and his voice was so unsure of itself that his English accent lost much of its polish. "We need to talk. But I must be certain that you will remain calm, that you will listen to what I have to say."

It struck Thorne that he might not be headed directly to his death or mortal agony. It was like waking a second time.

"You want me to be calm? After you just sent these two jerks—" he watched the back of the short Greek's head, looking for a response, but couldn't detect the least interest—"into my hotel room to stick guns in my face?"

Katsovakis looked directly at him for the first time. Even in the charcoal shadows of the car Thorne could see that the man was genuinely in bad shape about something.

"Leedom's dead," the captain said. "He killed himself."

It was Thorne's turn to look away. He laid his head back against the seat and shut his eyes. Leedom of Kinshasa, Leedom of Saigon, Leedom of Athens. Traitor and friend.

"I told you not to do that," Thorne said quietly. "That was my one condition. There was no reason for it."

"We didn't kill him," the captain said. It seemed to Thorne almost as if they were having a contest to see who could speak in the softest voice. "I give you my word."

At that, Thorne had to raise his voice slightly. "Your word doesn't mean shit to me. Nobody's word means anything in this business. We gag when we even think about telling the truth."

"We didn't kill him," Katsovakis repeated.

Thorne laughed, in sorrow and disgust. "Then who did?"

"We thought . . . perhaps . . . that you did. That this whole affair had been turned into a housecleaning operation by your side."

"You couldn't really believe that."

"No. Not so much. It's been a long time since American Intelligence has done anything in this city that wasn't common knowledge. Still, an outside possibility existed. That was why I thought it wise to send you an escort."

Thorne shut his eyes again. "Screw all that. Tell me about Leedom."

"Through the temple. Quick. No pain." Katsovakis hesitated, then forced himself to continue. "Leedom . . . was a bit wary of pain, you know."

And something odd in the tone of voice opened up an entirely new perspective for Thorne. The captain's voice had an authentic sense of loss. And Thorne realized that there was no reason why Katsovakis and Leedom couldn't have become friends over the years. They'd had the time. More time than Thorne and Leedom had spent together. And men in intelligence work were lonely by occupation.

"Physical cowardice is the easiest kind to forgive, I suppose," Thorne said slowly. "I've always been afraid of being tortured myself. Interrogated, I guess I should say. I always wondered how I'd do."

"I suspect," Katsovakis said, "that you'd hold up pretty well. You can tell about some men."

"From experience?" Thorne backed away, suddenly revolted by his softening. "You know, if you did kill Leedom, you'd better kill me now. Because I'll find out. And I'll kill you."

They were back in the center of the city again, running between the great squares. The street cleaners were out, and a few dark figures hurried on their way to miserable-houred jobs.

The captain looked off through his side window for a little while. Then he spoke to the glass. "I didn't kill him. He'd become too unimportant to kill. And we wouldn't have done anything that might've distracted you." He whispered a laugh to himself. "I was tempted not even to tell you about it. But I had to see you, to set my own mind at rest, to know you hadn't killed him. Your friendship with him could've been a ruse. To trap me."

Thorne felt his own private laughter aching inside. It was as though he were listening to himself. So hard to ever know anything for sure in the intel world. It was always a matter of bits and pieces and intuitions.

"And how did you find out he was dead? He call you up to ask permission?"

"His neighbor called us. It's always important, of course, to keep a close watch over anyone in Leedom's situation."

"Sure. Double agent, triple agent. The possibilities are endless."

"The neighbor's an innocent sort. Just picking up a few drachmae for keeping an eye on a foreigner. Rather patriotic."

Dead Leedom. Finally the other agony had become greater than his fear of physical pain. Thorne remembered the change that had come over the man the evening before, the sudden calming as though he'd resolutely solved a great problem. It was becoming easier to believe that Leedom had killed himself. In a way, it was surprising he hadn't done it years before.

But where was the *proof* that the captain's bullyboys hadn't killed him? For some unknown reason?

"I talked to our man last night," the captain said. "After you left."

Thorne looked at the captain. "Becker?"

"Yes. Are you still going to go through with the operation?"

Sometimes, when there was no one to trust, you had to satisfy yourself with going through the motions of trust.

"I'll come back afterwards," Thorne said, "and, if I find the least indication that your people killed Lee, I'll kill you. And I'll make it hurt. I swear it."

The captain let the threat glide by, proceeding with business. "Becker had a little more information. Krull *is* working virtually alone now. He has only the one last follower I mentioned, a man who simply does what he's told. Nonetheless, Becker insists that Krull's getting ready to make a big move. Soon. And it seems he's going after another NATO target. He's been trying to get his hands on NATO security passes." The captain faced Thorne with a look that had become earnest beyond calculation, the look of a worried man who had gone too long without sleep. "Becker's afraid Krull's becoming suspicious of him. But he assures me that he'll do all he can to have the complete details of Krull's little operation by the time you get to Bad Sickingen."

"And when will that be?"

The captain shrugged. "I wish I knew. As soon as possible. Certainly we'll get you out of Athens immediately. Just in case. Just in case your American Intelligence did kill Leedom. In case they're after you now." The captain smiled. "My sources assure me there's nothing of the kind in the wind. But one can never be too sure."

"Where will I go?"

"Istanbul. There's a morning flight. You'll have reservations at the Europa Palace Hotel. Tell them you are Mr. Delaney. There will be no problems. But keep close to the hotel. We'll make the quickest, safest arrangements we can for the rest of your journey, and we'll contact you."

"All right."

The captain huddled in his exhaustion for a long minute, and Thorne assumed the discussion was over. But he was wrong. Katsovakis turned to him again, leaning slightly toward him, as though he wanted to touch him but wasn't sure how it would be received.

"Leedom thought very highly of you," he began. "He didn't want you brought into this at all. Perhaps that isn't worth much. But we're meeting here in this strange place between the lines of battle, and I offer it to you."

Thorne didn't answer. There was much to think over, little to say.

"Professionally," the captain went on, "I'm glad we

brought you in. Another man in your place wouldn't have gone so far. You have a great deal of determination."

Thorne coughed a laugh. He felt exhausted, not determined. "You know who I am? I'm the last man on earth who gives a shit. That's what Leedom said to me once. Just in passing, in the flow of conversation. But I cherished it. Still, he was wrong. I'm not going through with all this because my middle name's Galahad. I'm doing it out of hatred. I *hate* Krull. It's that simple. I don't think I've ever genuinely hated any man or thing before. Not like this. And you know why I hate him? Not so much because of all those dead wives and kids in the commissary. Not even because the girl's dead. Because of something that bastard did to her, something he made her do, when she was still alive. Before I even met her. She told me about it, then said it didn't matter. And maybe it didn't matter. But I can't get it out of my mind." Thorne threw back his head and stared through the roof of the car. "You had to know the girl. She was . . . worthwhile."

"The German left is making quite a martyr out of her."

"They're shits."

The captain smiled wearily. He leaned forward and told the driver to head for the airport. Then he looked at Thorne and lowered his voice again. "I shouldn't tell stories on my brothers-in-arms. But I think you might be interested, and somehow I feel I owe it to you. Anyway, I don't think we'll ever meet again, you and I, so perhaps it won't matter so much. Would you like to know exactly why the underground arranged to hand the girl over to the government for the slaughter?"

"I think I already know. It was getting too hot for them. The manhunt and all. The only way to put a stop to it was to surface the girl."

"Yes. But there's more. It was more cynical than that. This martyrdom nonsense didn't suddenly occur to them after the girl's death. They saw immediately that she was more use to them dead than alive. Dead, she became irrevocably the fiery terrorist the government and the media had created. Alive, she was just a frightened girl in trouble not of her own making. They thought it through quite carefully, and even asked for outside advice. The actual transactions involved were carried out on a government-to-government level between East and West Germany, with East Germany playing honest broker for the underground." Katsovakis gave Thorne a moment to consider, then asked, "Does that shock you?"

The sea appeared at the end of a street. Steely, with black ships at anchor out in the bay. Thorne stared at it until another rush of buildings shut off his view.

"I wish it did," he said.

=== 16 ===

The Europa Palace sat directly across the street from the university. It was a small hotel with broken fixtures that cheap labor kept polished, the sort of establishment that made its faint profit from budget tour groups. The man behind the front desk wore a wretched suit that had been beautifully pressed and he stood with the posture of a French director of protocol. "Yes, Mr. Delaney." Without needing to look at the register. "You are reserved." A slight bow and snap of the fingers that Western Europe had forgotten generations ago.

The bell captain reported. He stood before Thorne, with a look of awful disappointment. Thorne had no luggage, only an armload of newspapers and magazines he'd bought—a reflex action—at the airport.

Thorne handed over the bundle of reading material.

"Ah, par*don,* Mr. Delaney," the desk clerk said. "I make apology for the lift which does not work. A sorry inconvenience of the moment."

"No problem," Thorne said. "Listen, can you get a

few things for me? I need a razor, shaving cream and a toothbrush." Not wanting to offend the dignity of the man, he didn't specify, as he often did in the Middle East, that he wanted everything new and still wrapped. The bazaars and street vendors sold everything second- and thirdhand, and, once, a request for a toothbrush in Karachi had been answered with a scummy nub-bristled horror and a bellboy's good-natured smile. "Also, some food, please. Sandwiches and some fruit. And coffee."

The clerk looked at Thorne with intense sympathy. "No coffee this week, I am sorry. Tea, perhaps?"

"Tea."

Thorne followed the bell captain up the stairs. The hotel was very quiet, a bad time of year. The bell captain looked back repeatedly, as if making sure Thorne hadn't run off. He smiled a great deal and finally tried his bit of English on Thorne: "Very pretty, Istanbul. Sightseeing."

Thorne nodded. "Pretty" was one word that did not describe Istanbul.

Thorne's room had a picture window that looked out onto the university gate. Two armored cars sat there, surrounded by loitering soldiers with automatic weapons. Probably there'd been disturbances in the night. An assassination, or the bombing of a politicized faculty. Or perhaps the soldiers were there as a precaution. Thorne tried to remember whether Istanbul was under martial law at the moment, but couldn't. Flip a coin.

The bell captain called Thorne's attention to the plumbing in the small bathroom. The toilet worked, if lethargically. Then the man turned on the taps and gestured for Thorne to run his hand under the water.

"Hot," he said. And it really was warm. The hotel had fuel at the moment. This was great luck. On the way in from the airport Thorne's bus had passed long snakes of stilled cars and trucks leading to streetside gas pumps. They weren't simply waiting their turn. They were all waiting in hope that gas would be delivered to that particular pump. Only once did the bus pass a tank truck making a delivery, and that operation had been conducted under the protection of a platoon of soldiers.

Thorne gave the bell captain fifty lire. Too much. But he wasn't saving his bit of money for anything. It was bad luck for a soldier to be stingy. Tradition had it that soldiers who saved their money were always the first to be killed.

He tried to read the papers. It was part of his job, his duty, he told himself, as though proceeding routinely could by itself force a return to normalcy. But he just didn't care anymore. What did it matter who was trying to govern Italy at the moment? And he didn't give a damn whether the French were selling a weapons package to Iraq or to the Navajo Indians. He read the "Situation Wanted" section on the back page of the *Herald Trib* and muttered to himself because it was so full of raw dreams. He tried hard to read about the petrodollar crisis as perceived by *Die Zeit*. But German was the wrong language to inhabit at the moment. Only twice did any of the headline articles briefly capture his interest: an article over riots in Teheran, and an interview with the CINCNATO about the ongoing autumn maneuvers in Germany.

The exercise was wonderful, successful and vast, the Chief said. The man was just spewing more of his soldier-statesman stuff. But the thought of the maneuvers made Thorne briefly nostalgic for the simplicity of uniformed service, with its clear-cut miseries.

His food arrived. Cold mutton on hard rolls. Withered apricots and a thimble of tea. He ate hungrily and drank tap water. Afterward, he stared out the window for a long time, abandoning the newspapers and skipping the stack of magazines. The bored soldiers down below huddled together, but didn't seem to talk much. The students kept their distance. The soldiers' close-cropped hair and crude woolen uniforms made them look like convicts. While the students looked like the hope of the nation. But it wasn't so simple, Thorne knew.

Leedom had known a great deal about Turkey, and he'd loved to tell funny stories about it, little parables, really, that always had a firm point. Thorne had learned from him. Now Leedom was dead and nothing was simple. Thorne tried to manufacture an illustrative anecdote for the complexity in the street below. But it was hopeless.

When he couldn't stand thinking about Leedom anymore, he thought about Maria for a while. Then he thought about Leedom again. Leedom and I made each other laugh, Thorne thought, and I can't forget it just because he betrayed our country. The idea of a country was too big, incomprehensible at the moment. But Leedom came very clear.

Thorne accepted that he was not quite sane anymore. Sane men were not obsessed with murder. And he was obsessed with killing Krull. It had gone beyond the rules of his profession, and beyond his cherished code of personal behavior. He had never understood revenge, neither in literature nor in Lebanon. Revenge had always seemed sick to him, one of the worst perversions of the human spirit. He didn't think he believed in God, but if anything in the Western tradition seemed worthy to him it was the example of Christ. Forgiveness. Now he'd finally come up against that which he could not forgive.

He let himself picture Maria on her knees before the big orange-haired cop. A fat, slopping girl. The face of a cow. There was nothing about her that you were trained to love. He imagined the scene in fierce detail. Then he thought of her on the last day, with the makeup and the permed hair. It was terrible that they'd made her go through that. That was the cruelest part of the whole betrayal. They should've just let her go die as she was. The thoroughness of it all had been inhuman. It made him want to drive his fist through the big window.

Despite what he'd been told, Thorne left the hotel.

He knew where he was going. He strolled in the direction of the bazaar. The streets were lonely of cars, but the sidewalks brewed with humanity. Men in worn suits, with tieless shirts buttoned to the neck, argued intently as they rushed along together. Turkish was not one of Thorne's languages, and he always wondered at the seriousness of the people. Probably they were only discussing lunch, but it always seemed to him that each pair of dark eyes weighed the difficult future of the country. The Turks were genuinely dignified, and hard-working. But the first attribute was often the enemy of the second. A Turk would literally break his back laboring, but his pride was incapable of accepting externally imposed compromises that would've lightened his load. As Thorne went down along Yeniceri Cad he was offered great bargains in leather and suede, tempted with things to eat, and promised imcomparable shoeshines. But no Turk begged. On one corner, before an indifferent hotel, an old man with a filthy dancing bear entertained a tour group. The bear was a diseased rag, his trainer vicious. Yet the man was in business, he even had an employee. The Turk longed to earn his way. He was conditioned to struggle. But, at the same time, his was the classic third-world tragedy of expectations that had outstripped realistic possibilities. A few good years had ill prepared him for a harsh decade. Turkey was a land of enormous potential slowly collapsing in agony. At the moment, the number-one export product of Turkey was Turks, contract laborers sweating in a dozen countries. They sent home hard currency, keeping the economy in wheezing life. But then they came home. And it was hard for a man who'd lived years in northern Europe to come back to the living death of central Anatolia. And this old, old city. It was always terribly busy, with men and more and more women in a hot Western rush. Except that all of the hurry was only a stupid and superficial imitation. Because all the energy was spent on little return, almost no productivity at all.

There just wasn't enough to go around. And his people had it, and these didn't. What were you to do? Did it help the wretched of the earth—he thought of the French paratroopers rifle-butting starving villagers in Chad—if you joined them in their lot? So many times he'd felt himself on the verge of helpful answers. Now he was a blank. He could only observe the misery of these foreign human beings.

The storefronts offered so much, and all of it was of such small value. Barrels and burlap bags of nuts and raisins and dried figs, postcards and tin treasures, and clothing that was actually very expensive when you considered how badly it was made. The Turk had wonderful amounts of the nearly worthless.

Thorne dodged a lonesome cab, an ancient Studebaker, that was drifting downhill with its engine off, and followed the current into the bazaar. Here the Turks mixed with tourists and terminal hippies. Boys, "junior partners," dashed along swinging round tin trays with small glasses of tea. In better times, when the country had not been so utterly bankrupt, the bazaar had been spiced with the fragrance of Turkish coffee. Thorne went along the sheltered twists and turns, past hundreds of tiny shops where the only items of any value were a few middling rugs. He listened to the ambitious attempts of salesmen to coax and amuse in English, German and French. Middle-aged tourists threaded their way with exaggerated caution—which they would abandon at the only point they might need it, in the act of buying. Once, Thorne had enjoyed the spectacle of it all, loving the exoticness at the same time he was determined to rescue the inhabitants from it. Now he simply wished he were someplace else.

He finally found his way out of the rump end of the bazaar and went down into Sirkeci, where everything got tougher fast. Here men voluntarily stumbled uphill under huge loads of leather that would've embarrassed a slave driver. And in cafés the size of closets they took quick tea breaks between burdens. Thorne eased along until he spotted one of the dives where the clientele was a mix of Turks and shabby, long-haired Westerners, and he went in.

Everyone looked at him distrustfully. Thorne figured that with his short hair he had international narc all but tattooed on his forehead. He smiled close-mouthed and nodded to the half-dozen customers leaning against the counter, taking a spot for himself. The customers drank tea or drink-yogurt scooped from a big iced pot. One longhair sipped a Coke. The Turks were dressed in patterned suits with shirts and ties in hard colors, while the young wanderers wore sweaters or faded sweatshirts with the seals of universities they'd never been to.

The Turk who was squeezed behind the counter leaned slightly toward Thorne, eyes a question.

"Efes," Thorne said, and he laid down a handful of lire.

Without a word the Turk reached down into an old wooden cooler and brought out a brown bottle. Efes, the only beer in town and barely drinkable. The Turk dusted the bottle with his apron, popped the cap and served it to Thorne with a white-stained glass.

It didn't take long before Thorne's neighbor, a kid of maybe twenty with long chestnut hair and a bridge of blackheads across his nose, asked, "Where are you from?"

Dutch, Thorne would've taken a serious bet on it.

"You don't want to know, brother," Thorne told him, and he turned to meet the kid's curiosity head on. The kid's eyes were dead, yet functional, with the meanness of the always-stoned. "You know, you look like one hell of a guy. So I'm going to be blunt. I'm looking to score. Just hash. I am a man in need and I'm willing to pay you for the risk of trusting me."

The kid looked away for a moment, but didn't make any alarmed denials.

"I'm not going to coax you," Thorne added. "If you're not interested I'll drink my beer and go." And he raised his glass a few inches toward the kid. "Long life."

The kid looked across the counter to the Turk on duty. Then all of the Turks took turns looking at each other. The formality of it was almost laughable. No nodding of heads, just the repeated question and answer of brown eyes. Thorne worked on his pissy beer and waited.

The Turk behind the counter said something abrupt to the kid. Thorne didn't understand it, but it sounded like a negative. He was surprised when the kid straightened away from the counter and said, "Come on."

He led Thorne back past the unstoned eyes of the Turkish gangsters and through a curtained doorway into a stairwell that stank of accumulated filth. But by the time they'd reached the first landing Thorne could smell something else too. And he could hear music, an old Bob Dylan album.

"It's all right, ma," Thorne half sang, with a soured little swagger.

"What?" the kid asked. The kid, so young and slender, was in terrible shape, gasping his way up the stairs.

"Nothing. Just time-tripping."

The kid looked at him blankly.

"The music," Thorne said. He pointed upward to help the kid understand.

"Yeah." The kid nodded. But Thorne still didn't think he'd got it, and didn't much care. They turned back to the climb, with the reek of hashish and incense thickening the air around them.

The kid stopped after the third flight and knocked on a door. The atmosphere slumped with meandering smoke while Bob Dylan sang very clearly, distressingly out of date in his bright young anger.

There was no answer.

The kid knocked again, calling, "Suleiman, it's me, Jan." He spoke English with a fair accent. English was the language of world business, and the dope trade was no exception.

A voice approached them from behind the door.

"I'm coming, you little twat."

A big-chested man in an Indian blouse opened the door. He had curly whiskey-colored hair and a thick beard and looked like an Irish barkeep. His alert blue eyes cut into you as though he'd learned a lot of things the hard way, as though he'd survived decades on the road, and Thorne wouldn't have chosen to fight him for adventure.

"Suleiman, a new friend," the kid—Jan—said.

The Irishman looked Thorne up and down. "He doesn't look so damn friendly," he said. Then he suddenly smiled and thrust his hand at Thorne.

"Suleiman," he said.

Thorne shook the strong hand. "Bob."

Behind Suleiman's shoulders Thorne could see a

shabby attempt at an Arabian Nights dope den. A room of piled ragged carpets, tired cushions and sprawled young Westerners. There was an ancient Beatles poster on the wall and another advertising Afghanistan.

"Bob wants to get high," Jan said.

"I want to score," Thorne corrected. "I'll get off somewhere else."

The Irishman nodded once and through some trick of personality clearly dismissed Jan from any further part in the transaction. The kid turned away and fuddled off down the stairs.

"Come on in for a bit," the Irishman told Thorne, "and we'll see if we can't put you onto something good."

Inside, with the door shut behind him, Thorne felt suddenly ill at ease. He felt like an old man. The Irishman was probably the older of the two of them, yet the years had counted less for him, leaving him finally much the younger being. Certainly he mixed better with the drowsy-eyed children who were scattered around the floor.

"Water pipe?" Suleiman asked.

"No. I've got places to be."

The Irishman shrugged. The air in the closed room was so heavily seasoned with dope that Thorne felt giddy already, if only from the shortage of good oxygen. The Irishman pulled a neck chain with keys out from under his shirt and bent to a chest of wooden drawers under the view of Kabul. Thorne squatted down beside him like an old gook granny.

"Suleiman," a ghost voice called. "Styx, man. Play some Styx."

"Pee off. If you don't like my music, go bore somebody else." He pulled open a drawer neatly packed with hashish in slabs of black, green and various browns.

"Blend? Or have you got a favorite? You know, these little twats don't even know who Bob Dylan is? D'you realize that?" He laughed, stirring dust from the drawer. "Of course, nowadays Dylan doesn't even know who he is himself. So, what'll it be, pilgrim?"

Thorne had never been confronted with this problem before. He hadn't smoked dope in a long time, and most of his smoking had belonged to a cruder era when you gratefully accepted what little was available. Later, he'd been duty-bound, with only occasional desperate lapses.

"I don't know," Thorne said honestly. "Whatever kicks ass."

The Irishman grinned. "Oh, they all do that. This is old Stamboul, man." He pulled a small brass pipe out of the pocket of his blouse and broke a nibble off a rust-colored slab that was already half gone. He tucked the pipe full to the brim, then made a flaming wooden match appear from nowhere, doper equivalent of a card shark.

"Poke this up."

Thorne took the pipe and drew off a slow toke while the Irishman made the match dance around the bowl. Thorne was unused to any kind of smoking and he nearly choked, then couldn't hold it down very long. His bad lung burned. But the second toke went better.

"Work on that a bit," the Irishman said, "while I put on some sounds for the silly little twats."

Soon the room was ablaze with hard music. Thorne

smoked down the pipe, smirking to himself about nothing at all except a general sense of wrongdoing that had nothing to do with laws or even the customs of his peers. He'd seen the laws buggered so many times he was operating on bare conscience anyway. And he wasn't sure how many peers he had at the moment. The Irishman came back and matched off the last grains for him, and Thorne let himself slip off his heels and against the wall. The slight thud closed his eyes and made him suddenly aware that he was on an express train to Stoned.

"That's fine," he said from behind shut eyes, "fistful of that."

"Thought you'd like it. Of course, it's a bit more expensive. That's Leb, that is. Hard to come by, what with all the troubles down there."

Troubles? In Lebanon? You don't *know* about troubles, brother. I was there the day the Phalange boys killed Tony Franjiyeh. They lit up Beirut like the day of judgment that night. The windows blew out and I laid down on the floor of Benny's apartment with a bottle of cognac. And I was in Germany the day they shot Maria Burckhardt, the notorious terrorist.

"Just give me enough," Thorne said, "for the high of a lifetime."

Back out on the street a nomad wind had come raiding down off the Black Sea. Grit and dust flew before it. Thorne's eyes narrowed and he tasted filth on his lips. It was time to go back to the hotel, to begin waiting again, this time with the little brass buddy the Irishman had thrown in with the deal. So cheap, even at the Irishman's rip-off prices. For five hundred lire he'd bought himself enough dope to make him sleep for a week.

But he didn't turn back toward the hotel. Not yet. He walked on down the street, into the slap of the dirty wind, toward the Golden Horn. He felt pleasantly dead and he let the dope trance lead him. He believed he had all the misery at a remove now, television news.

He passed by the scummy railway station that had figured so often in romantic mysteries and it gave him a tickled sense of roaming through one of history's sorriest dumps. Then he caught sight of the black waters of the Golden Horn.

In the off-season slack the sight-seeing boats looked haggard. They sailed some of the most polluted water in the world. Thorne wandered slowly toward the Galata Bridge, out of tempo with the purposeful crowd. The wind blew pocks of oily spray. But no one other than Thorne seemed to pay any attention. The black water bubbled with garbage and spat at the tethered boats. You just had to get used to it sooner or later. Why hadn't he ever gotten used to it?

Thorne was disappointed. It had been good for nearly half an hour. But the high was already wearing thin. The city was too much. The world was too much. He wanted to pull the pipe out then and there and cram it with nuggets of crumpled hashish and suck away. Temporary suicide. Nothing serious, Jesus. The old man just needs a little rest.

A gust full of cold blades blew off the water, and the Turks lifted the collars of their suit jackets. Thorne turned away at last, heading up alongside the gray mosque that perched over the street like a huge man-eating bug. It was an ugly, *ugly* city, and Thorne wondered, despairingly, why he couldn't love it.

He hiked up unfamiliar streets, aiming roughly back toward the heights where his hotel room waited. As he passed a shabby banking office, a gendarme in a robin's-egg-blue beret watched him with moronic eyes, sex-fingering an old Thompson gun. They were all over the city, the soldiers and gendarmes, standing alone or in pairs, waiting for terrorists in a passing car to cut them in half with machine-gun fire. Or blow them into bits of kebab.

Thorne turned a corner and nearly stepped on a dead rat the size of a rabbit. It lay stretched in the middle of the sidewalk. He wanted to run, since he'd had bad experiences with rats in Nam. When a firebase was under siege the rats ate the dead out in the tunnels and on the perimeter, then came in for the living. At night young kids went crazy and shot off their feet trying to kill a nibbling rat. Sometimes they shot up whole bunkers. Of course, the rats had an effect on the other side, too. Bitter vets swore that it was the plague and not U.S. firepower that lifted the siege at Khe Sanh.

Thorne didn't run. He forced himself to squat down and consider the perfection of the rat. The claws looked tormented in death, the fine hair lay greased back like a Latin lover's. The eyelids were pinched shut as though the creature had taken fright at some dreadful scene. Now, there was something you could do to ease the plight of the least-developed countries:

find a good use for rats. There were always plenty of rats. Exploit the rats. Turn them into foreign exchange, into energy, into protein. Someday men could look back and marvel at the way their ancestors had squandered a valuable resource for so long. Eventually, young people might even have to band together in a campaign to save the rat from extinction.

Thorne was sorry now that he'd gotten stoned, that he was still stoned out of all competence and emotional control but without the good death of it. He was sorry, and yet he knew that as soon as he got back to his room he'd light up and keep smoking until he'd obliterated the world.

Someone tapped at the door of the hotel room. Thorne had been sleeping thickly, with no awareness even of dreams, but he came up hard at the intrusion. The small sound flashed him a last stoned vision: an undersized hand, squeezed into a sharp fist the size of a snake's head. At the same time he felt that he was lying in wet. A beer bottle nestled against each movement of his thigh. Lot of beer, he remembered. He'd ordered a dozen bottles from room service. And he remembered how he'd promptly lost the opener and how he'd levered and chopped at the caps, using the lip of the night table. He remembered smashing a bottle or two as his clumsiness increased.

He shut his eyes again, lazing a last moment before getting up to answer the knock. His brain flirted with death images. Dark things behind the door. Then he laughed out loud. What a joke it would be if they were going to bust him for dope. Who, me? Surely not me,

Jack Thorne, an officer in the U.S. Army, once-removed? The hotel room stank gruesomely of hash and spilled beer. Thorne puckered his lips at the ceiling and blew off an imaginary toke. Probably smell it down in the lobby.

The faint knocking came again.

"Yeah," Thorne called. "Hang on." And he lifted himself from the slop of bedsheets.

He plowed his fingers back through his shorn hair and tugged up his jeans, approaching fate with a last nod to dignity. But he didn't bother putting on a shirt. His scars were honorable. He stepped luckily, forgetting to regard the broken glass on the floor, and didn't bother with the door's flimsy safety chain. If anyone wanted to do him serious harm, it wasn't going to make a difference.

He opened the door.

It was a woman. Tallish, she appeared remarkably thin despite the big discolored sheepskin vest she wore. She had sparse blond hair that was badly cut or terribly managed and a long face. Unmistakably English, no need to hear her speak. *Not* a woman, Thorne decided. An aged girl. Indoor skin and tiny hips from which her jeans seemed to shy away. She carried a huge shoulder bag of rose carpeting, and its weight gave a tilt to her stance. She wore sandals, and her toes were filthy. Thorne thought suddenly how cold it was to be wearing sandals, and he looked her in the eyes. A wild mix of intelligence and jaundice. There was hardly a ghost of old prettiness about her. Yet looking at her was like having a cunt rubbed up against your bare leg.

"Ahmed sent me," she said finally. She was looking him over, too. The arabesque of ruined skin.

"I don't know any Ahmeds."

"Oh," she said. "Oh, shit." She seemed unreasonably startled, as if she'd gotten the wrong room entirely, the wrong hotel. Then she went hunting in her enormous purse. "Wait."

Thorne stood patiently. Her hands were lost in the big bag. Then it slipped off her shoulder onto her wrist, and its weight seemed to pull her onto her knees. She knelt over it, slapping at a ragged curtain of hair with a shivering hand, trying to gather the waxy strands behind her ear. A junkie, Thorne realized. Absolutely. That gruesome sexuality.

She found what she'd been looking for. A manila envelope that looked as though it had seen prior service. She thrust it at him with a smile of accomplishment, rising toward him.

Thorne took the envelope. There was no address on it, and it was sealed. He put it under his arm and leaned against the doorframe.

The girl made no move to leave. She looked at Thorne with the old junkie blend of doubt and canniness.

"You could say thanks."

"Thanks."

She looked him over again. The scars like some crude alphabet. Book of Thorne. But she wasn't afraid. He figured she'd probably seen a lot worse.

"Going to invite me in, then?"

"Why?"

She smiled, revealing moldering teeth, and giggled a

little at his obstinacy. "Well . . . you know, dear. If
you wanted to fuck me. Or anything. Anything that
doesn't hurt too much. It's been paid for." She
hesitated for a moment, expression not nearly so sure
as her words. And Thorne realized that she was lying,
that nothing had been paid for yet. That she would
be paid according to how long she held his interest
and for how many incisive impressions her coked-up
brain could keep in order. Then he warned himself
not to assume her brain was as far gone as her body
looked.

She looked nervous. Thorne wondered how many
days' worth of heroin he was to her. Normally, he
didn't pity junkies. You had to work at becoming one,
you had to *want* to be a junkie. But neither did he have
any special wish to harm before being harmed. He
imagined pulling the white, bony flesh against himself. Why not? It would be better than being alone
with his monsters just now. And who would be hurt?
Shit, it was even on somebody else's tab.

His caution was a strain on her. Her eyes were
terrible now, an old woman watching her last young
lover go. "I do special things," she said suddenly.
"And I love fucking white men."

Thorne twisted away from the door, heading back
into the room.

"Come on," he said quietly.

Her sandals slapped after him, and she shut the
door.

Thorne stopped in the middle of the room, amidst
the littered glass, and turned to look at her again. She
dropped her bag by the side of the bed, more careful

this time. Probably had her works in it. Hell. She probably carried her whole life around in it.

"I'm Bev," she said, letting the matted sheepskin drop away from her skeletal shoulders. "You want to get right on with it?" She was ready to draw her sweater up from her waist.

"No mad rush," Thorne said, putting down the envelope. "Like a warm beer? Hungry?"

"Beer, thanks. I've got a thirst."

"This Ahmed. He give you a name to call me?"

He took one of the last full bottles and lined it up against the rim of the night table, then chopped a few times at the cap until he popped it.

"There's an opener on the floor," the girl said. "Under the chair, see?"

It startled Thorne to think that this junkie was more aware of their surroundings than he was.

"He told me to ask for Mr. Delaney. And he described you a little."

"Well, my name's Jack." He gave her the beer.

"And you're an American."

"Yeah. Who's Ahmed?"

"Oh . . . Ahmed. Well, he *pays* me."

"Salary or commission?" Then he caught himself. Why be a wiseass? Because a junkie spotted a goddamned bottle opener you couldn't find when you were stoned and half crazy?

"Commission, I suppose you'd say." She was giving a serious answer. "You're a fat job, I'll tell you that. You're to have whatever you want. Daddy must love you."

There was a slight change in her voice now that she

was safely inside. She sounded almost self-assured. And much more intelligent. She sat down on the bed and laid one filthy sandal on the sheets. The split of her scrawny legs led the eye back to their weak jointure. She was worrisomely erotic, in a way that meant no health of mind whatsoever.

"You have scars," she said.

"I'll order you food, if you want. Relax. You don't have to do anything you don't want. You can hit up, I don't care."

"It's very apparent, isn't it?"

"Familiar territory."

"The Turks don't mind, you know. It rather interests them." She grinned, displaying the lines of rotten teeth again. "I won't mind being here with you at all. It'll be a nice change."

Thorne retrieved the opener from under the chair and uncapped another beer for himself. Then he picked up the envelope and sat down in the only chair, cornered away from the girl.

"The Turks really are pigs," she went on, in the tone of assumed camaraderie that all cultures used against the foreign. "Especially with blonds. They love to put you through the whole course. More psychological than physical. Of course, I really shouldn't complain. It's my bread and butter."

Thorne inspected the outside of the envelope, putting off opening it. For no good reason. "Been here long?" he asked, without looking at her.

"Forever."

"You don't sound as though you like it much."

"Oh, I'm a bit of a complainer. It's got its advantages and disadvantages. One makes compromises in life."

"Lousy boyfriends but good junk."

She smiled, close-lipped, a smart cat. "Exactly. Tell me . . . Jack . . . do you believe that you're a happy man?"

"Do I seem happy?"

"No. Silly question. Ahmed never has dealings with happy men. And it's none of my business. But what I wanted to say . . . was that you needn't feel sorry for me. Oh, it's apparent that you do. And I traded on it. My drowned-cat look. You see, it's important for me to make you happy because that'll make Ahmed happy. And I need for Ahmed to be happy. But I'm really all right. I've found the thing I wanted to do in life, and I'm doing it. You really needn't feel sorry for me."

Thorne was forced to regard her. "All right. You made a conscious decision to do junk. And you're happier than me. Feel better?"

"Oh, I feel fine. I want *you* to feel good. That's what I'm paid for."

"I'm okay."

"And so am I. We're both o-kay." She giggled. "Wow. It's super to be with you, speaking good English—am I speaking well?"

"Incomparably."

"But I'm bothering you. I'm just so starved for talk in English. I should be paying you. You need to read what's inside your envelope, don't you?"

"It'll keep five minutes. Talk if you really want. I like that just now."

"Good. I'll tell you about myself, then. It's a good story. It fascinates most people. White girl gone to hell in the East." She sat up straight, doing it right, almost like a schoolteacher beginning a lesson. "I have chosen to live a short vivid life. I was what passed for a talented girl. Bit better-looking once, too. Soon a man like you won't even consider me. But once I was constantly coaxed. Anyway, I was bloody well bored with it. Sex was grand. But I haven't had to give that up, you see. Then I got boosted the first few times. And I knew immediately that the golden light of God had shone down upon me. I decided to accept revelation with open arms. I love junk. The prospect of life without it has worse than no appeal. That's my idea of hell. I'm really very lucky. I've found the thing I love. My life will be short, but rich." Her lungs made scraping noises of amusement. "I think I have another year or two of physical appeal. And even after that the Turks will do me. As long as I have a few scraps of blond hair left. Then the day will come when I won't even be able to work the docks in the dark. But I'm clever. Temperate, actually. I put a little money by. I'll run out of life before I run out of junk. I've got four, possibly even five years left. Five years of wonderful, wonderful dreams. That's a long time. How many good years do most people have in a lifetime?"

Thorne smiled, looking into her eyes now. "Selling?"

"Oh, no." Then she raised a sly eyebrow. "You want to get loaded?"

"No. Thanks."

"Hash and beer. That's like fucking for thirty seconds."

"I've made a conscious decision, too," Thorne said. Wondering if he really had.

"Then you're one of the rare ones. You know, I'm a good junkie but a bad whore. I get off with the customers a lot. They say you're not supposed to. But I can't help it. Touch me and I go off. That's why I don't mind the Turks so much. I'm in my own world. It drives them wild."

"You don't have to do a riff for me."

"Oh, I know. I can tell a lot about you. First of all"—she grinned—"you want me to have a bath. You keep looking at my feet. A Turk would never do that. They don't much mind a woman's feet."

"Sorry."

"No need. Besides, I'm clean where it matters. Thank God for modern medicine. Do you have hot water here?"

"Yes."

"That's super. I'd really like a hot bath. You know, you're lucky to have hot water, fuel's scarce."

"It's more warmish than hot."

"Still nearly heaven. Would it be all right if I do that . . . and hit up just a little? We'll have a good time."

"Be my guest."

"Positive you don't want to boost?"

Thorne shook his head.

The girl raised her dying body from the bed. She closed her eyes to slits and smiled the cat smile that was so much better than her grin. She moaned as she stood up straight, and the moan became words: "Sex and dreams," she said to herself, half singing it. "I like that."

She shut the door and turned on the taps. Thorne made a small rip in one corner of the envelope, then tore it open with great, arbitrary care. The girl came back out to retrieve the forgotten shoulder bag, but didn't disturb him.

First there was a note. "To my dear friend." Best wishes for a pleasant stay in Istanbul. Thorne was to fly to Rome the next morning, then take a train to Ancona. He was to stroll along the waterfront until he saw a lorry marked Lincoln Overland. The vehicle would take him to Munich, where he would make a telephone call and receive further instruction. Very best of wishes, Ahmed Nazilli. And there was a ticket, with documentation, as well as a bit of money. Thorne was glad at the thought of getting under way again. He felt as though he'd been in Istanbul a very long time.

The girl came back out wrapped in a towel. Wet, her hair looked even thinner, her face an elongated skull. The flesh of her shoulders and thighs was white almost to phosphorescence, bluing along the pronounced ridges of bone. She had a long back, and the towel, bunched tightly over her faint breasts, only partly covered the coppery mush of hair between her legs. Her movements had a wonderful slowness, and as she came closer Thorne could see a spatter of dead places on her arms and the inside of her thighs. He hoped, for her sake, that heroin was as sweet as she said it was.

She sat down on the feeble arm of Thorne's chair, towel splitting away from her belly. She reached for his beer, then, after she had wet her mouth and lips, she touched his chest with fingers like broken pencils.

As soon as her hand touched him, her flesh seemed to color. She made a slow search through hair and over bumps where his skin had healed like gnarled wire. Her thighs broke open an inch, then more.

"Terrible," she said.

Thorne flopped the papers onto the floor beside the chair. But he sat a moment longer, letting her fingers search over him. Then he slipped his hand between her legs, and at the first touch she shuddered and fell against him.

He reached back underneath her, up along her back, then slipped his other arm around her shoulders and picked her up and carried her over to the bed. She shuddered and moaned, yet her skin was cold, even the warm bath hadn't been able to soak life back into it. She bit dreamily at his shoulder, in her own world. He tried for a moment to imagine what bizarre reality he held for her now, then gave it up.

When he eased her down onto the bed, she opened her eyes and they briefly flashed with pre-junk intelligence.

"Turn out the light," she whispered. "You'll like me better in the dark."

In the long, long darkness he sometimes thought she was completely insane. She made love in freak twitches that reminded him of the way snakes jerk for hours after you cut off their heads. She muttered to herself in half-languages, straying now and then into Turkish that he couldn't understand but knew was vile. When she came she twisted up until he was sure her poisoned bones would snap. Then, instead of dying off into a junk swoon, she sucked and licked and bit at him, wandering randomly, but always, always clutching. She was like a vampire, he thought. And yet he responded, sinking into his own dreams.

He thought of the girl on the boat. He let himself imagine the sweet, bright flesh, the thick dark hair. Then he drove on greedily, conjuring a long parade of girls and women, old lovers, faces that had flashed by for an instant, never to be forgotten. At last he made himself tired with the weight of them all. No more sex left. And he thought again of the girl on the boat. Kate. That had been a last chance there.

Suddenly he started shaking. He saw Maria. Tangible flesh in the room. Her head exploded over and over again, yet she never stopped looking at him. She wore the look of a lover to whom you've broken every promise. He could *smell* her.

The crazy girl went on chewing at him, trying to draw him back into sex again. The earthquake was all inside him, and he thought: *this* is what death is like, knowing all the while it was nonsense, just the tension, the last veil of hashish and the contagion off this half-person gone out of control in his arms. But he desperately wanted it to be morning.

Finally the girl sensed something, and she crawled back up along his body. Her breath was full and horrible with the spillage of their bodies.

"Have you ever been in love?" she asked, in a lucid, shocking voice.

She so surprised him that he began to try to answer, to say yes and no, that he'd been a little in love several times but life had always moved too fast.

But she interrupted him. She hadn't listened at all. She was talking to herself. She went off into a driveling chant, breathing obscenities against his face. Then she abandoned English for some growling song from the brothels of Babylon. She sent a hand writhing back between his legs, and the eagerness of his response shocked him.

In the morning he woke to find her sitting up in bed, spotted hip beside his face. The room still stank of stale hashish, and he felt a little sick. But the girl was feeling fine. She stroked his hair, ever so gently. In the gray light her face looked healthy and wise, no different than scores of lovers he could recall.

When his eyes finally stayed open, she spoke to him in a voice that carried a slight blush. "You were like a crazy man last night. I was a little frightened of you."

Thorne looked up at the ceiling, trying to force some order into his thoughts.

"It was fine, though," she said, and now she used the curious matter-of-fact voice that genuine lovers use the morning after their first night of sex. "So fine that I couldn't help wondering something."

Thorne looked up at her. He didn't know where this person had come from. There had been another person the night before. And he hadn't known where that one had come from, either. He only knew that he had to be on a plane at ten. He jerked up on his elbow and looked at his watch.

It was still early.

His sudden movement had stirred up clouds of sex smells from the sheets. He dropped himself back down and closed his eyes. He was getting on a plane and flying to Italy. And of course there was a great deal more in life. He had a purpose. He had made a conscious decision to have a purpose.

Nobody ever made a conscious decision, it occurred to him. It was all needs, all needs.

"You know what I was wondering last night?" the girl insisted. "I wondered who it was you were pretending to make love to."

Thorne wanted to turn on her and slap her hard. To really hurt her. He wished she'd stop this senselessness and start acting like a junkie or a sex-nuts witch again.

"What makes you think I was fantasizing?" he said gently.

The girl smiled one of the smallest smiles he'd ever seen. You had to look very closely to see it in the fragile light.

"Oh, I don't flatter myself so much," she said.

=== 17 ===

The sun was shining as the big truck headed north out of Italy. Small cars with black plates shot ahead, rushing toward the Brenner. The truck, with its load of produce, climbed slowly. It was a British truck, underpowered, with a quiet, steady driver who doused his sweat with aftershave and played tape after tape of American country-and-western music. The cab was filthy with bits of old meals, candy wrappers and beer cans, grimy maps and blankets, and the overstrained speakers crackled with the very worst of Nashville. But everything was all right. They were headed in the right direction. Hard by the side of the highway, late harvesters snipped at ruddy vineyards. But the chalky mountains were steadily closing in.

They passed easily out of Italy and through the Austrian customs, listening to Charlie Rich and Faron Young. The quality of the houses improved immediately over those left behind in Italy. Everything looked recently painted and determinedly picturesque. Already, there was no more of the accidental splendor of the south. These mountains were beautiful, without liveliness or folly. Such beauty was as boring as it was visually impressive. The truck downshifted for the long descent and, despite the loud music, Thorne fell asleep.

He dreamed. He was younger, though not a child, standing in wonderful sunlight in his back yard. Everything was very clear and exact. The white frame house on the greener side of a coaltown, the black flat-topped hills of waste whiskered with birches, even the silky sound of fine coal rushing down a basement chute, each detail lived. The dream had the sort of superreal presence that couldn't be contained in sleep, but haunted the dreamer with a sense of loss all day. Then the dream shivered into motion. Thorne wasn't standing in the sunshine to no purpose. He was waiting for the snakes, watching for a rippling of grass. The snakes threatened the house, they threatened everything, and had to be gotten rid of. The first one came. Thorne tracked its progress. It headed toward the fringe of flowers and shrubs along the side of the house. Then, as it left the grass and thrust its head out over the dirt, Thorne got his first good look at it. Fat and brown, with black tracings. It headed into a hole under the azaleas. The hole was huge for a snake den. A small child could've crawled down it. Thorne couldn't understand how he'd never seen it before. Still, he wasn't afraid. He had a big blowtorch, damned near a flamethrower, and he was going to burn the hole out. But first he had to wait. There were two of the snakes, he knew. Suddenly, the other came furrowing through the grass, quite close to him. Then it passed off toward the hole, which seemed even bigger now, a small cave. As soon as the snake nosed into it, Thorne blasted the den with a cloud of fire. The snake reared visibly, a dark form writhing agonizedly up into the red storm. It made a noise like a gnashing of teeth, then wavered and collapsed. Thorne went cautiously forward to the mouth of the hole. Everything was scorched black. The hole was steep, shaftlike. Thorne put a long burst of flame down it, straining to burn it as deeply as possible. Then, over the hissing of the flame, he heard a greater hissing behind him, all around him, like the rushing in of the sea. And there came the sound like the gnashing of teeth, vastly multiplied. There were huge snakes, serpents, rising from the grass all around him. But Thorne didn't panic. He turned the flames on them, scorching first one, then another, scorching tangled bunches of them. He felt capable, strong, determined. Only there were so many. And he had to keep turning because there were more trying to rush up the shaft at him now. And the flame was weakening, shrinking with each burst.

"Wake up, man. Wake up."

Thorne hurried out of the dream, alert to a world of dangers. The sun was gone, and swirling fog brought the horizon down under a hundred meters.

"Was I talking in my sleep?" Thorne asked quickly.

The truck driver looked surprised. "No. You were sleeping like a babe." He smiled at the highway, peering through gray. "Felt like a bit of a bastard, waking you, but we're only a few minutes out of Munich and I thought you might want to put yourself in order."

Thorne looked sharply at the man.

"We're in Germany already?"

His question was answered by a pair of blue-and-white autobahn signs popping out of the mist.

"They hardly looked us over at the border. I saw no need to wake you."

Perhaps it was only the bad dream, or the change from bright sun to this foggy gloom, but the suddenness with which Thorne found himself in Germany again had a feel of hard fate. If they were this close to Munich, they'd already been in the territory of the Federal Republic for over an hour.

Thorne looked at the truck driver, wondering again how much the man knew. He'd been waiting for Thorne in Ancona, along the docks, as promised. They'd exchanged maybe a dozen sentences. The announcement of a stop for a last cheap cup of coffee, a pair of comments on the desirability of a girl in an Alfa Romeo . . .

"Do you know who I am? Or what this is all about?" Thorne asked.

The truck driver didn't change his expression in the least. "You're a hundred quid in my pocket, friend. Where do you want me to drop you?"

It was after midnight when Thorne pulled into Bad Sickingen. First he drove to the train station, outside which there was a town map for tourist use. He drove up as close to the map as he could and kept the car engine running while he got out and checked the index for Becker's street. But all the traveling had spoiled his efficiency, and his tired eyes had to search the list several times before they caught the street name and its grid location. Finally he had to trace over the map with his finger.

He felt vulnerable, standing in the open, peering at the map like a drunkard. But there wasn't really much danger, he knew. Not here. If they were waiting for him, they'd be closer to the judge's house.

Coming back in had been so easy. He was tempted to assume there was no more interest in him. The truck driver had dropped him off at a filling station in the north of Munich. He called the number he'd been given and was told to go to Münchener Freiheit, then walk along a certain street toward the English Garden. There would be a light-brown Saab with Mainz plates parked in front of an antique store. The keys and other necessities would be in it.

And that was it. The car was waiting, as promised, a bland-looking machine with a good engine. And with a 9mm. pistol in the pocket.

The only surprise on the long drive from Munich to Bad Sickingen had been the convoys. He'd picked the first one up outside Nuremberg. From that point on, the military traffic had been constant, heading in both directions, bogging and blocking traffic. Serial after serial of muddy tracks and tactical vehicles crept along the autobahn at thirty miles per hour. In the darkness the evenly spaced red taillights could be seen snaking for tens of miles through the valleys of the Spessart. It seemed as though the entire might of the U.S. Army had been called out for a show of force. But what he was seeing was only a fraction of the total, Thorne knew. Finally he remembered the newspaper article he'd read in Istanbul, about the big NATO maneuvers. These were the player elements going home. Equipment would be stretched over the roads and rail lines for days. He drove by the flashing yellow lights of a wrecker. And there would be accidents. There were always plenty of accidents after the drivers had crisscrossed Germany for days without proper sleep. There were safety briefings by the thousand, to which no one really listened. Casualties were expected. He knew. He knew all about these convoys and the war games and the bleary kids who'd sell their souls for a beer or a Milky Way. He'd been part of it all once, and all the way into Bad Sickingen he remembered.

Thorne drove toward Becker's street. The route led away from the American barracks, through clean, silent streets. But in the background Thorne could always hear the drone of the convoys coming in, and he couldn't help comparing those raccoon-eyed kids in grubby uniforms with all these citizens who were sleeping so soundly, arms around well-fed bellies.

He hoped Becker had something for him. Katsovakis hadn't painted a very flattering picture. He could only hope that some pressure had been brought to bear and the judge had gotten off his ass. If not, Thorne always had his contingency plan. It was a very simple one. If the judge hadn't scraped up any more info on the planned Big Operation, Thorne would simply extract the names and addresses of everyone the judge knew to be involved. Then he would go immediately, beginning with the big orange-haired sonofabitch, and kill them. If there were only two, as Katsovakis had indicated was the case, it would be possible, with luck, to do the job and be in Luxembourg or France before the town had properly awakened. It was even conceivable that he might be back in the United States in less than twenty-four hours. There would be problems then too. A great deal of shouting and threatening and explaining. But he was confident he could get through all that, given the chance. There were so many gray areas in this one that he suspected they'd finally be glad just to let him walk away and never darken their vault doors again. And he would be glad to walk away.

Thorne drove slowly up Becker's street, watching for any sign of trouble. It was more than just watching —it was a mental attitude, a keying of all the senses. There was a good chance it would end right here, maybe he'd just get to see the first orange flashes before he was shredded. If they were waiting now there wouldn't even be time to draw the 9mm. out of his jacket.

The street was a perfect place for an ambush, too. It cut up across a hillside, with restraining walls, fences and shrubs thick along the uphill side. On the down-hill side there were clear fields of fire into back yards and vacant lots for better than fifty meters.

Thorne had to shift into a lower, louder gear. He read the numbers on the roadside garages and gates, always switching back to scan the steep lawns and gardens. The houses grew larger and larger, and they were spaced ever farther apart. These houses were each distinctively styled and, in West Germany, that alone announced wealth. The middle class and even the upper-middle class lived in identical concrete boxes, stoutly built and ugly. But here there were houses of stone and brick, some almost North American in the extravagance of their design, others built in the popular German version of mock Tudor.

The judge's house was one of the dark-brick-and-timber variants. Even in the darkness the lawn had a disciplined look. Thorne drove on past it until he found a break in the line of houses where a few undeveloped lots led up into hilltop fields and groves of trees.

He pulled over onto the shoulder, shut down the engine and listened.

The distant *om* of the convoys, nothing else.

Getting out of the car, he patted his jacket to make absolutely certain the pistol hadn't disappeared. The air was chilly, and a shiver passed over him. Down the hillside the town glistened in stillness. Off in the darkness of the valley the convoy headlights poked along. But here there wasn't even a stray car.

He stepped quickly up into the weeds. The nearest houses were about a football field away on either side. Three houses down, Becker was waiting.

Thorne drew out the 9mm. and jacked in a round. He began to walk up through the field.

Wherever the weeds and grasses thinned he could feel the earth hard as iron underfoot. It was still October, but the winter was coming in from every direction. Whenever he could, he avoided the shelter of the trees, their fallen leaves a noisy trap underfoot.

As he approached the first groomed property, he redoubled his efforts to go quietly. The damned Germans loved dogs. Big loud dogs. For a moment he wondered whether it might not be wiser to go back and walk openly down the street.

Instinct said no.

He slipped along the farthest edges of back lawns, skirting rear fences. It was so easy, really, to move about here. No wait-a-minute vines, even a sky directly overhead with no triple-canopy to rob you of its slight paleness.

There was a belly-high mesh fence all along the edges of Becker's property. Thorne squatted by a thicket, searching the yard's shadows for concealed men. When he didn't pick up anything, he made sure the pistol was on safe, stood up and vaulted over the fence.

He dropped low when he hit, absorbing sound and shock, and quickly drew out the 9mm. He clicked off the safety and stayed down low. But none of the dark shapes shifted or spit fire.

Becker was supposed to be waiting, he was supposed to know he had company coming. There were no lights on, but that was all right. No reason for the judge to sit up all night. Thorne's timetable hadn't been all that tight. Just so there was a door left unlocked, some provision made. Thorne didn't feel much like breaking and entering, and he didn't know if he'd have the guts to ring the doorbell, then stand there waiting.

He started down the yard. He walked at a deliberate pace, footsteps shushing in the damp grass, eyes snapping from side to side. He held the pistol up against the side of his chest, left hand locked on his right wrist.

His heart thumped as though it were trying to break out of its prison of ribs. He couldn't understand now how he'd ever had the guts to do some of the things he'd done. He'd been a brave man, he had the scars and badges from the days when he'd been able to nerve himself up to do the things the others were afraid to do. Now what had passed for bravery seemed like foolishness to him, insanity. So much had been changing so quickly. He felt as though his understanding had been left continents behind his actions. And he needed some of that old craziness now. But there wasn't any left. Maybe, he told himself, it was just being so goddamned tired.

Shit. He was praying no twig would snap within half a mile. He was afraid the least sound would start him shooting uncontrollably into the darkness.

Had he ever been brave? Really?

He made it into the shadows by the back door and leaned up against the house, resting his head back against the itch of brick. Despite the cold, he was sweating. He closed his eyes and listened.

Thorough stillness.

He tried the door handle. It wasn't locked. He opened the door halfway, quietly, then shut it again without going inside.

No lights flashed on, no automatic weapons ripped the walls.

He opened the door again and eased carefully inside.

It was much darker. The timid paleness of the window showed only a tabletop with a silhouetted salt-and-pepper set. Thorne considered turning on a light, then decided against it. Better just to feel the way for now. Becker's bedroom was probably upstairs, he'd hear the sleep-breathing when he got close.

Across the room there was an even blacker darkness that had to be a hallway. Thorne started moving toward it, probing his way with short gliding steps. When his shoe skidded half an inch in something wet, he stopped. When he tried to go on, his next step kicked into a soft firmness that was unmistakably a body.

Instinctively, Thorne dropped to the floor. He clutched the gun, fanning it in wild arcs, protecting himself against the haunted darkness. The girl from the boat, Kate, flashed up in his mind. He couldn't understand what he was doing here, why he hadn't stayed with the girl and begun a new life then and there, when he had the chance.

His first rational act was to make his shaking fingers put the pistol back on safe before he started blasting at spooks. Then he forced himself to feel back toward the spot where he'd kicked meat.

The body was dead, but the gruesome coldness hadn't had time to settle in yet. It was a man's body, big, muscle going to fat. Thorne hadn't seen any pictures of Becker, and from Katsovakis' half-assed description he'd been inspired to imagine the judge as a small, half-starved library prowler. But this aging sportsman's corpse was Becker, he knew it surely.

So the man had been right to be afraid. Now he was dead. In his pajamas, it felt like. Thorne traced his hand over the big chest up into the pulp of a shot-up jaw. He jerked his hand away, feeling down along the outstretched arms now, wondering if he'd find a pistol in one of the hands.

No. The hands were clutching a newspaper. They'd killed him while he was reading a newspaper in his pajamas.

Thorne's hand was repulsively wet and he wiped it

on the dead chest. He didn't know which feeling was the more dominant in him anymore, physical fear or despair. Even the contingency plan was all screwed up now. All he could do would be to sit somewhere near the police station until he picked up Krull, then try to track him to a good kill zone. But it all sounded so terribly difficult and painstaking now. He'd done much harder things, he'd waited months for minuscule returns. But he'd been different then.

It was time to move, time to un-ass the area. But he had it flickering in his mind that it was somehow important to have a look at old Becker. Something inside was pushing him to turn on the light, just for a few seconds.

It was stupid, unreasonable. His hand had picked up all the vital information. Even after being wiped off, it felt sickeningly sticky.

But he *wanted* to turn on the light, to see. He couldn't help feeling that it wouldn't be all right to leave until he'd *seen* the dead man.

Okay. If any of the neighbors happened to wake up at two in the morning and notice a light on, they'd probably just figure the guy was getting himself something to eat or drink. The only other concern was if someone were watching the house. But if they were they'd undoubtedly already picked him up on the way in.

Thorne reached across the table and pulled the curtains all the way shut. The room was nightmare black now. He felt back along the wall toward where the door had been. And there was a switch.

A big barefoot man, baldheaded, with a blasted jaw, in purple-and-black-striped pajamas. Blood all over the floor, chair knocked over when he fell. The dead man was clutching the newspaper with both hands, holding it away from him as though he was farsighted. It looked as though he'd been sprayed with small-caliber bullets all along his right side.

So that was that. The requirement to see it and make it true had been satisfied. Thorne cut off the light and let himself back out into the night.

He was still afraid. Goddamned terrified. And it seemed to be an awfully long way back to the car. He couldn't even think beyond reaching the car now. He had no idea what he was going to do, where he was going to go. He'd been relying on Becker, much more than he'd realized. He'd been depending on the sonofabitch to at least be alive. He'd been counting on bad-ass Jack Thorne, too, who seemed to be nothing but a memory now. It was all he could do to keep himself from running all the way back to the car.

When he finally reached the Saab he didn't even take a few seconds to sniff around before he jumped in and started the engine. He drove hurriedly up the hill, away from the dreadful town, the body.

And he'd seen so many bodies, they were the detritus of his profession. He'd lain beside the bodies of men and boys he knew well and cared about. He'd dragged them, carried them. He'd seen men beaten to death in cement rooms and he'd seen them beheaded by dancing swordsmen under a raging sun. He'd killed without spoiling his appetite, a great warrior, champion of patchwork causes. Even Maria's body had only made him angry, not afraid. Why should this bald-headed corpse eat at him? Was he cracking up in the clinch?

The car tore past stripped vineyards. He didn't know these black country roads, he was driving much too fast. But it was impossible to slow down, the only option was to go faster still. The car screamed through lifeless villages. Random streetlamps were like candles in a crypt.

A sensible man, he thought, would find a dirt road where he could pull off the park out of sight. A sensible man would try to get some sleep and wait for the daylight when everything would be so much more clear.

But he knew he wouldn't be able to sleep. He felt as though somebody had hit him up with meth in the eyeballs. He couldn't stop thinking, yet couldn't think clearly. Something was nagging and nagging at him. But he couldn't pinpoint it. He felt that he was somehow failing to understand something important, but whether it had to do with his fear or the dead man or the whole situation he couldn't tell. He only knew that something was tremendously wrong.

Had the body been left there for him to find? No. No, absolutely not. If these people had had any idea he was coming they would've waited and finished with him too. And Becker hadn't been dead for more than a few hours. Whoever had done the job on him had gotten out quickly, you could feel that.

Well, not all that quickly. They'd been at least half-assed methodical, they'd had the sense to turn out the light. They must've turned it out. Becker hadn't even had time to loosen his grip on the newspaper before he died. And he certainly hadn't been reading in the dark.

What was wrong? Thorne tried to picture the kitchen scene in detail. Was he missing something obvious? He was practiced at taking a hard, quick look, and he could see the room clearly. Green tile halfway up the walls, the positioning of the spotless white appliances. Dishes in the drying rack. Blood all over the floor.

Back up.

Blood all over the floor.

Back up farther.

There'd been no blood sprayed over the walls. None on the tile or the goddamned spotless white appliances. And he didn't remember any pattern of bullet holes, no splintered tile. What angle could they have shot him from? If he'd been sitting at the table, the window would've shattered if they'd shot him from behind. But Becker hadn't been shot from behind, anyway. They'd laced him down the side, from the jaw to the thigh.

It wasn't a big enough room. If they'd come up beside him, he would've seen the killer or killers. He would've at least dropped the damned paper and tried to put up a fight. Or to run. And whether they'd shot him while he was sitting or on the move there would've been a mess of bullet holes and blood over the walls and furnishings.

Becker had died in the kitchen, all right. But he hadn't been shot there. They'd surprised him in another room. And the most likely room in which to surprise a barefoot man in his pajamas would've been the bedroom. Which would also explain the track of wounds right down the side of his body. Horizontal spray, horizontal man. So a man full of bullets had dragged himself from a bedroom, probably upstairs, down to the kitchen.

Why? Why the kitchen? Thorne already knew, of course. His mind was finally functioning again. But he was so furious at himself for his thickheadedness that he forced himself to go through all the steps of interrogation, leaving nothing out. There had been something in the kitchen that the man had wanted to get to before he died. And it hadn't been the telephone, Thorne couldn't remember seeing a phone in the room.

It was the newspaper. The paper had been on the kitchen table, that even explained the knocked-over chair. Besides, a man didn't hold on to a newspaper with both hands while stumbling downstairs in agony.

So stupid, so stupid not to have picked it up immediately. There hadn't even been any blood on the newspaper, except where the hands had smeared it a little.

Katsovakis had been wrong. Becker certainly hadn't been a coward. He'd been the only man who'd understood the extent of the danger all along. And when his superiors had pushed him—at Thorne's urging—he must've pushed the killers beyond good judgment. When he learned too much or finally asked the wrong question, they killed him.

But even full of bullets the man had incredible presence of mind. And a determined sense of duty. Christ, what visions must've been driving him? To make him drag himself out of bed after the killers had gone and stumble his way downstairs in darkness so they wouldn't know he was still alive if they were watching the house from outside. Then he'd forced himself on into the kitchen where he knew he'd left the paper. And he'd clutched it in both hands, holding it carefully away from his soaking body so the man who was scheduled to come would be able to read it. Doing all this while his body must've been screaming grab me, hold me, cringe and howl. No, Becker had not been a coward. He'd been a believer. Even to the point of believing that the man his people were sending would have the quality of intellect to realize what effort had been made and why, the sense to look at the goddamned paper.

Thorne stopped the car in the middle of the road, between skeletal ranks of vineyards, and began to turn it around.

It still wasn't easy to force himself back through the fields and yards and into the house. It seemed unreasonable to him to hope that his presence hadn't been detected—*sensed*—by now. Only his anger at his stupidity, at his cowardly rush to leave the scene earlier, strengthened him to it.

The dying fields and dark homes had grown a morbid look. There was moonlight now, straining through a thin membrane of cloud, and it scalded the grasses to a pale glow. Bare trees clawed the sky, with scrub huddled around their trunks like pestering wolves. The frosty dew was thickening, sopping through Thorne's shoes and jeans.

There was nothing left in this world. Thorne felt as though he could choose any door at random and enter to find corpses going stale. Blue plague flesh and crosses. Wheels, skulls and crows.

He would almost have welcomed the reality, the liveliness, of gunfire. It was strange how you graduated to an ever higher perfection of nightmare. Once, night fighting had seemed the ultimate horror to him. And not just because it made you so afraid for life and limb. No, the flashes and bursts all deviltry and dragons' tongues, the confusions of direction and distance, the shouting, the insane running and the precious skills reduced—in that first bearingless paralysis—to sheer chance, all that did something else too. It made you hungry to kill any living thing that might touch you, to slaughter anything that even came near.

Now the memory of postmidnight firefights in the jungle seemed like an affirmation of life to him.

He sent himself back through Becker's kitchen door, actually nauseous with fear for the first time in a dozen years. He didn't turn on the light, but got down on his hands and knees, feeling toward the spot where he remembered the body to be lying.

There wasn't much smell, and it surprised him. In his freaked-nerve imaginings he'd pictured a blooming stink of death by now, the infestation by maggots.

But the flesh, when he suddenly struck it with his paw, remained supple and firm. Death was still so recent. He hadn't been away an hour. It only seemed longer.

Thorne tugged the newspaper out of the dead hands. It tore somewhat, even hours into death Becker's grip held on.

The answer had to be in the paper, it *had* to be. It was the only way things made sense. His immediate urge was to fold the paper up, put it into his jacket and sprint for the car. Instead, he got to his feet and forced himself toward the remembered hallway, carrying the precious paper into the guts of the house.

He was hoping that one of the first doors would lead to a powder room or a closet with a light, somewhere that wouldn't spill too much light to the world outside. He was determined to follow up everything on the spot this time. No more chicken-shit running.

He felt along both sides of the wall, arms extended like a scarecrow's, pistol back on safe. The first door opened to yet a deeper shade of blackness, and Thorne hoped he'd found a closet. But his foot found only air.

He pitched forward, losing his balance, grabbing desperately for the wall, before his heel finally caught on the first step and he pulled up.

Cellar stairs. He wouldn't risk them in the dark. A broken leg under the circumstances would've been a hard end.

He moved on. And even before he opened the next door he heard the gurgle of water shifting in a toilet tank.

He went into the room carefully, feeling the wall for a light switch. At this point the light was a chance that had to be taken. Anyway, he couldn't spot any window paleness.

It was a very clean modern powder room, blue and pink. The only window was small, high and heavily curtained.

Maybe, he thought, luck was finally starting to run his way. As soon as his eyes had settled out the pain of sudden brightness, he looked at the paper.

And everything was clear. It was all right there in the centered photograph.

Thorne tried to read the caption under the photo, to make certain. But his hands couldn't hold the paper steady. Christ, Katsovakis—Becker—hadn't been exaggerating. The sonsofbitches *were* going after big game this time. The biggest fucking elephant in the jungle. Finally, Thorne sat down on the floor and flattened the paper on the throw rug.

The lead articles were all about the end of the largest exercise in NATO history. Over sixty thousand soldiers, from half a dozen nations. There were tales of mock battles, blue and orange forces, statistics about equipment, maneuver areas, accident rates. Every article was interspersed with the standard pronouncements about Allied brotherhood and interoperability. And there were paragraphs about student demonstrations against the exercise, some past, others still to come. It was regarded by the left as an outrageous provocation, a betrayal of the years of *Ostpolitik,* a virtual prelude to nuclear war. But all these details only served as a frame to the photograph of the NATO Commander in Chief inspecting the turret of a tank.

The caption said the Chief was going to hold a conference the next day—no, that very day, it was already the tomorrow of the paper—in the heart of the maneuver area, in the university town of Ramburg, and this conference would mark the formal end of Exercise Ready Guardian. The Chief would be meeting with high-ranking representatives of the various militaries who'd participated in the exercises, for the purpose of assessing the training results.

Thorne looked at the photo. The neat border of white hair around the edge of the four-starred baseball cap, those eyes an arctic blue in the memory. Thorne could hear the statements for the press, see the handshakes sustained until the last flashbulb popped. The conference, like all such publicized affairs, would be self-congratulatory theater, great political wampum back home, with nothing really accomplished. Differences over budgets and strategy were discussed under different circumstances entirely.

For an instant Thorne was tempted to let the sly old bastard outwit himself this time.

But he couldn't. He knew that.

But would there even be time? How far was Ramburg in a good car? Three hours? Four? The one time Thorne had made the trip, it had taken nine or ten hours. But that had been in convoy, long ago.

And what if they hit the Chief on the way in? The newspaper said it was a morning conference. There'd never be time if they were going to hit him before it got underway.

The sensible thing would be to get on a phone and call everybody he could think of.

But he wasn't going to do that. The sonsofbitches weren't going to walk away from this one. There wasn't going to be any cover-up by a nervous government. At least not until Krull had been taken care of once and for all.

He'd do his best for the Chief, goddamn him. He'd do his duty. But he'd do it his way.

Thorne snorted. It was really a tiny bitter laugh. The damned thing was that the Chief might even wind up getting more political mileage out of it this way, if he survived the attempt.

And he *would* survive the attempt. These bastards wouldn't get him. And the Chancellor and his cabinet would remain securely in office. Because Thorne hated Krull far more than he despised the Chief. Because the smug German government really was the best that could be expected. Because there was no real choice.

Thorne was a good soldier.

18

In the breaking light the highway resembled a battle-field. Ditched vehicles littered the roadside. Huge, mud-encrusted tanks, their tracks thrown wild, slanted through guardrails, where a flatbed trailer had overturned. As Thorne swerved by, a medevac chopper lifted noisily up through the mist. On both sides of the highway, pointed in opposite directions, long convoys were pulled over for piss stops or awaiting road clearance. Other convoys rumbled slowly past, roaring and grinding, with their vehicle commanders popped up through top hatches, filthy and dead-eyed. Long .50 cal. machine guns hung off camouflage-painted armored personnel carriers. Huge SP guns rode tractor trailers, going a long distance. There were always convoys straggling off in every direction at the end of an exercise. Assembly areas and all routes of travel outside the designated maneuver area had to be prescheduled with the German police, then timetables had to be adhered to down to the minute. So, at the end of a far-ranging maneuver, units would gather themselves together, then drive a hundred kilometers north to an approved start point so they could drive south a hundred and fifty kilometers to their garrisons. And already-exhausted soldiers would sit in the rain for an extra day, eating still another ration of cold canned shit, in order to leave on a midnight journey. And drivers of fifty-ton monsters fell asleep at the controls, unstable jeeps blew tires and flipped, big guns tore into houses along twisting village streets and, all the while, day or night, insane German drivers wove their stubby cars in and out of the convoys at high speeds, infuriating the kids who were already overflowing with hatred, and occasionally killing themselves.

Thorne, in his own special hurry, sped past a convoy of two-and-a-half-ton trucks with blue triangles and chalked convoy numbers on their sides. It would be days before the roads were free of convoys, months before all the damage had been repaired. The list of combat and logistics vehicles involved in these maneuvers ran into tens of thousands. Crawling along the road.

Just ahead of the trucks a column of M-60 tanks had stopped in the middle of the autobahn. German drivers flashed recklessly past them, hurrying to work. As he raced along with the stream Thorne glanced over to the tankers again and again. Dirty burned-out kids, they stared at the civilian traffic with sullen resentment. It wasn't hard to imagine one of them suddenly veering his enormous monster of a vehicle hard to the left, letting half a dozen fragile cars squash themselves against its flank. It was beyond all reason, the hatred you could feel in such a situation. Thorne could remember how the bitterness tightened up the skin around your eyes when you were cold and hungry and scabbed with grime, held in place on some idiot technicality while fat men blasted by in their BMWs, their country grown rich in the security you guaranteed with your own deprivation.

Nor was it only the Germans you grew to hate. Once, as a young platoon leader, Thorne had ridden for twenty-six hours in a roofless jeep in winter rain. Traveling from assembly area to start point in detour, traveling in loops. Some high-ranking character had had the brainstorm to take off all the removable vehicle roofs that year, for safety reasons. Theoretically, with no canvas to block your vision, you could drive much more safely. But the colonel or general, who'd long grown used to flying to and from maneuvers in his private helicopter, had forgotten what it was like to drive with freezing rain whipping in your face. That blocked your vision, too. The Army had taken a lot of peacetime casualties on that one. Yet the canvas roofs stayed off the vehicles for months. To put them back on immediately would've been to admit a link between a flag officer's inspiration and a dozen deaths.

At the end of the long line of halted tanks there was a good reason for this particular delay. One of the lead tanks had overstrained a track and when the treads broke apart the tension had slashed one end of the track into the passing lane, where it cut a Volkswagen in half.

Still the commuter traffic merely skirted the mess.

None of the Germans stopped to help the glazed-eyed GI medics. Time was money. Low overhead, a pair of tank-killer aircraft made a practice strafing run over the line of vehicles.

The final stretch, between Frankfurt and Ramburg, was even worse. Here there were not only U.S. Army convoys but German, Canadian, Belgian and French convoys as well. For half an hour all traffic on Thorne's side of the autobahn came to a complete stop. Thorne sat helplessly in his car, half crazy with sleeplessness and time-worry, while impatient Germans honked their horns nonstop and temporarily avenged GIs stabbed up their middle fingers at them in the first sparkling burn of sunshine.

Thorne rubbed his hand over his face, feeling at his whiskers and the dead area around his eyes. He hadn't slept since his nap in the Brit truck, his filmy skin craved a splash of water. The world around him was very clear, yet not quite real. The colors were too harsh.

Unexpectedly, he found himself grinning. One weirded-out mother, he thought, going in to rescue Western Civ. He felt his second wind coming on. It always came when you just kept on marching. It made him feel giddily optimistic. There'd be time, the traffic jam couldn't last forever. And he'd put things straight. Fate was on his side, it had to be if he'd made it this far.

The Saab was wedged between the median strip and a big APC fitted with an antitank-guided-missile launcher and a machine gun. Two GIs, one black and the other white under all the soot, sat on the vehicle's top deck, legs dangling, buzzing on the sunshine and watching the show. Thorne finally shut off his engine. The Germans were getting out of their cars now to peer ahead. Thorne stayed put behind the wheel. He looked away, across the flow of the opposite lane and into the fields beyond. The mist was burning away and he could see deep dark furrows ripped across meadows and smashed fences. It looked as though an entire battalion of armor had attacked through there. The U.S. Army paid exorbitant maneuver-damage fees to the Germans, and there were successive campaigns to encourage the troops to be more careful. Some listened, others didn't. When you were broke and lonely and shunned, it was a great release to drive a tank in a perfectly straight line through every obstacle in the way.

Thorne turned around quickly, as if he'd heard his name called.

The two GIs up on the deck of the track broke into tremendous smiles. They'd swiveled the .50 cal. machine gun around and they had it pointed down at him. The white kid yelled something Thorne couldn't quite hear, then made the gun shiver as though firing. He and the black kid looked at each other and laughed. Dead German motherfucker. And the traffic began to move.

As he neared the Ramburg city limits, Thorne began to notice another kind of presence. Now there were parked convoys of police. The *Bundesgrenzschützen* were out, too, with their green armored cars equipped with water cannons and decked barbed wire. The BGS were border guards, but they also worked internal-security missions such as riot control. Before he got anywhere near the center of town Thorne had passed a small army of police and paramilitary forces waiting in side streets for the call to action.

Ramburg was a small clean city, dreamy in the international style of communities whose existence centered around a university. The atmosphere was instantly recognizable. Shaded streets of good homes, the fragrance of blooming lives. Only now a flock of police choppers curved overhead.

Thorne had no idea where to find Tannenberg Kaserne, the site of the conference. He was watching for Army vehicles or any of the small dark signs used to guide military traffic, when the first ambulance howled by him.

Panic overcame him. It was done, the assassination had gone off. And maybe history had taken it up the ass because he'd been too pigheaded to make a phone call to tell his own people what he knew. It had been childish of him to cowboy it out alone, greedy for personal vengeance. Whatever he did anymore was childish and wrong. It seemed this crampheaded, hangover feeling had been with him for weeks. And now, for lack of clear thinking, he'd let something terrible happen.

But, even as the second ambulance came charging through the traffic, Thorne had begun to rethink. They wouldn't take the Chief anywhere in an ordinary ambulance. If he stubbed his toe he'd be medevaced out in his private bird. And, if they did have to take him anywhere in a normal rescue-the-peons-type ambulance, he'd have one hell of an escort of MPs and German cops.

German cops. Thorne shook his head.

Of course, if it had been a bomb, there could've been a lot of casualties. The way it had been with the commissary. And these people liked to use bombs.

But he hadn't heard a blast. And the police choppers overhead were still flying their surveillance patterns, there were no scooting medevacs.

Thorne turned a corner and found traffic backing up at a newly imposed roadblock.

He tried to do a quick backup or turn. But he was instantly boxed in by the traffic behind him.

There was no more time to waste. And the thought of more car-sitting was intolerable. He pulled the Saab up on the sidewalk at a loading zone and started to jump out. Then he dropped back into his seat.

If the police were regulating access to the area surrounding the conference, it wouldn't do to have a pistol stuffed in his jacket.

Thorne threw the 9mm. into the dash pocket. Then, on impulse, he threw in the passport and identification papers he'd been given. He didn't trust any of it.

He locked the dash pocket, then got out and locked the car. The volume of noise multiplied. Underneath the pulse of the choppers there was a distant rise and fall, like the sound heard outside a crowded stadium. Somewhere in this town there were a lot of excited people. Then he saw the first streaming gas grenade arc across the street several blocks down.

The police by the roadblock wore riot helmets and carried batons and clear-plastic shields. Their faces were expressionless, as though it made no difference to them whether they'd be called into action or not. They weren't holding up pedestrian traffic yet. At least not all of it. They were making a great fuss over the identification papers of a cluster of long-haired student types. But they let Thorne pass unmarked. As he went around the barrier Thorne heard a police officer explaining politely to a well-dressed man that traffic had been stopped for the citizens' protection. There was some slight difficulty with a demonstration that had gotten out of hand. He promised that it wouldn't be a significant delay, just as another grenade spilled its arc of yellow smoke across the horizon.

Thorne passed by another skirmish line of cops in riot gear. There were dogs too, and vans to transport prisoners. But this group as well remained at ease.

Now some of the shops were closed up, with night fencing drawn across their windows. Others were in the process of closing. And there were fewer and fewer workaday pedestrians.

Thorne crossed the mouth of an alley packed with more armored cars mounting water cannons. The crews sat on the turrets, drinking thermos coffee.

The noise was suddenly much louder. There was a loud wail or cheer, it was hard to tell which. Up ahead, beyond parked cars, in the slow curve of the street, Thorne could see part of the action now. Ranks of police marched on an invisible enemy, their backs to Thorne. A head turned to the side in the attitude of command, and Thorne saw the snouty profile of a gas mask. The cops were going in shoulder to shoulder, lined straight across the street, not using the standard riot-control wedge formation.

Maybe they didn't need it. These were tough cops. And there were more of them in every side street now. It seemed as though they must've drawn the police from all over the state of Hessen.

With a huge throb, a police helicopter swooped along the street, so low Thorne felt the prop-wash on his face and in his hair. A few blocks down it began broadcasting over loudspeakers. But the message was unintelligible from Thorne's position.

He heard the *thupthupthup* of a volley of gas grenades being fired, but couldn't see them this time. His pace had slowed almost by half now, he was one of the last civilians on these sidewalks. Then, at a corner, he was jarred by chanting down on his right, somehow an unexpected direction. It was a very simple chant, easy to understand even with the distortion of distance and so many voices.

"Amis raus, NATO raus, Amis raus, NATO raus . . ."

Suddenly there was a bloom of color amid the green police ranks moving up ahead of Thorne. Despite the density of police, despite the gas, some demonstrators were breaking through.

Some of the demonstrators had gas masks, too. And motorcycle helmets. They fought with ax handles and chains. The police smashed back with their batons, blocking blows with their shields. But their ranks were degenerating into a disorganized street fight.

On Thorne's right, the chanting from the other, still-unseen element grew louder.

"Amis raus, NATO raus, Amis raus . . ."

Another police chopper thundered in, its huge noise resounding in the canyon of the street. This bird didn't bother broadcasting warnings, it fired gas grenades right down into the disintegrating ranks where the demonstrators were slugging it out with the cops.

Behind Thorne, armored engines growled to life. A moment later the first armored vehicles began rolling out of the side streets.

Up ahead, the demonstrators had punched a clear hole in the police ranks and they were coming through at a run. Many of them had gas masks on, others ran red-faced or stumbled drooling off to the side. The kids who'd taken in too much gas looked comical in their staggering, faltering misery. But Thorne knew the kind of determination it took to last as long as they had in the yellow cloud that the end of the street had become.

It was a race now. Behind Thorne, three armored cars were coming along abreast of each other, followed by several ranks of police moving at a slow run, a German version of the airborne shuffle. Ahead, the demonstrators were running as fast as they could, as if to meet the armored cars and cops head on.

Thorne stopped, bewildered. What the hell were they doing? Where were they going? He couldn't believe they just wanted to mix it up with the cops. Was the *Kaserne* behind him? Had he passed it in a stupor?

The armored cars picked up speed, leaving the trotting police a bit farther behind.

Dozens of demonstrators had broken through the defense line now. Meanwhile, the street fight continued, and it looked merciless. When anybody from either side went down, he was immediately surrounded and beaten until he stopped moving.

"Amis raus, NATO raus . . ."

The spearhead of demonstrators reached the corner just ahead of Thorne and suddenly changed course, turning to their right, Thorne's left.

The *Kaserne*. That way.

The armored cars rumbled past Thorne, a football field ahead of their supporting infantry now, hurrying to cut off the demonstrators.

The chanting from the flank exploded into a shout of elation. A breakthrough on that front too.

The water cannons opened up, blasting demonstrators off their feet, interdicting their passage into the cross street. A pair of choppers came diving in, like Cobra gunships going in on the NVA. More gas.

Thorne had it in his eyes now as he jogged across the street. He was in the dead space between the armored cars and the advancing lines of riot police. He moved up behind the spray of the water cannons, keeping to the sidewalk, tight along the building. He could hear a chaos of sirens in the distance now. The reserves were moving in from the edge of town.

Across the street from Thorne a kid with a gas mask and long hair gathered into a ponytail ran from a doorway, arching his arm to throw a clump of fire. As it left his hand Thorne saw it was a bottle. It exploded on the side of an armored car's turret. Then there was shouting and screaming behind Thorne and he stopped running just long enough to turn and see more demonstrators crashing into the advancing ranks of police at the intersection he'd left a minute before. And then came the first tattle of gunfire.

Thorne moved out. His eyes were streaming tears, eyelids batting shut on their own. The water cannons were clearing the street ahead, blasting the streetfighters indiscriminately. The armored car that had been bombed had a small fire burning on its upper deck, but its operation didn't seem to have been affected.

Thorne peeled off from behind the armored cars as soon as they passed the intersection where the lucky first few demonstrators had turned off. He could see them ahead of him now, a handful of gypsies running free. He trailed them at a run.

They were in another dead space. In a pocket of silence between distant shouts, clashes and sirens. The gunfire had stopped, but the reeking air echoed with it.

He ran past a girl who was hacking and retching air. She was very thin and she leaned into a doorway, rocking in fits.

"Don't rub your eyes," Thorne shouted. She looked pitiable, in need of help. But there was no time.

Anyway, she'd be all right. The air was already better here.

The demonstrators who'd made it through had only a sixty- or seventy-meter lead on Thorne when, in a beautifully coordinated ambush, police burst from both sides of the street. Surprised, the demonstrators froze for the long second that might've saved them, and the cops swarmed over them. The demonstrators were so thoroughly outnumbered that their colored sweaters and parkas and jeans soon disappeared completely in a big huddle of green men swinging clubs.

Thorne slipped into the recess of the nearest shop entrance. The door was locked, gloomy windows offered arrangements of small electrical appliances, in white and orange plastic, for purchase some other time. Thorne hoped the cops hadn't noticed him. He was convinced that he was finally on the road to the *Kaserne.*

But what the hell was he going to do, even if he got there? He'd left the 9mm. in the car. And there probably wouldn't be much of a chance to go after anybody with bare hands. The notion made him think of Krull with his little orange beard. The big face haunted him. It would've been a pleasure to have him in a basement room, to painfully rebreak the already broken arm.

He should've killed him, should've killed him.

But he'd let the man live. And somehow, unreasonably, that made him responsible for all this gassing and clubbing, as though everything had broken down to the point where there was no longer a logical connection between cause and event, only a bond of emotion. Hadn't things come completely apart, anyway, when murder was a solution?

Doubt, depression, weakness. It was so hard to keep on going. His eyes still burned and his skin itched from the gas. What was the good of talking tough? The only real possibility left was to tell the authorities what was going on, to plug into the system again and try one more time to make it work.

But he *still* wouldn't tell the goddamned Germans. He had no faith left in them at all. When—if and when—he got to the *Kaserne,* there'd be American MPs, the Chief's escort. They'd be paranoid as hell with all this mess in the streets, well disposed to wild-sounding tales. With any luck, he might even get to the Chief himself.

Staring vacantly at hair dryers and toasters, Thorne realized he'd played a whore's trick on himself. Without noticing it, he'd changed his primary focus. He still wanted to get the pigs who'd blasted the commissary and caused Maria's death. But the most important thing, after all, had become keeping the Chief alive.

And you could come up with good, rational reasons. The assassination of the NATO Commander in Chief, whether it too got cynically blamed on the left or not, would have fearful repercussions. But in his heart Thorne knew that this wasn't exactly what was so important to him. It was far, far stupider than that. It was an infuriating, helpless mix of emotions. With all his intellect Thorne despised the man and feared the effect he might have on their country as a politician. But so often in life it was impossible to implement the conclusions of the intellect.

It was funny. Ferry had been right after all. The girl hadn't been all that important.

But she *had.* And remained so. Every goddamned human life was important. You had to believe that. You had to fight to believe it.

But was it true? Was it true? Didn't the fate of nations, of millions, honestly deserve precedence, just like the sonsofbitches said?

Thorne thought of Maria, alive, with her big ass and her dreams.

There was a clatter of running boots in the street and on the sidewalk. A squad of police ran past the storefront where Thorne had taken shelter. Then one of the trailing men spotted Thorne tucked in the doorway.

"There," the cop shouted, "there's another one of them."

And in an instant the cops were on him as a team, swinging at him with their batons. Thorne tried to break out, but he barely had time to double-punch at one of their shields before they smashed him to the ground.

Vi...the sun...

=== 19 ===

Thorne never completely lost consciousness. He was dazed from being struck on the head, and the world had a dreamy ambience, alternately telescoping and magnifying, but he was always at least faintly awake. The cops dragged him, streaming blood, along the pavement. He understood that there was now a hole he could slide his tongue through where his upper front teeth had been, but he wasn't yet quite clear as to why. He kept his eyes shut much of the time because the sun had become so stunningly bright. He was aware of being cursed, but the voices remained a little outside the place he was in, distinct but distant. He floated.

They threw him into the back of a van, further complicating its tangle of bodies. A female voice shrieked obscenities, and the metal door slammed shut. The blackness was complete, an ink storm in outer space, sour with the gas residue that clung to hair, clothing and skin. Thorne realized he was being a burden to the others sharing the crowded space. But he couldn't quite move. He was nudged, shoved lightly. A limb drew out from beneath him. Ghost voices whined and coughed and swore. He managed to roll over on his side. The small of his back hurt awfully. And radiating from his left ear came a pain as big as the Rocky Mountains.

He tried his fingers, suddenly he was very worried about his fingers. He moved each one carefully.

Okay.

It was soothing to know that his fingers were all right. Somehow it guaranteed recovery. Encouraged, he tried to lift himself off the floor of the van, hands grabbing and slapping at shoes and boots. But he managed only to lift his shoulders a few inches.

The pain in his back was really something. A special category of pain. A challenge.

He went tramping uphill at a rugged pace, between memory and imagination, carrying a fully loaded pack. In wonderful weather. It was warm, but clean breezes kept it from being hot, and he felt invincible. The way the packstraps tugged at your shoulders made you wonderfully aware of your strength, your marvelous capabilities. The hill was very steep. But there was no hill steep enough to stop him and his men. *Up jumped a monkey in a coconut grove.* Their voices came up behind him, full of bravado. They hadn't been there yet, hadn't seen. *He was a mean motherfucker, you could tell by his clothes.* Loud, sad voices. But it was contagious, it always made you want to sing, too. You knew you were part of something greater than yourself. They ran up the hill with their packs and rifles, North American dust rising around their combat boots. They hadn't been there yet and he didn't want them to go. *Lined a hundred women up against the wall, made a bet with the devil he could. . . .*

He'd been hurt worse. This wasn't going to stop him. No shitbird Germans were ever going to stop him. Because he'd been there. And he'd come back.

He tried to tell them, to holler it out at them. But his mouth wouldn't perform properly. He listened to himself groaning at words. There was no hill, no pack, no singing of cadence.

Cadence was wonderful, though. He loved barking cadence. Functional poetry. *Hold your nose and bow your head, we are passing by the dead.*

How we strained to exalt ourselves, how we struggled to fill our lives with some meaning.

Thorne tried to lift himself up again, and managed to do half a sit-up. But he couldn't lift his back any higher, it just wouldn't go. And he wouldn't give up. He held himself there, halfway, shaking with the pain.

Just when he was about to collapse, strong hands found him. They lifted him the rest of the way up to a sitting position. The pain in his back filled the darkness with dizzying flashes of color. But he would not let himself sink down. He was going to be all right now. He had a mission, and they weren't going to stop him. Not these bastards. He'd been hurt worse than they knew how to hurt you.

Thorne collapsed sideways against a pair of upright calves. He laced his arms around them so he wouldn't fall all the way down again. He was not going to fall back down. He clutched the denimed calves, resting his cheek on a bent knee. The pain ricocheted from his back to his ear now. But he was not going to go down. He held on. He didn't know whether he was clutching a man or a woman, and it didn't matter. It was wonderful when the big hands touched him again, careful in the dark, it was the most heartbreaking decency he could remember when the arm slipped around his shoulders and helped him support himself. The inside of the van was much quieter now, calmed to low sobbing. Then the floor shook as the engine started up.

As they pulled out, the arm realigned itself, making sure it had a firm hold on him. It was a strong, capable arm, and he let himself relax a little. They were never going to stop him. It was only that he needed a little rest.

He managed to stumble out of the van, with a little help. The hard light hurt his eyes and made the pain brutally clear, but it let him see his Good Samaritan. The strong hands and kind arm belonged to a tall young man with long black hair and a full beard. But all the hair couldn't hide the puffed lip and discolored cheekbone. He looked like Rasputin after a prizefight. Thorne tried to pronounce a few thank-yous. But his mouth was a mess, and the police were hurrying them along. Still, Thorne sensed that this helpful Rasputin understood, and he was glad.

They were herded down a gauntlet of cops leading toward a large building with high windows. It looked like a gymnasium. Startled, Thorne realized they were on a military installation. Behind the police, gray-uniformed German soldiers had gathered to watch what was happening. Unarmed, loitering just beyond the perimeter of the action, they looked like new conscripts. Then Thorne saw the first Americans.

U.S. Army MPs in gleaming jump boots and glossy black helmets with big white letters. There were half a dozen of them clustered around a jeep.

They'd delivered him to his desired destination, brought him right inside. He was sure this was it, it had to be.

But, if this were the right *Kaserne,* wasn't it terribly stupid to bring the prisoners right into the same compound with the Chief?

There was no time to waste. He had to talk to the MPs.

Thorne could read the sign above the door to the gym now. Building 2557, Tannenberg Kaserne.

He pulled all his strength together and lifted his hand to wave at the MPs before it was too late, before he was driven inside.

The tip of a baton stabbed him in the solar plexus and he crumpled to the pavement.

It was incredible how you could feel pain on top of pain. The body was remarkable in its capacities. He lay clutching himself across the chest, knees drawn up, quivering.

The police let him stay there while they crowded the others into the gym. Then the ranks broke up and two of the cops came over to him. He expected them to pick him up and throw him inside. But they only stood over him. Thorne could see them very clearly. They were grinning.

"He's got a pair of memories to take with him," one said. And they chuckled.

One of the cops kicked him in the side.

"Come on, asshole. Get up."

Thorne didn't get up. He held still. But suddenly he felt much stronger, almost able to run uphill with a rifle and pack.

This was the enemy.

The cop kicked him again, harder this time.

"Come on. Up. Don't make problems."

"Maybe he really isn't able?"

But Thorne was already rising. Slowly. He curled his shoulders up off the ground, rising angrily through the layers of pain. When his chest was all the way up to his knees, he eased himself forward, planting his knees solidly on the ground.

"That's right. Up we go," the cop said, making no effort to help him.

Thorne was looking straight at the MP jeep. It wasn't more than forty meters away, with a clear field.

He raised one knee, digging in the foot. He groaned, but calculatedly this time, and held still for a moment. Then he began raising himself, mentally cataloguing damaged parts, testing feet and legs. As soon as he'd gotten partway up, as far as a football hike position, he took off.

His body hurt outrageously, it didn't want to go. But he forced it. Dizzy, puking-sick, he kept his eyes locked on the jeep. Last play of the game and fucking Green Bay needs a touchdown.

This was where it mattered. This was why they sent you to Ranger School, why they tortured you and taught you all about the body's nearly endless willingness. It was the damned brain that let you down first. You had to overcome the preconceptions, the caution, the reasonableness of the brain. With proper training you could keep on fighting an hour or two after you were dead.

The jeep was much closer. He could even hear the crackling of the radio.

One good ear left, anyway. And what the hell did you need two for? He ran on clumsily and exuberantly, not giving a damn about the pain. They weren't going to stop him, not those bastards.

Startled, the MPs stood watching him. They had dumb, beautiful American faces. Thorne raised his arm to wave. He called to them as clearly as he could through the pulp of his mouth.

Then a great weight hit him from behind and he went down under it. But he crashed onto grass this time, it was a pleasure to fall down on grass instead of concrete.

He continued yelling as best he could, ignoring the big fist that began slamming him between the shoulder blades.

"I'm going to kill you, you shit," the cop gasped.

But suddenly the MPs were running toward them, and they were shouting now, too.

The big fist thumped down again and again. This was the enemy, this was why and wherefore.

The MPs grabbed the cop, dragging him off Thorne. The cop got in one last kick. But it didn't matter. Thorne closed his eyes and dropped his face onto the cold, dry grass.

He couldn't rest. They were rolling him over, straightening out the twist of his body, shaking gently at his shoulder to make him open his eyes.

They weren't speaking English to him, though. They spoke in pitiful GI German, asking him if he was okay. And he realized that they hadn't understood a word of his yelling, that they had only come to his rescue in a burst of human decency.

"The Chief," Thorne said, struggling to form the words clearly, "they're after the Chief."

In the background there was an argument going on, with Americans speaking pidgin German and Germans shouting in broken English.

"They're going to kill the Chief," Thorne said.

"What'd he say?"

"The . . . Chief . . ." Thorne said, speaking very slowly, fighting his excitement. "They're going to kill him."

"Kill who? Holy shit, Marty, I think he's a goddamned American."

"Yes," Thorne said, *"yes.* American. Listen to me."

"Captain Walker, sir. Hey, Captain Walker. The cocksuckers beat up an American."

Thorne was aware of more figures crowding around. They tugged him up to a sitting position and he looked at them all.

"Going to try to kill the Chief." It was much easier to talk sitting up.

"Who?"

"The Chief. Going to kill him."

"Who's going to kill him?" This was the captain, the man with railroad tracks on his collar. He spoke with an even drawl, maybe West Texas.

"German police. The German police."

The captain stared at him. He had a disgusted, disbelieving look on his face. It wasn't a very intelligent face. More of a stubborn one. Thorne realized that this was going to be another battle.

"Major in the United States Army. Major John Thorne. Believe me. This is important."

"You got an ID? Clark, see if he got an ID."

"No. Listen. Don't have anything. I'm undercover. You've got to believe me. Isn't much time."

"You just tell me what's all this business about hitting the Chief," the captain said.

In the background the argument between the Americans and the Germans was escalating. An urban voice shouted:

"You take a flyin' fuck, dude."

Thorne fought to speak clearly. It was like speaking a hard foreign language for which your muscles weren't developed. He wondered what his mouth looked like.

"Captain," he said, "if the NATO Commander in Chief dies today, it's going to be your fault." That made the smart bastard think. "I'm telling you, they're going to try to kill him. *Today.*"

"The German police?" the captain said. "The German police are going to try to kill the Chief?"

"Small group of plotters. The people who bombed the Bad Sickingen commissary. Big cover-up."

"You know, you look like they got you pretty bad, friend."

"Goddammit—" Thorne raised his voice—"take me to the Chief. Please. He knows me, he approved this project."

The captain was thinking, you could tell. But it was a slow process. The man's brain needed a crank that could be turned from the outside.

"I swear he knows me. Just get me to him for one minute."

"Well," the captain said. "I couldn't do that even if I wanted to. He ain't here."

It was Thorne's turn to be surprised.

"He's miles away," the captain went on, "out in the boonies. Don't you worry about him, buddy."

"But it said . . ."

"Oh, all the stuff in the news was a decoy. Tannenberg Kaserne, my ass," the captain grinned. "Why, we got every Commie cocksucker in Germany trying to fight his way in here. While the Chief's off having himself a quiet little working lunch."

"But you're the Chief's bodyguard, aren't you?"

"The Chief's in good hands. We just have to sort of sit here and stay visible."

"Whose hands?"

"The German police are taking care of him."

There was a quiet then, the captain suddenly thinking about what he'd just told Thorne. And about what Thorne had been trying to tell him.

Thorne pounced on this beginning of self-doubt. "I say again, Captain: If the Chief dies today, it'll be your fault. There is a plot by German police to kill him. And he's with the German police right now."

The captain was thinking very hard now, figuring odds in mental slow motion. If anything was going to save the Chief at this point, Thorne decided, it'd be the old Army rule about always covering your ass.

The captain looked away from Thorne, then looked back to him.

"What'd you say your name was?"

"Jack Thorne. *Major* Thorne."

The captain took one last unhappy look at the situation, then said, "You know who these guys are, sir? You'd recognize them?"

═══ 20 ═══

The jeep sped over country roads. Thorne sat in the tiny back seat, bunched against a husky MP who smelled faintly of marijuana. Both this MP and the driver were thoroughly stoned, Thorne had picked it up right away. It didn't surprise him. MPs had a reputation for being the heaviest dopers in the Army. And, up front, the captain studied his acetate-covered map, looking up now and then to yell at the spaced-out driver and point a direction. Thorne ignored the occasional fuss. He was resting, saving whatever reserves he might have left.

The pain in his back was phenomenal, getting worse instead of better. They'd done him serious damage. He'd pissed blood all down his pants without realizing it.

His face was bad, too. It looked deformed. He'd wiped away some of the blood with canteen water and a handkerchief, only to find a silly monkey's face staring back at him in the jeep mirror.

But he'd expected his face to look bad. It was easy to

make a face look bad. Besides, it'd look much better as soon as the swelling went down. He'd even had a pleasant surprise. His nose wasn't broken. Incredibly, it remained straight, changed only by the puffiness around his eyes. Pissed him off about the teeth, though. He could accept the smashed ear, somehow. But he'd always had such good, straight teeth.

Shit, it was almost a luxury to be able to catalogue your injuries so soon after the event. In Nam he'd stayed conscious just long enough to get a thorough appreciation of what pain meant, then he'd crashed and stayed out for three days. This was just the Saturday-night fights at the corner bar.

He felt very much alive in the cramped back of the jeep. There were no doors on the vehicle, and the wind currents managed to encircle you and chill you on all sides at once. But he didn't mind. He was glad the doors were off, he was grateful for the cold wind. The air cut hard into his torn lips. But it was a beautiful feeling, once you'd stripped away your preconceptions.

The captain twisted around in his seat, poking his head back toward Thorne.

"Nearly there," he said—then grudgingly added, "sir." He still hadn't completely made up his mind about Thorne, that was clear. But he was hedging his bets. "Uh, I'm not really sure . . . just how to handle this."

"How you mean?" Thorne asked, leaning forward against the noise of the jeep. He hadn't spoken for some time and his lips had begun to seal. Speaking again opened them painfully.

"Well, these fellas you say want to kill him. We can't just go arresting German cops. We have no authority."

"No problem," Thorne said. "Our job is to cover the Chief. Get him out of there before anything happens."

The captain put on a thinking look. He was searching for words. Finally he said, "Well, the Chief might not like that."

"Why?"

"He just might not like it."

Thorne was getting irritated. This man was a captain, in his Army. Acting like some dumb goddamned motor sergeant. Then Thorne realized what was actually on the captain's mind.

"You still don't believe me worth a shit. Do you? You're afraid of making a fool out of yourself in front of the Chief."

"Listen, mister—*sir,* I've gone along with you this far. Because it's my job not to take any chances. I got to cover all the bases. But you ain't even got an ID. All you got's a story. I think I'm doing all right by you just taking you there. This location's supposed to be secret."

It hurt Thorne's mouth too much to argue. "Okay," he said. "All right. Tell you how we'll handle it. Just take me there and let me look the German cops over. If I spot the guys I'm looking for, we'll play it by ear. If not, you can just look out for the Chief any way you want. Sound fair?"

If they were there, he'd spot them. The big bastard would be hard to miss, with his orange beard and a broken arm besides. And, if he spotted them, he'd make sure they were taken care of. Somehow.

"Sounds fair," the captain said.

As they were climbing the last hill, an observation helicopter broke low over the crest and buzzed them, checking them out. Dark-green belly with big white letters: POLIZEI. Then it lifted away from the road and whooped off, followed across brown fields by its shadow.

"I hate helicopters," the captain said. "Something so smart-ass about them."

From the top of the hill they looked down on a classic village. On a knoll just off to the side of the clustered houses stood a country inn, surrounded by armored cars and uniformed men deployed in nearby fields. Two brown U.S. Army choppers and a small flock of other NATO birds rested in a level meadow. The machines were guarded by a double cordon of police. Along the road leading up to the inn, dozens of green-and-white police vehicles nudged each other's bumper.

"Jesus," the captain said, "looks like a damn firebase."

"You going to have any trouble getting me in there?" Thorne asked.

"Naw, I got that all figured out." The captain smiled his first smile. "Tell them you're a reporter's been in an accident. The Chief's always got reporters with him these days, they're used to it."

The first checkpoint they had to pass through was at the entrance to the village. The guards there waved the Army vehicle through. At the second checkpoint, leaving the village on the road up to the inn, they were stopped. The guards stared at Thorne. But the captain's story worked.

They drove slowly uphill along the line of police cars and buses. Thorne strained to see inside each vehicle. But he didn't see Krull.

"Listen," he told the others, "I'm looking for a big guy—a real big guy—with light reddish hair. Last time I saw him he had a Vandyke."

"You mean a little beard, like?" the driver asked. "Like all the rads wear?" It was the first time he'd spoken and he even sounded spaced out. But he sounded interested too. Stoned at the movies and part of the action.

"Yeah. A little pointy beard. And he should have a cast on one arm, if there's any justice. Listen, if he's here, this guy's going to be hard to miss."

"Sounds like it," the captain said. "Major—or whoever you are—you better not be shitting me." But he didn't sound very sure of himself now. It sounded as though he was finally starting to consider all the possibilities in the situation, including the implications for himself if Thorne happened to be telling the truth and he blew it.

There was a dense crowd gathering around the entrance to the inn. Police, reporters, military aides from a bouquet of nations. Bunching, chatting, waiting. It looked as though they expected the meeting inside to break up at any moment.

"Anyway," Thorne said, as they drove slowly past, "we got here before anything happened. But we're going to have to get into that crowd."

He expected the captain to give him a hard time

about that too. If only as a matter of principle. But the captain's mood was definitely changing now that they were on the scene.

"Park it," he told the driver. "Just pull it off the road."

The driver obeyed immediately, taking them right across a little gulley and into a field. The jolting sent pain stabbing up from the small of Thorne's back.

Thorne let the burly MP climb out ahead of him. It had hurt like hell scrambling in, and he knew it wasn't going to be any better on the way out. He lifted himself into a crouch by grasping the seatbacks.

The driver leaned back in to padlock the steering wheel. He looked doubtfully at Thorne, appreciating the other's pain with mellow concern.

"You going to make it, sir?"

"Sure as shit, pal. Thanks."

Thorne dropped himself forward into the passenger seat, and the impact closed his eyes. You just had to keep on marching, he told himself. He swung his legs out onto the ground and shoved off from the jeep.

"Come on," he told the others. "Let's go."

German cops, armed with automatic weapons, were all over the place. But not the right German cops. In a sense, he realized, he should be glad. Maybe it meant the attempt wasn't going to come off after all. But he wanted so badly to make an end to this.

"The sonofabitch has to be here somewhere," Thorne said.

Pain made you angry, made you mean. Pain made you want to cause pain. He was able to walk at a decent pace, but he had to twist his torso to the right with each step, to keep a tension in his back. And he looked ridiculous, he was sure. Smashed face and freak walk, pants pissed bloody. The German police all watched him go with frozen faces.

Probably thought he was some sort of prisoner, Thorne realized. Wedged between an MP captain and two enlisted MPs with M-16s slung over their shoulders.

Screw 'em. Let them think what they wanted, let them laugh if they wanted. He'd soon be done with their loathsome country.

The crowd in front of the inn was spread over a large patio, from which one set of steps led up to the inn and another half-dozen steps, on the opposite side of the terrace, led down to the road. In warmer weather, guests would sun themselves and eat cakes. Today the patio hosted loosely ranked border guards and police around whom the international assortment of military men stood in small fluid groups, chatting in English, German and French. Unlike the police, these officers generally ignored Thorne's hammered face. They were all old hands at seeing only what they chose to see. As Thorne and the MPs poked by the clusters of beautifully tailored uniforms, these captains and majors and colonels, aides and adjutants to the great men inside, carried on with their conversations about armaments and expenditures, the neutron-warhead fiasco and the approaching ski season. A happy circle of Belgians laughed about a woman who apparently couldn't say no under any circumstances, while beside them a German, master of technical data, advised a Canadian major not to buy an Italian sports car.

Krull wasn't there. Thorne led his three companions all the way around the inn and its complex of sheds and garages, hoping desperately. But there were only more of the border guards, who watched the group's progress with strict eyes.

They wound up back on the patio, at the rear of the crowd.

"I've got to get inside," Thorne said. "There's a chance they're already in there." More and more fully, his concern for the Chief's safety was being overtaken by the fear that Krull would *not* show up. He *had* to be in the area. It was unthinkable for him not to be.

"I'm sorry, sir," the captain said. "I can't let you do that. I've gone along with you as far as I can."

"But they could be in there with him. They're going to try to kill him, I tell you."

"Calm down. There's nothing else we can do." He looked at Thorne. He'd become a little caught up in the spirit of the chase. Now he was almost sympathetic, in his way. "Maybe these fellas you're worried about suckered for the bit about the Chief being back in Ramburg, just like you did."

But Thorne wouldn't give up.

"We can't take that chance. It won't cause any trouble for you. The Chief knows me, he'll understand."

Thorne stood with his back to the crowd, and the captain suddenly looked past him.

"Well, it don't make any difference now. Looks like he's coming out."

Thorne twisted around to face the entrance just as the ranks of guards were called to attention. All conversations abruptly terminated and the officers turned toward the steps leading up to the doorway of the inn. In the road below the patio, a small convoy of military and police sedans rushed up and halted, their drivers leaping out to open rear doors in preparation. The function of the sedans would be to carry the Chief and his entourage the hundred and fifty meters to the helicopters.

The Chief appeared in the doorway, a clear target above the crowd. The world cracked to attention.

Frantic, Thorne looked from side to side, expecting sudden movement or the serial flash of automatic weapons. But there was only the rasp of the breeze in the dried-up garden and the low idling of the sedans in the street.

The Chief paused at the top of the steps and slowly scanned the crowd. As if he wanted to present a perfect target. He wore his dress greens today, and, on his left breast, ribbons climbed from pocket to collar, topped with the blue-and-silver Combat Infantryman's Badge and silver wings. He looked heroic and wise, with his fine posture and the blue eyes that condensed the color of the sky. This was the man who'd put those endless convoys on the road, who'd begun his service by dragging a platoon across northern France, then driving a company through the snows of Korea, who'd commanded first a brigade, then a division in Vietnam before receiving an appointment to the White House, where he'd apparently gotten a taste for the neighborhood. This soldier, who'd risen so high during his country's exasperating and unreasonable decline, stood tight-lipped on the landing at the top of the steps, charged, more actually than any other man, with the defense of the West.

"At ease," he finally said, in the clear voice of command, "everybody, please." He waited while subsequent commands followed in a pride of languages, then, when the formations had relaxed slightly, he continued:

"I'd like to take this opportunity to thank each one of you, and I hope you will pass my thanks on to your comrades-in-arms who are not here today.

"I'd also like to add a note of warning to those thanks. Gentlemen, we are standing at the crossroads. We have come to a point in history where nations must intelligently *will* their fate. For thirty years, we have followed the currents of history together. But we can no longer afford to follow. We must lead history where we want it to go, where the survival of democratic values requires that it go. We remain strong. But yesterday's strength cannot match the greater strength the East-bloc armies will possess tomorrow. We are opposed by men who have the power to implement their wills without argument or opposition. And we must outstrip them, not only in armaments, but also in this power of the will. Already, we've fallen behind in certain areas. We must not let these inroads become a trend that might then become history. We must revitalize our nations and ourselves, and we must do it now.

"This great exercise, the largest in NATO's history, has been extremely encouraging. Never before in peacetime have so many men from so many nations cooperated so fully in the military sphere. Certainly, many problems were identified. But none of these problems is insoluble and we have made a great beginning toward eliminating them over these last few weeks. So take my congratulations home with you. And take this message as well: Though we be strong today, our mission requires that we be even stronger tomorrow. And the only viable means to achieve this greater strength is through unity—and relentless determination. Thank you, gentlemen."

As the Chief broke his stance to descend the steps, a half-dozen voices barked commands, and formations cracked back into rigid discipline. The big huddle of staff officers parted to make a path through their midst and as the Chief passed among them he turned his head from side to side, offering swift personal thanks and pumping hands like a candidate. His personal staff followed him down the steps and across the patio toward the sedans, trailed, in turn, by the inner circle of correspondents. None of the pressmen crowded the Chief or pecked at him with questions. Their interviews were guaranteed.

Thorne pushed forward into the crowd, followed automatically by the MPs. The captain touched at Thorne's arm, but Thorne shook him off and headed for the steps leading down to the sedans, where his path and the Chief's would intersect. From the foot of the hill Thorne could hear the deep flutter of the choppers getting ready to go.

Thorne felt another tug at his arm. He tried to shake this bother off, too. But the hand clutched him.

"Sir, hey, sir," it was the jeep driver talking, "is that the guy you're looking for?"

Thorne whipped around, forgetting all pain now. The kid had become very serious, no longer playing stoned games. He pointed along the line of sedans.

A police cruiser crawled along the line, heading slowly toward the Chief's sedan. Peering out of an open side window was the big orange-haired chunk of face. A white cast rested on the windowsill, supporting the just barely visible muzzle of an automatic weapon.

The Chief was near the top of the steps, still turning his thanks from side to side. For a split second he and Thorne looked into each other's eyes.

But there was no time. Thorne turned again and tore the M-16 off the unprepared jeep driver's shoulder, then launched himself forward between two guards, fingers going automatically, almost with homesickness, to the necessary points along the weapon, even as he was hitting the ground and rolling down the short bank toward the oncoming car.

Make sure the safety's off and it's on auto, cock the fucker and lock it in against your shoulder as you come back up.

Thorne rose from the foot of the bank and put a short burst through the front window of the car from a distance of ten meters. In a lightning pause he saw the clumsy jerking of the cast and the chest, the outraged look of surprise on Krull's face. The big cop's own weapon spit wildly into the air. Thorne put the next burst into the driver and was drawing his aim back across the veer of the car, across the devastated windshield, when the first rounds hit him.

He'd known they were coming, still it was like being

hit by iron baseball bats. Every bodyguard and security man with a clear line of fire had reacted automatically to the violence outside. They'd been well trained. The successive impacts made Thorne's shoulders jig, knocking him against the nearest sedan. But he wouldn't go down. The shot-up car meandered into the ditch by the side of the road, and Thorne saw, with perfect satisfaction, the slumped bodies and the great big hanging head, but he was determined to make use of the last half-second of possibility that remained to him before a dozen more bursts chewed him up, and he emptied his weapon into the big head, making it dance, exploding it over the inside of the car.

The M-16 trigger went dead. But Thorne wanted to sing. Got you, you fucking bastard. I got you and I'll goddamned well always get you. Every goddamned time, you hear me?

The expected storm of bullets threw Thorne up on the hood of the sedan, then rolled him onto the pavement. He landed on his back, arms thrown wide, the M-16 lost forever.

But he wasn't dead. He was still perfectly conscious, looking up at the blue, blue sky. There was no more firing now. Only the throbbing choppers. Somebody hated choppers. Who was that? Thorne wished he could remember, so he could tell them how wrong they were. The choppers were on our side, they were your friends. They came and picked you up when you were scared half to death. They brought you back to life when you should've been dead. They brought you food and firepower and carried you over the jungle like a god.

Thorne couldn't see the sky so well now, men were kneeling over him, blocking it. Their faces were dark, all shadows, strangers. Then Thorne heard a Texan voice.

"He said he was a U.S. Army major. He said there was a plot to assassinate you, sir. He said he was working undercover."

The captain sounded so afraid. There was no need to be afraid. We were all strong together, going forward together to build a New Jerusalem. Then Thorne remembered that it was the captain who hated helicopters. He filled with pity for the man and wanted to tell him that everything was going to be all right. The poor bugger didn't even know the choppers were on his side. What kind of officers were they getting these days? Where were the bright young men? How were they ever going to win the war with men like this?

Suddenly the dark faces drew back and Thorne saw the sky again. The wonderful Pennsylvania sky. They didn't have skies like this anywhere else in the world. Even in the dead of winter the sunsets wept with color, color, color. The slanting light blazed across the snow, and between the car and the warm house there were frosty kisses, dry lips and hot wet mouths. Women in wintertime, the pleasure of working down through the layers of clothing. Winter nights.

Another face bent over him now. He could see this face clearly, with no one blocking the light. It was the Chief. Now everything would be all right. The Chief knew, he understood. Those blue eyes possessed more knowledge than the eyes of an ordinary man. Oh, you might not like him. But he was definitely on your side, this father of armies, and that was important. You had to be on the right side. Sure, there'd be compromises. You'd have to do bad things, because the world was a terribly complex place. But it would be all right in the end.

The Chief stared down at Thorne, slowly narrowing his eyes, considering him. These were, Thorne felt, the eyes of an entire nation, the best of nations. They were hard eyes. But history . . . history . . .

"Nonsense," the Chief said, drawing his face away, standing back up. "This man's a well-known leftist, a scribbler. He's suspected of involvement in several terrorist operations in Europe. We've been keeping tabs on him. Oh, he's an American, all right. But he certainly isn't in any way affiliated with the United States Army."

It didn't matter. That's what the girl had said: it didn't matter. The lies were necessary. So many lies. The Chief knew what he had to do, you had to believe that. It didn't matter if your part went unrecognized. You didn't do it for medals. You did your duty, and all that mattered was the result. But it was hard sometimes.

Other faces hovered over him again. But he didn't care so much about the sky now. It wasn't a Pennsylvania sky. And the faces were trying to help him. He was their fellow soldier.

Why weren't they touching him? Comforting him? Inspecting his wounds? Why couldn't he feel their goddamned hands? Was it that bad?

He didn't even try to raise his head to look at

himself. He knew he couldn't. It was bad this time. Worse than in Nam. The thought of going through all the hospitals and the inching therapies again made him tired. And he hadn't slept for such a long time.

But he'd been more tired than this. Trudging through the jungle valleys. It was a shitty war, and its weight had fallen on sorry shoulders. But you had to keep going. Somebody had to do the job.

It wore you down, though, used you up. The sleeplessness, the constant need to pay attention, to watch for tiny points of light. It was a terrible war. But it was over for him now.

Don't give up. Just don't you ever give up, motherfucker. The enemy don't give up. Come on, I want them moving. I know they're tired, McCallister. We're all tired. But you just can't ever give up.

Pick up your weapon and follow me.

I am the infantry.

Oh, you could keep going forever. You just had to learn about pain, how you could march right through it.

Somewhere the helicopters were rising. They were coming for him, he knew. The choppers are your friends, pal.

The birds are coming, they're on their way. Let's wrap this one up.

Battle jacket hanging open like John Wayne's vest. Walking toward the smoking elephant grass. Going in to shut this one down.

The important thing was not to despair. Don't worry about here and now. Someday you'll be back where it's safe and they got more women than they can use. You'll understand it all then. It just takes time and a little distance.

The choppers were coming. Wonderful choppers. Soon big hands were going to pick him up.

The last thing Thorne heard was a voice shouting for a medic, shouting and shouting, in the familiar accents of home.

Author's Note

This book was written in Bad Kreuznach, West Germany, in 1979. I hoped to capture the feel of a specific time—the end of the '70s—and of specific places during the Hamlet years of United States foreign policy. NATO struggled with doubts, while West Germany was obsessed with the ingratitude of terrorists who were an even greater threat to German values than to German lives. Istanbul had a fever begging for a radical cure. Greece had freed itself from military rule only to imprison itself with rhetoric. In *that* Europe you could endure the café monologues of young German leftists and the old irredeemable conservatives, dine with a Greek Communist banker in a souring paradise . . . or digest the latest political murder along with your breakfast in Turkey. It was a fascinating time to be young and abroad, without the financial wherewithal to insulate yourself from the impatient world around you. Writing now, at the end of 1989, I am astonished at the difference a decade has made in our world.

There were, however, two respects in which this novel proved more prescient that I would have wished. The early '80s did indeed see the realization by European terrorists that the easiest way to strike the U.S. military was to attack the commissaries, family housing areas, and private automobiles of services members. Bombings such as the grim Ramstein incident made reality out of a scenario I would have preferred to lock safely in the realm of fiction.

Further, the resurgence of the German right under the leadership of the "Republican" Franz Schoenhuber and others simply makes me shake my head and marvel at how willfully Americans misunderstand Germany. It has become fashionable in Washington to adore Germany, even as the Federal Republic turns its back on so many of the interests its leaders once reverently professed to share with us. While Germany (and Japan) certainly pose no *military* threat to the United States, the modalities of warfare are expanding, and, in the elegantly violent sphere of economic competition, rehabilitated enemies are beginning to look like enemies once again. Meanwhile, even the dramatic and promising metamorphosis underway in East Germany is accompanied by annoying undertones of right-wing extremism —which receive little mention in North American news coverage—while the left is increasingly discredited on both sides of the crumbling border. A decade ago, the Greens were the nightmare of career men in Bonn, while today those fears have shifted across the political spectrum to Herr Schoenhuber's Republicans, for whom the only good American is a distant and impoverished one.

Certainly, the demagogic right wing in the Germanies commands only a small minority of followers at present—but, in the Federal Republic, it is already sufficiently resurgent to send mainstream politicians scrambling after lost votes. If nothing else, we shall all hear a great deal more in the coming decade about how divine it is to be German.

Such ruminations aside, I can only hope that the reader of *Bravo Romeo* has been entertained by this first novel from an angry young man who was utterly unable to admit how happy he really was.

—RALPH PETERS